Titia Sutherland was brought up in the country and has spent much of her adult life in London. She had a patchy education at various day schools, and English was the only subject in which she received a good grounding. As a child she started many novels which were never completed, and she and her brother wrote and acted in their own plays. In her late teens she spent two years at the Webber-Douglas School of Drama and a short period in repertory before marrying a journalist. The birth of a baby put an end to acting. Following a divorce, she had a series of jobs which included working as a part-time reader for a publishing firm, and designing for an advertising agency.

She started to write when the children were more or less adult and following the death of her second husband. Her three previous novels, *The Fifth Summer, Out of the Shadows* and *Accomplice of Love,* are also published by Black Swan. She has four children, enjoys gardening and paints for pleasure when there is time.

Also by Titia Sutherland

THE FIFTH SUMMER
OUT OF THE SHADOWS
ACCOMPLICE OF LOVE

and published by Black Swan

Running Away

Titia Sutherland

BLACK SWAN

RUNNING AWAY
A BLACK SWAN BOOK 0 552 99620 3

First publication in Great Britain

PRINTING HISTORY
Black Swan edition published 1994
Black Swan edition reprinted 1994

Set in 11/13pt Linotype Melior by Phoenix Typesetting, Ilkley,
West Yorkshire.

Black Swan Books are published by Transworld Publishers Ltd,
61–63 Uxbridge Road, Ealing, London W5 5SA,
in Australia by Transworld Publishers (Australia) Pty Ltd,
15–25 Helles Avenue, Moorebank, NSW 2170,
and in New Zealand by Transworld Publishers (NZ) Ltd,
3 William Pickering Drive, Albany, Auckland.

Printed and bound in Great Britain by
Cox & Wyman Ltd, Reading, Berks.

For Philippa and Emma
with much love

Chapter One

After the girls had departed for school, Laura stood at the window and watched them walking slightly apart and in silence, until they reached the corner of the road and disappeared. Then she turned abruptly and resolutely, preparing to work her way through the list of things to be done before she left home. She felt in that moment a wave of remorse and self-disgust at deserting them. But the urge for solitude was stronger still. Allowing herself no time to stop and consider, she fetched her coat, searched her bag for the car keys and let herself out into the fine October morning.

Autumn was late this year: the trees on Barnes Common had scarcely changed colour. Laura did not notice them as she drove to the garage, her thoughts taken up with practicalities. The Metro was far from new, and she was about to ask it to carry her some six hundred miles. Staying alone in an isolated house held no fears for her; being stranded on a motorway filled her with horror. She listened intently for any strange knockings from the engine, but the car purred along as if looking forward to its prospective journey. It was 9.30 and the garage forecourt was empty. Ted Fowler himself came to attend to her, wiping his hands on an oily rag.

'Morning, Mrs Snow. You're up bright and early. What can I do for you?'

'Petrol, please, Ted, a full tank. And I'd like the oil and the tyres checked.'

'Going a fair way, are you?' he asked, one eye on the pump while he dealt with the first request.

'As far as – to the West Country.'

'Should be nice down there if the weather holds. Make a break for you and Mr Snow.'

'I'm going alone. To friends. Richard can't get away.'

''Course, you'd be driving the Volvo otherwise, I daresay.'

She had not expected such well-meaning interest in her plans. Rick used Fowler's garage, they both did. It might have been wiser to go elsewhere, but Ted was reliable.

'Your rear left-hand is wearing a bit thin,' he said, looking at the tyres.

'Oh Lord!' She peered anxiously. 'Should it be changed?'

'No, no, it'll see you through a good many miles yet. Better bear it in mind, though, when you get back.'

In the shop she paid her bill and bought two large slabs of Cadbury's Fruit & Nut, finding it surprisingly difficult to look Ted in the eye as she thanked him. She felt as shifty as an escaped prisoner. But that is exactly what I am, she told herself as she drove home, realizing simultaneously that her reasons for escape would seem negligible to the average observer. She was not a battered wife; Rick was neither an alcoholic nor a womaniser. He was the soul of kindness. His objective was to take all the stress from her life, to compensate for the rough ride of a first marriage; a commendable aim, on the surface, she supposed. But a certain amount of stress was necessary if one was not to become a vegetable, and the lack of it had sapped her initiative, leaving her mind as bland and soggy as a bowl of rice pudding. Sometimes she felt he would be happy to stop her thinking processes altogether. Time and again she had tried to explain this to him; time and again he had failed to see her point of view. The car

8

behind hooted her, and she shot forward with a grinding of gears over the green traffic lights.

It is my own fault, she told herself. I married him for the wrong reasons, for refuge, a solid base, a man of my own and a father-figure for Hannah. It had been easy to pretend to herself she had fallen hopelessly in love. She had been given all those things, and Annabelle, her stepdaughter into the bargain, whom she loved as much as, and occasionally more than, her own daughter. And now, contrariwise, she wanted to overthrow the shackles; not for ever, but just for a while, she wanted her independence. I need space, she muttered to herself, wryly conscious of echoing the often perverse Hannah.

If only Rick were not so competent, but in some respects the helpless male, rather than holding down a responsible job and more or less taking over the running of the house besides. It was years since she had paid a household bill or changed a plug. He was a far more imaginative cook than she, teasing her tolerantly for her basic efforts. At weekends he did most of the cooking. Little by little she had less and less to occupy herself; only the occasional script to be reviewed in her part-time job as reader for the firm of publishers where once she had been fully employed. She missed the cut and thrust of office life. There should have been all the time in the world for writing, but the atmosphere was wrong, the incentive lacking, and her folder of poems lay in a drawer, unadded to for months.

It was Rick's amused and gentle condescension towards the poetry that riled her most. 'Scribbling?' he would say, putting a smiling face over her shoulder, so that she involuntarily covered the page with her hand. She used to write while the girls did their homework, forgetting the time so that he would arrive home to find her bent over her desk, the preparation of supper forgotten. It was this thought that made her put on the brakes with unnecessary force as she parked in the drive of her home. Where she was going, there would be the peace and isolation to write whenever the mood so moved her. She opened the front door with a surge of renewed resolution. The house was very still and quiet as she climbed the stairs, pulled her packed suitcase from its hiding place in the spare room cupboard and carried it to her bedroom to put in the last items. She was not taking much in the way of clothes; life in Cornwall would demand little beyond jeans, tracksuits and jerseys.

Zipping up the case, she took her letter to Rick from the desk and placed it in Annabelle's room, propped against the legs of a scruffy teddy bear, as prearranged with her rather reluctant stepdaughter. The room was meticulously tidy as usual; the sight of it caught at her throat in a sudden stab of conscience. I am not running away for good, she said to herself, only for as long as it takes. At the window she looked down at the back garden. The table and chairs on the little paved terrace were rusting: she had been meaning to give them a coat of paint before she left. Rick would most likely have taken the paint brush from her hand had she done so, doubting her ability; just as she, too, had seriously begun to doubt it.

Laura had decided to leave it as late as possible to tell the children, not wishing to have them brooding for days over her intended absence, although in Hannah's case she need not have worried. Hannah had painted her room scarlet. One wall had footprints walking up it and continuing across the ceiling; she had used a pair of old trainers for the purpose while the paint was still wet. Every inch of remaining wall space was crammed with posters and weird objects collected from markets and Indian junk shops. The floor, with its piles of discarded clothes, resembled a stall at a jumble sale. Hannah herself was lying on her bed reading, wearing an elongated T-shirt, Walkman earphones strapped to her head. She peered at her mother between pale curtains of straight, shiny hair.

'What did you say?'

Laura reached out and turned the music off at the base. 'Take those things off. I want you to hear properly.'

Hannah obliged, Laura sat on the bed. 'I'm going away tomorrow for a while.'

'With Rick?'

'No, by myself. For a sort of holiday.'

'Why?'

'Because I need the break, time to think.'

Hannah lay back on the pillows, eyes narrowing to blue slits. 'Are you getting a divorce?'

'No,' Laura said, more emphatically than was necessary, 'certainly not. Whatever gave you that idea?'

'You never go anywhere without him. Usually we all go. Family unity,' Hannah recited in imitation of her stepfather.

'We're very lucky,' Laura said firmly. 'I need space, that's all. Just for a short time. You should know about that – it's your favourite subject.'

'Well, I think it's rather mean, leaving us to slog away here while you have a fab time somewhere.'

'One day before long you'll be doing just that, and I'll be slogging in your place. Besides,' Laura said, 'you don't work that hard.'

'Who's going to do the cooking? And the shopping?'

'You can work that out between you. There's enough food for a siege in the freezer, and all of you are capable of wheeling a trolley round a supermarket, and grilling chops. And don't leave everything for Annabelle to do,' Laura told her. 'Fair shares, please.'

11

'Annie's seventeen, older than me.'

'You're quite old enough to do your bit. Annabelle's got "A" levels to worry about.'

'Does Rick know about you going?' Hannah asked suspiciously.

'Only in theory. He will tomorrow.'

'Curiouser and curiouser,' Hannah observed. 'Where are you going, anyway?'

'The West Country,' Laura said quickly. 'I shall ring each day to make sure you're behaving,' she added more or less as a joke.

'There's a pop concert coming up in a week's time. Michael Jackson at the Hammersmith Odeon. Can I go?'

'I think not, in the middle of term,' Laura decided. 'Don't forget your flute lessons. And you're staying with Daddy and Trish for two days at half-term.'

'That's two and a half weeks away.' Hannah looked shocked. 'Won't you be back by then?'

'Probably, I'm not sure.'

'The brace is being taken off my teeth then. I shan't have anyone to go with me and I hate the orthodontist,' she moaned, having a shot at pathos.

Laura ignored it. 'Annabelle will go if I'm not here.' Hannah made a face. 'Don't bait her, Hannah. She's working flat out and it's not easy for her. Promise?'

Hannah lowered her eyelids secretively and nodded.

Laura sighed. 'I'd better say good night.' She bent, put her arms round her daughter's thin shoulders and hugged her. 'See you in the morning.'

'You are coming home, aren't you, Mum?' Hannah asked carelessly, flicking through the pages of her book.

Laura turned by the door. 'Don't be silly, darling, of course I am.'

Annabelle was still working, slumped over the little Victorian kneehole desk which Laura had bought her

12

in a sale. The top was somewhat stained, but she had renewed the embossed green leather square and the wood had polished up quite satisfactorily. Telling Annabelle was not going to be easy. Her outward appearance, a little overweight and with a peaceful face, gave a false impression of placidity. Besides, she was no longer a child, and her reactions would be quite different to those of Hannah at fourteen. Her mother had died ten years ago and remained only as a dim memory. Laura, from her position as an unsure substitute, had moved to becoming the real thing in Annabelle's consciousnes: a dependable entity who was unlikely to vanish. She heard Laura out more or less in silence, a small frown forming two lines between her eyebrows.

Laura said, 'Something's worrying you. Is it being left in charge, the cooking and so on? Daddy is competent, and I've told Hannah she *must* help.'

Annabelle doodled absently on a piece of foolscap. 'It's not that.'

'What, then?'

Annabelle glanced up and away. 'I don't understand why you haven't told Daddy. You're not splitting up, are you?' she said, asking the same question as Hannah, but in tones of trepidation.

'Of course not. It's nothing like that.' How much easier it would be, Laura thought, if she could explain the whole situation. 'I have talked it over with Daddy, and he doesn't completely understand. If I tell him I'm leaving tomorrow, he'll try to reason me out of it, that's why I'm explaining by letter. Sometimes a *fait accompli* is the best way.'

Annabelle ran a hand through floppy brown hair, shifted on her chair nervously. Laura could read her; she was thinking it was the coward's way out. 'He'll get an awful shock.'

'I don't think so. I've been very careful to word the

13

letter so he won't panic. I'm only going for a week or two, after all.'

'But this thing of not knowing where you are—' Annabelle's voice tailed away dubiously.

'I shall be in a small house in the West Country. And I shall ring every evening to make sure you're all all right.' Laura searched for words to explain herself. 'This is something I have to do, darling; please try to understand. Nothing to do with disagreements or rows – you know we don't have many of those. It's really a matter of changing the scene, just for a while,' she heard herself saying. 'The poetry is important to me, you see, and somehow, here, it seems to have dried up.' She looked at Annabelle, hoping for a degree of empathy, and finding it in the dark brown eyes. 'Do you think I'm being very selfish?'

'No,' Annabelle shook her head. 'But I wish I was going with you, because I feel the same. Not about poetry, but about getting away from everything.'

Laura glanced at the desk covered in half-finished writings; her heart ached for the child. 'I'd take you with me if it wasn't term-time.'

Her eyes took in the room with its striped blue-and-white wallpaper, chosen seven years ago when they moved in. Nothing had been altered since, there had been no demands from Annabelle to do so. None of the mess that ensued from Hannah's decorative endeavours had cluttered up this pretty, sedate room. Even the teddy bears and worn woolly animals lay in the same order on the bedcover. Sometimes Laura felt that a little more chaos in her stepdaughter's way of life would have been a healthy sign.

'If you're going to worry yourself into the ground, I shan't go,' she said. 'It wouldn't work out.'

'I'll be all right,' Annabelle said. 'Fine, in fact,' she

added with a visible effort. 'I'd better finish this paper, I suppose.'

Laura stood up. 'You shouldn't be working this late.' She kissed the top of Annabelle's head. 'Ease up a bit, darling. "A" levels aren't the end of the world.'

'I have to slog. I'm not brilliant like Hannah.'

'And don't let Hannah make life hell for you. You have full permission to hit her if necessary.'

Annabelle rolled her eyes up to Heaven. 'I shall, if she's a pain. Where's the letter to give Daddy?'

'I'll leave it on your bed in the morning. Sure you don't mind? I'd rather not just leave it for him to find.'

'He won't believe I don't know where you are.'

'He will. I've made it absolutely clear.'

'Oh well, then—' But it was not well. When Laura had hugged her closely and left, Annabelle finished the page with difficulty and tidied the desk. Her mind had temporarily swapped niggling her over her work, for worry over Laura. She was far too intuitive to imagine she had been given the entire story behind Laura's plans. Her unsatisfactory shape that showed in the mirror as she undressed proved a distraction, but it was only momentary. Unsaid things bothered her. In bed, she put the light out straight away, certain she would not sleep, but she did, because she was young and very tired.

The desire to abscond had been with Laura since the summer holidays, spent this year on the Isle of Wight in an unsuccessful attempt on Rick's part at teaching the girls to sail. The place to escape to had dropped into her lap quite unexpectedly, during lunch a fortnight ago with Gerard Wyatt. Gerard was an editor with Laura's erstwhile employers, a self-confessed homosexual and as such, approved of by Rick as a lunch companion. Although Rick's objections to other male friends of Laura's were never voiced, he none the less managed to make them felt.

On this particular occasion Gerard's purpose, besides the genuine enjoyment of Laura's company, was to persuade her to return to the firm. He had hopes of succeeding, having listened to her description of the holiday and noted a desperation in her tone that far outweighed such a trivial topic. She was not happy with her lot. He waited until they had both finished their *moules marinière*, refilled their glasses, and put the suggestion to her. For a moment she was overjoyed by the idea; and then the realities started to impinge. Rick's opposition to the scheme, the demands of children and house, doubts about her own ability to cope by now with a proper job. She sagged back in her chair and produced this dispirited list of reasons for declining.

'So you see, Gerry, it's not on. But I'm very flattered to be asked.'

He said, one eyebrow raised quizzically, 'I had no idea you were so firmly under the estimable Richard's thumb.'

'That's not fair.' She might have guessed Gerard would go straight to the crux of the problem. 'I'm my own woman,' she said positively, sounding unconvinced even to herself. 'Rick's the kindest of men, but you know how it is in a relationship. You can't just ride roughshod over your other half's feelings on a subject.'

'It depends,' he replied, 'how self-serving those feelings happen to be.'

Laura reddened. 'You've never really liked Rick much, have you?'

'Darling, not true. I'm mad about him, but then I don't have to live with him.'

She knew this was a cue for laughter, but she did

16

not feel like it. 'I have no right to grumble. I live a comfortable life. I have two great daughters and I'm cosseted and protected. *Over*protected by Rick, but that's no great crime; hundreds of women would give their eye teeth to be in my shoes.' She took a sip of wine. 'I'm beginning to feel hemmed in. I want to scream and then run away. How's that for gratitude?'

'Understandable, in my opinion,' Gerard said comfortably. 'A change is in order. That's why a job amongst friends would seem ideal.' He leant forward. 'I'm not offering you your old slot back. Dawn Pryce is leaving us and we need a replacement.'

'Replacement for an *editor*?' Her eyes widened in a mixture of disbelief and pleasure. 'I couldn't do it, Gerry. I'm not qualified.'

'Nonsense. I wouldn't suggest it if I didn't think you were suitable. Your children are old enough to take care of themselves.' He looked at her in mock severity. 'Where's that old self-confidence you used to be renowned for?'

Suddenly she wanted to cry. 'Gone,' she said. 'Drained away. I suspect it was only youthful bumptiousness, in any case.'

'Marriage!' Gerard snorted in disgust.

To her horror a tear spilled from each eye and rolled slowly down her cheeks. Gerard's round, pink face puckered in dismay and sympathy. She scrabbled in her bag for a tissue. He ordered brandy while she blew her nose and recovered herself.

'I'm sorry,' she said. 'Stupid of me.'

He patted her hand. 'Mid-life crisis, perhaps?' he suggested cosily.

'Some sort of crisis, but not the sort you mean.'

He sighed. 'What are we going to do with you? What do *you* think you should do to break the cycle?'

'I should like to go away and be alone for a bit,' she

17

said promptly, surprising herself. 'Write poetry and go for long walks and just have time to think.' She drank some of her brandy. 'The trouble is, I can't afford a hotel, and anyway, it isn't the answer. Perhaps a cottage somewhere. It shouldn't be expensive, out of season. If I can get myself organized,' she added with a smile.

'No need to bother. The house at St Merric is sitting empty. How do you feel about Cornwall?'

She stared at him, unable to believe her luck. 'But you and Oliver always go there in October, don't you, when the tourists have left?'

'Not this year, dear girl. Oliver has a yen for Florence, so he's dragging me off. One must let the boy have his head occasionally.' The 'boy' in question was Gerard's long-standing partner, marginally younger than Gerard himself. 'It's better for the place to be lived in,' he said. 'We never let it, of course, it goes without saying.'

'Oh, I couldn't just stay there for nothing,' Laura protested, already seeing herself installed.

'Nonsense! I'm not going to break the rule for you. You can give me something towards the telephone bill. You've never been there, have you?' She shook her head. 'It stands alone, a short way out of the village. You'll only have the seagulls for company, but that's presumably what you need.'

'Oh yes,' she breathed, 'yes, it is.'

'Then, if you want it, it's yours. I shan't be down before Christmas.'

They finished lunch with a discussion about details such as keys and how to find the house on arrival, and excitement welled up in Laura and flushed her cheeks.

'I can't begin to thank you, Gerry.'

'Don't try.' He looked at her quizzically. 'I hope this isn't the break-up of your marriage, because I won't be held responsible.'

'It's more likely to be the making of it,' she reassured him.

'My original offer of Dawn's job still stands. We'll see how you feel when you get back.'

Following her slight figure and pale blond head as they left the restaurant, he wondered how much Richard appreciated his wife, and whether he had the vaguest inkling of the silent battle going on inside her. He rather thought not.

'At least Richard won't imagine you in the arms of a lover,' he said with a smile, as they stood together on the pavement, 'when he realizes whose house you are borrowing.'

Laura smiled back. 'I have an idea I may not tell him,' she said.

She had come to this conclusion only the previous weekend, when the idea of escaping was still in its embryo stage. The girls had gone to play tennis on the local courts with two of Hannah's friends, a reluctant Annabelle having been press-ganged into making a fourth. Rick was preparing *coq au vin* for supper, while Laura peeled potatoes. The sight of the ingredients and implements laid out in orderly precision, and the sound of his humming made the irritation rise in her throat to boiling point. The knife slipped, slicing her finger and turning the potato water pink. She muttered an expletive.

He glanced up. 'Cut yourself?' Handing her a handkerchief, he said, 'Better to use the peeler. Go and put something on it. I'll finish off for you.'

'The day I'm incapable of peeling a bloody potato,' she said furiously, throwing the knife on the draining board, 'is the day I leave home.'

'Hey! Hey! Hey! What's all this?' he asked mildly above the chopping of mushrooms.

19

She drew a deep breath, pulled herself together. 'How long will you be, doing that?' she said as calmly as possible. 'Because I meant what I said, and I'd like to talk about it.'

'All right. We'll talk about "it", whatever "it" is,' he said amenably. 'I'll be about ten minutes. Could you turn on the oven to 300° before you go?'

Ten minutes, while she found a plaster for her finger, gave her time to think about what she was going to say to him. There was not much point in going over old ground which had been covered more than once in the past. A flat statement of intention was what she decided upon, against which he could argue as he liked, but she would stand firm.

In the kitchen, Rick put the casserole dish in the oven, tidied up methodically and considered meanwhile the strange phenomenon of pre-menstrual tension, from which Laura was undoubtedly suffering. It seemed to affect her badly; he might suggest she consult someone about it. Then he poured himself a drink and went to find her in the garden, where she was sitting in the dusk.

'It's a bit dark out here, isn't it?' he said.

'It's warm, and we won't be able to sit outside much longer.' The fact was that she found any sort of confrontation easier in the open air.

'I'm arranging to go away for a while,' she said without preamble.

'I see,' he said calmly, thinking how well the new climbing rose had done in its first year. 'Why didn't you tell me you wanted us to have a holiday on our own? The girls getting you down, are they? I agree Seaview wasn't an unqualified success.'

'Not us, me, alone.'

He was silent a moment. 'Why?' he asked finally, sounding curious rather than hurt.

'Because—' she searched for words which would explain her feeling succinctly and in one sentence, 'because I want to be in control of my own life for once.' Now she had said it, it sounded incredibly pompous. 'I've tried to explain it to you several times,' she added.

'This is all to do with going back to work, isn't it?' he said. 'I can't stop you, darling, but it would be better for Hannah and Annabelle if you didn't, in my opinion. Anyway,' he drank some of his whisky, 'it would make me feel inadequate, unable to take care of you properly.'

'That's just it. I feel inadequate,' she said, 'but it's not to do with work or no work. I've lost my sense of identity and I want to find it again.'

After a pause, he said, 'I rather thought identities melded together in a real marriage, as in all good partnerships.'

'I know you think that, and that's where we differ. Someone always has the upper hand.'

'I didn't realize I'd given you such a bad time,' he said huffily. He was hurt now, her words getting to him.

She touched his arm. 'You haven't. I'm not trying to be difficult, but I must do this soon or I'll become impossible. I won't go for long, and I'll come back a nicer person.'

In the gathering darkness she saw his well-shaped, pleasant face turned towards her thoughtfully. 'There isn't someone else involved in this?' he asked. 'You haven't met someone, have you?'

She shook her head, almost laughing. None of her explanations had made sense to him. 'Nothing like that.'

'I don't understand,' he said heavily. The girls had returned at that moment, arguing volubly about who was going to get the first bath.

21

Supper was eaten in the kitchen round the large pine table and conversation became general and mainly dominated by Hannah. Only she did justice to the *coq au vin*, which was as delicious as ever; Annabelle had a headache, and the appetites of Laura and Rick had dwindled. Later, despite the unpromising atmosphere which she had created, they made love, and Rick cheered up considerably. He lay for some time with his arm round her, talking. He quite agreed that she needed a break, he told her in warm loving tones; it wouldn't do him any harm either. It was too long since they had spent time on their own. The girls could stay with friends, or maybe his mother could be prevailed upon to hold the fort while they were away. He would get some brochures on Monday.

Laura lay awake long after he had fallen asleep, hopeless in her failure to explain herself to him. Psychologically separated from him, her lovemaking had been purely mechanical, but he had not seemed to notice the difference. Wide-eyed with sleeplessness, she stared into the darkness. It became increasingly clear to her that if she was to achieve her objective, she must up sticks and go without further warning. There was no alternative.

Laura put the suitcase in the boot of the car, together with a rug, a thermos flask of coffee, a bottle of whisky and her gumboots. From the driver's seat she made the mistake of glancing upwards at the house, at its unpretentious Victorian façade, mellow and friendly in the morning sun. It had been home for seven years: her hand hesitated over the ignition before starting the engine, her resolve wavering badly. Then she backed into the road more precipitously than usual and headed for the river with a lump in her throat. It was not until half-an-hour later on the M4 that the effect of her solitary leave-taking started to subside, to be replaced by a nervous elation. She had made a decision and carried it through: the beginnings of a new emancipation. Exhilarated, as if about to attempt the ascent of Everest, she slipped a tape into place, and the music of Vivaldi filled the car, until city became country and the Berkshire downs rolled away on her left.

It was a long time since she had driven any distance on her own. She had forgotten the monotony of it, leaving the mind empty to toy with the past, both immediate and far away. She found herself thinking of the previous night: lying in bed, her plans laid, dreading the effort of appearing normal in front of Rick. She was spared the strain. He had stayed up late, working on a speech for the firm's annual dinner; it was one o'clock before he climbed in beside her and she had feigned sleep. Her duplicity returned now, shaming her and taking the edge off her spirits. He was essentially good, he did not deserve such churlish treatment. His only sin was his obtuseness, a blank refusal to recognize a cry for help when he heard one; and even that applied solely to herself, it seemed, for he bent over backwards to understand Hannah's capricious behaviour.

Laura tried to remember if any of this had been apparent in the early days of their being together. They had been introduced by a friend who had gone to live in the country. Laura, who was waiting to be divorced from Patrick, and whose self-esteem had been dealt a crippling blow, had reluctantly accepted an invitation to stay the weekend.

'You should move to the country, too,' her friend Sarah had advised. 'That's where you'll meet the men.'

Recently released from her own marriage, she suffered none of Laura's bruised confidence; Laura had privately sworn never to get emotionally involved again. Richard Snow had been asked to lunch with his small daughter Annabelle, and Sarah behaved towards him as if she already had proprietorial rights. Laura was relieved: the man was claimed, there was no match-making intended. The day was sunny and geared to the children, who ran in and out of the garden sprinkler and the paddling pool, shrieking hysterically. Sarah produced a huge lunch and an equally large tea with calm efficiency, yelling at her two sons when their behaviour went over the top. Laura and Rick lay in deck-chairs making desultory conversation. Annabelle, three years older than the others, sat close to her father, shy and silent, and made tentative advances to an elderly spaniel.

There was no shyness in Rick. He talked easily and asked questions with the same eager facility. Laura did not encourage delving into her private life; Patrick's defection had left a raw place which did not bear touching. When her reticence slipped, a certain acidity crept into her answers which she was aware of and could not check. Richard Snow had broad, comfortable shoulders, eyes that sloped at the corners and crinkled pleasantly, and nice hands. He was knowledgeable about a lot of things and he leapt up whenever there was something to be done. Watching him take a loaded tray from Sarah, Laura decided they would be good for each other: two competent, uncomplicated people who had adjusted to bereavement and divorce respectively without fuss. She wondered if she would be asked to the wedding.

In the end, Laura recalled with a faint smile, Sarah came to hers.

She stretched, stiff from driving for an hour and a quarter. Pulling into the next lay-by, she unscrewed the thermos, poured coffee into the cap and stood by the car, drinking it while the traffic thundered past her to the west, casting its pollution in her face.

She had never known how much Sarah minded about Rick. If she felt any animosity towards Laura for usurping him, it never showed.

'By the way,' she had said when Laura rang to thank her for the weekend, 'Richard asked me for your phone number. You've obviously made a hit. Shall I give it to him?'

'No,' Laura replied unhesitatingly. It made no difference. Her name was in the directory, and over the following months he had pursued her with tenacity: a kind of obstinate persistence, she decided, screwing the top of the thermos back in place, that was in itself a clue to his character. She had no-one but herself to blame, allowing herself to be gradually wooed into security. The sheer luxury of being cared for had seduced her and drawn her into the final step. She had gone down, if not exactly fighting, then at least clinging feebly to the last remnants of her independence. It was eighteen months before she married him, on a wet day in January at Chelsea Register Office.

She sighed, re-seating herself behind the steering wheel. They had not lacked romance, those pre-nuptial eighteen months; the affair, conducted between her flat in Chiswick and his in Cadogan Gardens, had been exhausting but exhilarating. Cohabiting was out of the question with two small children; instead, they had driven hectically back and forth from one establishment to the other, dodging child-minders and forever leaving their toothbrushes in the wrong place. Days of wine and roses, she thought as she eased the car on to the motorway; and yet it had been a relief to be settled finally under one roof.

'Come and look,' Rick had called from upstairs.

It was their first visit to the house since it had been vacated by the previous owners. The empty and curtainless rooms echoed the sound of their footsteps and the excited voices of the children running from room to room. Laura found him standing by the window of what was to be their bedroom, looking out on to the garden.

'It's a bit of a mess,' he said, 'but there are some nice shrubs. I think we should do away with that awful bright pink patio and lay York stone.'

'Oh look, there's a sundial, covered in ivy,' she said, enchanted. 'I never noticed.'

'Don't you agree?' he insisted. 'About the stone.'

'What? Oh yes, I suppose so. Terribly expensive, though.' Her mind was half on furnishings, trying to visualize the walls stripped of their present insipid wallpaper and replaced with something of her imagination. 'Still, I suppose with both of us working, we'll manage all right.'

He turned slowly from the window. 'I've been meaning to talk about that,' he said. 'There's no need for you to work, you know; no need to worry.'

'I'm not worried,' she answered cheerfully. 'I enjoy what I do.'

'It might be better,' he continued calmly, 'if you spent more time at home; better, that is, from the children's point of view.'

Warning bells sounded faintly in her head. She said defensively, 'I'm away from them four days a week only, I take them to school and I'm back for bedtime. They adore Gaby, who's very good with them. I don't think they're deprived, Rick.'

'I wasn't suggesting they were,' he said mildly. 'But it would be good for Annabelle in particular to have you around, as a permanent fixture.'

This was moral blackmail. She felt suddenly very angry, as if her delicately constructed role as a stepmother was being criticized.

'We'll talk later, anyway,' he added, maddeningly understanding. 'This isn't the moment.'

Unable to speak, she had gone in search of the girls on the upper floor; Hannah, seven years old and Annabelle ten. Hannah was jumping up and down on a squeaking floorboard. 'This is going to be *my* room,' she announced unequivocally, dragging Laura into the largest of the top floor rooms. Annabelle hung back silently in the doorway, biting a thumbnail.

'Oh yes? Who says?' Laura asked.

'I say!' sang Hannah.

'Well, I've news for you. This will be Annabelle's room. Yours is the one next door.'

'Why?' Hannah stopped hopping up and down and stood still, her eyes, bright blue and hard as agates, on Laura's face.

'Because this one is bigger, and so is Annabelle. She needs more space for her things. No arguments.'

'But we'd chosen!' Hannah burst into noisy tears and went to sob on the stairs.

'I don't mind which I have. Honestly,' Annabelle told Laura. Her pale face creased anxiously beneath its dark fringe of hair.

'You may not mind, but I do,' Laura put an arm round her and gave her a hug. 'What do you think of the house? Do you think you'll like it?' she asked, ignoring the howls from nearby.

'I expect so, when I've got used to it. I've never lived anywhere except Cadogan Gardens, so it feels a bit odd, really.' Annabelle moved to the window. 'It'll be nice having a garden,' she said politely.

'It won't seem so odd when it's furnished and painted. I thought we'd have wallpaper in here, blue and white as it's your favourite. All right by you?'

Annabelle nodded. 'Shouldn't we go and cheer up Hannah?'

'She'll stop if nobody takes any notice of her,' Laura said, adding gently, 'You mustn't give into her always, darling. She's quite a little bully when she chooses, and it's bad for her to get her own way constantly.' She knew while she spoke that there was as much likelihood of Annabelle turning aggressive as a nun taking up arms. It was a problem that would either get better or worse as the girls grew older.

Rick's voice could be heard, uttering words of comfort by the sound of it. Hannah's cries stopped abruptly. When Laura and Annabelle descended, she was sitting on his knees on the stairs, her tear-stained face bulging with a gob-stopper.

'You shouldn't spoil her,' Laura said sharply. 'She'll go on throwing tantrums till she's twenty-one if you do.'

Hannah leant against Rick and glared balefully from her secure position, wisps of pale hair escaping her ponytail.

'She'll grow out of it,' Rick said with equanimity. 'Won't you, you funny little thing? Lunch at McDonald's, everyone?'

Laura's memory of that morning was not a particularly happy one. Rick's broad back seemed gently implacable as they filed down the staircase, Hannah chattering again, her skinny figure in direct contrast to Annabelle's stocky one. Laura was full of vague forebodings over a future which appeared to have been mapped out for her: a direct result of the new wedding ring on her finger. For a moment she queried the purchase of the house itself, for all its large windows and sunny aspect, and longed for her flat in Chiswick, which had had a view of the river.

But they had settled in, made the house home, been happy there.

They were still happy there basically, Laura told

herself, dismayed at her thoughts slipping so easily into the past tense. All at once hungry, she drew into the next service station with a restaurant, ate a leathery mushroom omelette and checked the mileage to Exeter on her map, where she intended breaking the journey for the night. She tried, unsuccessfully, not to think about the moment when she must speak to Rick.

Laura was not the only one to wonder about Rick's reactions. Annabelle, who had managed to push such thoughts to the back of her mind during a busy day, came out of school with a leaden feeling in the pit of her stomach. She dreaded handing over Laura's letter; for the first time since Laura had become her step-mother, Annabelle felt resentful at having been put in an unenviable position. It was nothing to do with her, it shouldn't be her responsibility. To make matters worse, she could see Hannah at the bus stop chatting to her cronies and tossing her hair back in an affected way. That meant they would have to travel home together on the same bus. On this day of all days Annabelle could have done without Hannah's company.

Both girls went to St Paul's, Hannah by means of a musical scholarship and Annabelle by dint of hard work. Their differing ages meant they rarely met during school hours, but occasionally, and particularly on Hannah's flute lesson days, their return journey co-incided. Hannah, Annabelle noticed as she approached slowly, had turned her grey pleated school skirt over at the waistband to convert it into a mini: strictly against the rules. In the Sixth Form, Annabelle was no longer obliged to wear uniform and rather missed it. It had solved the enigma of what to wear, and when you were painfully conscious of your weight, this could be a problem. Laura had pointed out that she had good legs and should show them. Somehow Annabelle had seldom found the courage, and felt happier hiding behind the camouflage of long, full skirts and loose sweaters. Standing beside Hannah made her feel large and shapeless as a pillow. She pulled a paperback from her pocket and read until the bus came.

She had hoped that Hannah would remain in a giggling mass with her mates, but she slipped onto the seat next to Annabelle, unwrapped a Penguin and offered her half. She shook her head.

'What do *you* think about Mum taking off like this?' Hannah asked through a mouthful.

Annabelle shrugged, unwilling to commit herself.

Hannah in a friendly and confiding mood was extremely suspect. 'You don't suppose she's got a *boyfriend*, do you?' She stared at Annabelle with round eyes.

'Don't be a clot. Of course she hasn't,' Annabelle said forcefully. 'She isn't that sort of person.'

'I don't know. She's quite pretty still.'

'Why shouldn't she have a holiday on her own? We probably drive her up the wall at times. Besides,' Annabelle added, 'she wants to write. You need to be alone for that.'

'Well, she hasn't told Rick,' Hannah persisted, 'and that's weird, if you ask me. I think they've had a row.'

'They never do, you know that. Anyway, Laura told me they haven't.'

'She tells you much more than she tells me,' Hannah remarked peevishly.

'Only because I'm older.'

'I suppose she's left her address with you, too?'

'She hasn't left an address,' Annabelle said, watching the boys from St Paul's straggling across Hammersmith Bridge.

'Well, that's a bit much, I must say,' Hannah observed. 'What happens if one of us has a terrible accident?'

30

'Oh, shut up, Hannah,' Annabelle said wearily. 'She's going to phone us each evening.' Her head ached, as it always did when she was faced with a problem – which seemed to be practically every day.

Hannah stayed silent for a full minute, picking flecks of chocolate off her skirt before saying, 'Who's going to tell Rick? Rather you than me.'

'Neither of us has to. She's left a letter, explaining everything. She's only away for a week or two,' Annabelle said, reassuring herself with the words.

Having flogged the subject to death, Hannah remembered another equally important item on her mind. 'It's Samantha's birthday disco on Saturday. Can I borrow your gold hoop earrings, please, Annie?'

'I suppose so, but don't lose them.'

'Thanks.' Hannah jumped up for their request stop. 'Who's going to cook supper tonight?' she asked as they got off the bus.

'Laura's made a steak-and-kidney stew. There's not much to do.'

'Goody. And Rick always cooks at the weekends, and it's Friday tomorrow.'

'There's the washing-up,' Annabelle reminded her laconically.

'Here comes your boyfriend,' Hannah said in a piercing whisper, changing the subject once again. 'I rather fancy him myself, but I'll be really tactful and push on.'

She drew ahead, flicking her hair self-consciously over her shoulders as she passed the tall boy walking towards them, and shooting him a flashing smile. Annabelle felt the hated colour rise up her face in a wave as he reached her. He was wearing a St Paul's jacket over jeans and was clutching an armful of books and a battered briefcase.

'Hi.'

'Hi.'

'How are things?' he asked, sounding as if he wanted to know. He had a thin, clever face and dark eyes behind spectacles.

'Awful,' Annabelle said on impulse.

'Work?'

'That, and – oh, just everything.'

'Not to worry. You'll sail through when the time comes. Pity me with Oxbridge looming. It's the interview I dread, not the exam. I'm no good at interviews.'

'Well, that's something I won't have to face. I'm not clever enough,' she said gloomily.

'How about taking in a film on Saturday to relieve the blues?'

'I don't know, Ben. I've got a great wodge of stuff to get through—'

'I'll give you a ring,' he said. 'Must go. 'Bye, Annie.'

' 'Bye.'

She walked home with new-found optimism. Even a promised telephone call was something. The beat of music from Hannah's room reverberated through the house as she opened the front door. There was no Laura to make her turn it down. Annabelle sighed, and poured herself a glass of milk cold from the fridge. In an hour or so Rick would return from work. Until then she would not be able to concentrate anyway, in which case there was not much point in banging on Hannah's door and telling her to cool it.

In a small bedroom of the Forte Hotel in Exeter, Laura unpacked the necessary things for the night, washed her hands and gazed imploringly at the clock which seemed stuck for ever between six and a quarter past. For the past hour she had filled in time by walking in the town and looking round the cathedral. The hushed vastness of the interior with its atmosphere of permanence had soothed her, and at the same time made her guilty. She knelt in one of the back rows of chairs and tried to pray, without success.

'I'm sorry, God,' were the only words which came to her silently moving lips, and those were false, because she had no real regrets apart from possibly hurting Rick's feelings. Impatient with herself, she rose and made her way out, leaving a pound in the repairs fund box as she left. And now, with half-an-hour to go before it was any use phoning Rick, she took her bottle of whisky from the cupboard, poured herself a drink and switched on the television news to watch fifteen minutes of world tragedy.

When she finally dialled home, it was Annabelle who answered and handed her straight over to Rick.

'I'm going to another phone,' he said curtly, so that, between the click of one receiver and the lifting of the other, she realized this was not going to be made easy for her. 'Hello,' he said in the same tone.

'Hello, darling. I'm just ringing to make sure you're all right.' There was silence. 'Rick? Are you there? Do say something.'

'I would have thought it was up to you to do the talking.'

'I've tried to explain everything in my letter. Haven't you read it yet?'

'Yes, I've read it, and it explained nothing.' In a voice that shook with anger and wounded pride, he said, 'Laura, how could you do it? Take off like this without a word of warning. It's beyond comprehension—'

'I gave you warning; don't you remember? Told you I wanted time on my own for a bit – and you didn't understand then.' In the face of his censoriousness, her own temper started to rise.

'I thought we'd agreed to go away together. We'd started to plan it.' He added in a low voice, 'You

33

lay there last night, knowing you were leaving in the morning, and keeping utterly silent about it. Don't you realize how hurtful that was?'

'Don't *you* realize what it's like to lose a life of one's own, all sense of who you are? And to be patronized.' The words were out, too inflamed as she was to stop them.

'I've never patronized you in my life,' he said, violently for Rick. 'Perhaps you shouldn't have married me, if that's the way you feel.'

Perhaps I shouldn't, Laura thought, suddenly weary of this unaccustomed battle. 'Do we have to row?' she asked.

There was a short pause. 'When do you intend coming back?' he asked heavily. 'Or don't you?'

'That's not fair, Rick. I'm only going for a week, or possibly two.'

'And I gather you're not giving me an address or phone number,' he said, 'so that if there's a crisis I have no means of reaching you.'

Sarcasm had taken the place of indignation, so out of character it made her more wretched than his anger. 'So that I can be anonymous for a short while.' And in order that she should not be deflected from her course of action. 'It's no use even trying to make you see. But I'll telephone each day; I shan't be out of reach.' He did not answer. 'Please, Rick. Can't we be amicable about this? It's not much to ask. Are the girls all right?'

She heard him take a deep breath. 'As far as I know. I've only seen Annabelle. Hannah is belting out loud music in her room, if that's what you can call it.'

'Then make her stop. Be firm.'

'Do you want to speak to them?'

'Tomorrow, I think. Give them my love.' She paused, added, 'I do love you, Rick. You know that.'

'You have a funny way of showing it,' he said

34

heavily. 'I'd better go now, see what's happening about supper.'

'I left a stew to put in the oven. Annabelle knows. Good night, darling. I'll talk to you tomorrow.'

'If I'm here.'

'What do you mean?'

'I might be out. I might take them to have supper somewhere. After all, as you've so forcibly demonstrated,' he said, 'we should all be in control of our own lives.'

On this rather childish jibe he said good night and the line went dead. After the initial sense of guilt had worn off, Laura felt relief. The first call was bound to be the worst; his temper would cool. He might possibly enjoy being without her for a time. She asked for sandwiches in her room, poured a second drink and started to chart out her own directions for the following day from the map, using a sheet of hotel writing paper.

Chapter Two

Friday, the day after Laura's departure, had been one of the toughest to survive that Rick could remember. Not since the death of his first wife, Miranda, had a day at work seemed so long and tedious. Colleagues kept asking after Laura, or suggesting they both come to supper, as if there was a kind of conspiracy to worm the truth out of him; which was ridiculous, for how could they possibly know he had been deserted? He normally stopped on the bridge on his way home and gazed at the river, at the houseboats and the silvered water, and the white specks of gulls on the mud flats. Tonight he pressed on without looking, disliking the weather for being fine and still in its Indian summer, wishing only to reach his front door, forgetting for a moment that there was little consolation behind it. Facing him also was the effort of keeping up a façade of cheerfulness in front of the children; of hiding the fact that he was seriously disturbed by Laura's behaviour.

He could hear sounds from the kitchen as he stood in the hall: the chink of a saucepan lid, the voices of the girls raised in dispute, the splashing of a fast-running tap. 'Oh! You cow, Annie, you've showered me with water.'

'Well, don't stand in the way, then. I've done the potatoes, you chop the beans.'

'Hi,' he called, sifting through the mail.

Hannah came swiftly, giving him an effusive hug. 'You're in the nick of time. I was about to stab Annie. She's being bloody bossy.'

It crossed his mind to say something about her language, habitually awful, but he did not have the energy. Annabelle appeared in the kitchen doorway, her face flushed, reminding him strongly of Miranda.

'I've defrosted the chops. Is that all right for supper?' she asked.

'Fine,' he said, kissing her. 'But I thought we might all eat out, give ourselves a treat.'

'What about the chops?' she said dubiously. 'And I've peeled potatoes.'

'Great!' Hannah said. 'Can we go to "The Stable"? The food's something else there.'

'Everything'll keep in the fridge,' Rick said. 'We'll eat it tomorrow.'

'I'm going to Samantha's disco tomorrow,' Hannah said. 'All that slaving in the kitchen for nothing.' She sighed dramatically.

'You dried two spoons,' Annabelle told her witheringly.

'That's settled then,' Rick said with cultivated brightness. 'I'm going to have a bath. Seven forty-five take-off time, all right? What on earth are you wearing?' he asked Hannah, raising his eyebrows at black leggings, topped by a shrunken grey jersey with holes, and what appeared to be the tails of a man's shirt trailing beneath it.

'It's called "grunge". It's the in-thing, Rick, I always wear it. You just haven't noticed.'

'Well, change the sweater at least.'

'Oh, all right. If I *must*.'

He did not in fact want the bother of bathing; it was an excuse to be unavailable if Laura phoned. He was not trying to punish her by this evasive action; he quite simply did not know how to talk to her at present. Lying immersed in hot water, he tried, as he had done for half the previous night, to sort out his thoughts and to put the situation into perspective. He had made a serious attempt at this, and managed to divide her actions in two, reaching the conclusion that it was not what she had done that hurt, so much as the way in which she had done it. It pointed to insensitivity on his part, that he had not sensed her desperation. It showed an ever-widening gap in their marriage which he had not known existed. However hard he pursued the enigma, he could not make out when or how that gap began, and, therefore, how to close it. It seemed to him that their marriage had worked, looking back over seven years of it, considering each of their widely disparate children and the traumas of their previous attachments. He loved her, was in love with her still, and had lived under the apparently false impression that she felt the same for him. All he had set out to do, smoothing paths for her in order to erase memories of the abominable Patrick, had been flung back in his face. The word 'patronize', her choice of accusation, remained indelibly printed in his mind, wounding him painfully.

He stepped out of the bath and wrapped a towel round himself. The burr of the telephone sounded faintly above the noise of escaping water, and stopped after several rings. He imagined her voice speaking either to Annabelle or Hannah, and was seized with a sudden longing to hear her. Sitting on the side of the bath, he dried between his toes lethargically. Through his self-pity seeped the uncomfortable suspicion of his own shortcomings. He had gently but relentlessly persuaded her to give up her work. Was this where the trouble started? It had been from the best motives, but that did not alter the fact of his possibly dogmatic insistence. She minded, and he had not listened. Nor had he listened when she told him what she intended to do. He heard her and did not want to know; only half-believed her talk of needing space and losing identity. He had failed to understand because he did not wish to. The idea of her wanting to escape from him, even for a short period of time, frightened him deeply.

He took a long look at his face in the bathroom mirror, as if assessing its value, seeing well arranged features, apart from the nose – knocked slightly askew from a cricket ball years before – and a very square jaw-line which denoted determination. Or obstinacy, Laura had pointed out to him laughingly and not so long ago. We don't laugh enough these days, he said out loud, all at once aware of the fact.

Someone banged on the door. 'Mum's on the phone. Are you going to speak to her?' Hannah shouted.

'I'm dripping wet,' he answered untruthfully. 'Tell her I'll talk next time.'

Annabelle was listening to Laura. 'Part of the house is built into the cliff-side. And the windows look over the mouth of the harbour. I wish you could see it, it's so peaceful.' She sounded enormously happy.

Annabelle pictured it clearly, smelt the sea and saw the boats clustered by the quay.

'Are you getting on all right?' Laura was asking. 'No crises?'

'We're all right,' Annabelle said, trying to sound ordinarily bright. 'Daddy's taking us out to supper.'

'Lovely. Enjoy yourselves. Think of me eating scrambled egg in solitary state.'

How wonderful that would be, thought Annabelle: eating alone, looking out at the slowly darkening water, not having to listen to Hannah's interminable voice gabbling on. 'Do you want to speak to Daddy?' she asked. 'Oh, Hannah says he's in the bath. I have to get tidied up, Laura. I'm glad it's nice where you are,' she added with an effort. She handed the receiver over to

Hannah, feeling unaccountably lonely. Up in her room she changed one full long skirt for another in black, which made her look thinner. She concentrated hard on going to a film with Ben the following night.

While Rick dressed, he regretted not sending his love to Laura via the children, deliberately withholding it. It showed a meanness of spirit.

Laura sat at the round table by the kitchen window, eating toast and watching the cloud shadows on the limb of land across the harbour mouth. She could not stop looking at the sea; every window beckoned her to drop whatever she was doing and gaze from it in reverie. It was the second full day after her arrival, and the day before had gone by mainly spent in this blissfully contemplative way, while the embryo of a poem swam in and out of her mind at intervals. There would come a time, she supposed, when she would do something positive, but there was no urgency.

From the moment of her arrival, her surroundings had enchanted her. Driving into St Merric and round the harbour, she had followed the steep and winding street and stopped at the post office for directions. The house stood on its own behind white-painted gates, with 'Cliff House' inscribed in black. The sound of her car had brought Gerard's cleaner to the door, a woman with a comfortable bosom who introduced herself as April August. Forewarned by Gerard of the unlikely name, Laura was unastonished, following April's solid figure into the hallway and then into a double bedroom.

'The bedrooms are by the front door,' April explained in soft Cornish accents. 'The house is built into the cliff, see.'

'Upside down,' Laura said, smiling. There were bay windows everywhere, she discovered as April led her on a conducted tour. Reflections from the sea filled each one of the rooms with light, bouncing off the pastel colours of walls and ceilings. Gerard's Oliver was an interior decorator and it showed in the simple chintzes and the modern art displayed here and there. 'Hardly your usual seaside cottage,' Laura said to herself, thinking how good of them it was to let her stay.

'There's milk and butter in the fridge,' April was saying. 'The shops close an hour lunchtime, but they'll be open s'afternoon for what you want.' Her cloud of frizzy hair was the colour – artificial – of daffodils, appropriate to her first name. Laura liked her, she went with the place. 'I come Mondays and Fridays 'less you want me more,' she added. 'Got the keys safe now, have you, m'dear?'

When she had gone, Laura opened her bedroom window and leaned her arms on the sill. To the left she could see the harbour and the boats bobbing skittishly on ruffled water, the village street with its houses painted pink and white snaking downhill beside the quay. To the right was the open sea. Below her the only thing visible was a cluster of black rocks, the sea washing at them and slipping back with a sigh. She went downstairs and let herself out of a back door to explore.

There was a semi-circular flagged terrace with a table and chairs in front of the living-room. She peered over a low parapet and caught her breath, momentarily dizzy. The garden seemed to drop a sheer forty feet to the rocks. She realized after a second that this was an optical illusion, that it was in fact a very steep slope, built out in tiny terraces like vineyards in Italy seen from a distance. The miniature flower beds grew fuchsias and thyme and a variety of rock plants, bright against the grey of their supporting stones. It struck her how perilous it must be to garden there, balancing awkwardly against the incline. The cliff was not very high compared with the ones of her childhood holidays spent in North Cornwall, but enough to cause a nasty accident if you missed your footing.

A small jetty jutted out from the rocks; Gerard and Oliver owned a sailing boat, presumably moored further down in the harbour. Above her head seagulls wheeled and planed, uttering their plaintive, lost-soul cries. Here she would be able to write, here there was peace.

Later she had walked down to the village and bought a bottle of wine and a copy of *The Times* so that she could attempt the crossword. The bakery sold home-made bread, still warm to the touch, and the fishmonger who filleted plaice for her wore a straw hat, as had all fishmongers in years past. It was as if she had been transported back in time.

The summer crowds had gone, leaving the village to the locals, judging by the scraps of conversation of people in the shops and the street. Laura paused by the quay and took a closer look at the boats below her, knocking against each other's bumpers in the brisk, north-westerly breeze. It was several degrees colder than in London, and she was glad of her Arran sweater and an anorak as she walked home. It was a steeper climb than it appeared. Ahead of her the figure of an elderly woman in a felt hat toiled slowly upwards with a dog on a lead. By the time Laura reached the house, the woman was leaning on her stick and gazing in open speculation at Laura's car in the driveway.

'Good afternoon,' Laura said, amused.

The woman smiled, quite unperturbed. 'Hello, my dear. Staying with Gerard, are you?' She had a pink face framed in soft white curls, and wore the hat at a rakish angle. Her expression was ingenuous.

Nosy, thought Laura. 'Gerard isn't here, I'm afraid. He's kindly lent me the house.'

'How nice. I'm Eleanor Shawcross. I have a cottage

near the church.' She waved her stick at the hilly background of St Merric. 'Quite a climb for someone with arthritis, but we manage.' She watched Laura with small, bright blue eyes as she spoke, summing her up. 'Well, I must be going. Have a pleasant stay. I'm sure we'll meet again.'

'I'm sure we will,' agreed Laura politely, hoping it was not too often. Constant interruption from callers was not part of her plan.

She explored the house for the second time, peeping into the other two bedrooms, both immaculate. There was the pink room and the blue room; she had been given the yellow, with a bowl of late yellow roses on the dressing-table. There were books everywhere, on bedside tables and shelves, and a bookcase in the living-room filled the whole of one wall. It was unnecessary to have brought reading matter. Here the bay windows curved the length of the room, and opposite them was an open fireplace stacked with logs ready to be lit. Laura let out a sigh of sheer contentment, quickly followed by a stab of conscience. She had expected comfort, knowing Gerard, but not of this standard. It would have been easier to reconcile the conscience with an ill-equipped hovel. Once she started to think about Rick and the girls, a large proportion of her happiness evaporated, and the imminent telephone call she must make impinged still further.

When she did ring, she was secretly relieved to be spared the tension of speaking to Rick. He was in the bath by design, she was quite aware of that, which meant that he had not come to terms with her escape.

Preparing herself for Samantha's disco, Hannah gyrated around her room full of pre-party fever. She was dressed so far in psychedelic tights and T-shirt only; she had still to find the black hot-pants buried somewhere

43

in a mound of discarded clothing. 'Da-da-dee-dee-da, da-da-da,' she sang in time to the compact disc, beating out the rhythm on imaginary drums, letting her hair fall forwards across her face and tossing it back sexily.

She paused in front of the mirror and caught the hair back with both hands, frowning. Then she went to bang on Annabelle's door and open it simultaneously.

'Can I have the earrings, please, Annie?'

Annabelle handed them over. 'Don't you ever wait to be asked in?'

'I knocked. Thanks, Annie.'

'If you lose one, I'll kill you.'

'I won't.' Hannah da-dee'd her way back to her own room and set about seriously searching through the pile of clothes.

'And turn that thing down!' Annabelle shouted.

She was not, in fact, working, but doing the same as Hannah in a less flamboyant manner: trying to find something suitable to wear. Hannah would never have her problems, though, being thin as a rake. Annabelle envied her. She supposed it didn't really matter what she wore to a film, but going with Ben made a subtle difference. From a feminist point of view she knew this to be politically incorrect, minding what men thought; but then she wasn't much of a feminist. Ben had lovely dark eyes, and she found him attractive. It worried her that he had never kissed her properly, when most of the girls in her term had gone a lot further than that with people, if you believed them. She stared in the mirror as Hannah had done, but without the self-satisfaction, pulling her hair back so that only the fringe showed. Her face was oval, her eyes large and brown; they were the best part of her. If she half-closed them, she could just imagine a resemblance to the barmaid in Manet's *Folies-Bergère*. Laura had told her that she had a Madonna's face; Laura was always trying to boost her confidence. Annabelle could have done with a little encouragement right now, but Laura was missing.

She heard Rick come upstairs and tap on Hannah's door. 'Can you turn the volume down a bit, darling, please?'

Honestly, she thought, how pathetic. Doesn't he realize you've got to sound really furious to make an impact on Hannah? Then she felt suddenly remorseful because they were both going out and leaving her father alone. She started to apply mascara, to accentuate the best feature: her eyelashes glued together.

Rick, who had quite looked forward to an evening on his own, was feeling all at once unconvinced. He had watered the plants in the garden that he considered were suffering from the dry weather, and now found himself at a loss for something to do. This was a rare occurrence for him; he was a person who had a mass of interests at his fingertips. If there was nothing to be constructed, such as shelves, or taken apart and mended like recalcitrant toasters, there was always a new recipe with which to experiment. In between times, he read: biographies occasionally, but mostly history. At the moment he was delving into the American Civil War and had a pile of books on the subject by his bedside. Now he seemed to have lost the incentive for any of these activities. Laura not being there had rendered him curiously enfeebled, as if she had taken his powers of concentration with her. Thinking about it, he realized he missed her, not only for obvious reasons, but for her positive quality. She discussed things, argued with him, frequently disagreed. Miranda had been so very different, happy to go along with his ideas: the provider of a passive and contented background. He had grown used to her placidity, had never quite readjusted to Laura's positivity. Now it had been withdrawn, he was vaguely beginning to understand why, although he still felt it was a cruel way to make her point. He sighed. It all seemed so unnecessary: life was no fun without her. He poured himself a drink and switched on the television, tried all channels, switched it off again.

'Will you be OK on your own?' Annabelle asked from the doorway.

'Fine, darling, thank you.' He looked at her. 'You've done something to your hair.'

'Does it look all right?'

'Mmm. Nice. It suits you.' He knew Laura would have said something more, well, *positive* for want of another word. 'Ben will see you home, won't he?'

'Daddy, he always does.' She added pointedly, 'Hannah's the one who needs supervising.'

'I don't have to on this occasion. She's staying the night.'

'Why don't you ring someone up? Go and see someone?' she suggested.

'Darling, because I don't want to. Stop trying to organize me.' He gave her a kiss, grateful for her anxiety. 'I've planned my evening.'

Nevertheless, when Annabelle had left and he had driven Hannah to her party, he started to search through the telephone numbers in his diary. Laura's call caught him off-guard, he had momentarily forgotten the arrangement. He had meant to unbend towards her, to bridge the gap between them, but try as he might, all he could remember was the unfairness of her behaviour. The conversation was short and stilted. He was well, she was well, the children were well. The weather was good both ends of the line. Pride prevented him from asking how long she was staying. He put down the receiver on this unsatisfactory conclusion, and returned to his diary, realizing suddenly his need to talk to somebody. Not the ordinary discussions of the chattering classes on the government, or the stock market, or the state of the world, but only about his own world and how it seemed to be falling apart. He turned to the obvious choice in his list of numbers and phoned Sarah Pemberton, who had introduced them, and who was, after all, eminently sensible.

Laura had lost track of time. It was not until she heard the church bells that she realized it was Sunday. The sound drifted down from high up in the village and across the fields to where she was walking by the estuary. She had decided at last to make some sort of routine for herself before the slothful existence became ingrained: exercise in the morning, writing in the afternoon. To return home without having achieved anything apart from a change of scene would be degrading, and the poem in her head demanded to be put down on paper. Action would help to disperse her lingering attacks of guilt.

She had followed the cliff path to where it descended steeply and became pastureland, intersected by dry stone walls. The cliffs had dwindled in size, becoming no more than sharply inclined banks holding back the waters of the estuary. Here at its mouth the stretch of water was wide, perhaps a mile to the opposite side. Trawlers lay at anchor, along with the long hulk of an oil tanker in the distance. Small sail boats scudded before the wind; a power boat skimmed and bounced, heading for the open sea, bringing Patrick to Laura's mind. Patrick, who had worshipped anything to do with speed: cars, power boats, fast ski-ing. They had had no money to speak of when she married him, but there always appeared to be some aquaintance or other willing to lend him a boat or a car or a part of a chalet. Thinking back, it seemed to her he was forever wearing a crash helmet. There had been an excitement about those early days. They had practically nothing in common, but she had loved him with an aching intensity. When Hannah was born, things changed. Laura could not spend every weekend watching him pursue his hair-raising activities with a baby to look after. But there was no lack of other women happy to stand and applaud.

Eighteen months after Hannah, a second baby was born, a boy, who had lived only twenty-four hours. Laura felt it was all her fault: something had gone seriously wrong with the birth. She mourned for a long while. Patrick had loved Hannah in an off-hand sort of way, alternately cuddling her or ignoring her. Laura used to think the son they did not have after all might have saved the marriage. Now she knew better; children were not good material for creating emotional cement. Patrick had married a girl called Trish. He and Laura were perfectly amicable, and he had Hannah to stay each holiday, spoiling her rotten so that she came back rather more impossible than before.

James, the baby, had been christened by a hospital Sister. Laura thought about him from time to time, following his age in her mind. He would be almost thirteen. She pictured him walking with her now over the sheep-cropped grass, stopping to watch the boats, telling her endless technical facts as boys of that age did, knowing it all. He would have already grown taller than her, and soon his voice would be starting to growl and squeak. She thought about this quite dispassionately and out of curiosity, with only a twinge of original sadness.

Her musings had taken her across three fields, and the estuary had begun to narrow. The sharp, sweet air had a river tang to it now, the smell of mud mixed with the sea. Ahead of her lay woods coming down to the water's edge; it was tempting to explore further. But the calves of her legs already ached from unaccustomed exercise: another day, she decided, and started to re-trace her steps, the wind whipping her hair backwards like a blond flag.

Mrs Shawcross, the felt hat rammed firmly on her head, was sitting on a stone bench a few yards from the gates to Cliff House, where the path ended and the road began. She raised her stick in salute. Laura wished uncharitably that she had made her walk last longer; something warned her that Mrs Shawcross might be intrusive.

'Good morning, my dear. Enjoy your walk?'

Laura had the impression the woman had been lying in wait for her. 'It was wonderful.' She bent to pat the terrier scrabbling at her jeans. 'What happens beyond the woods?'

'Down, Tigger.' Mrs Shawcross yanked the dog's lead. 'There's a path of sorts all the way to St Just-in-Roseland. It's a long walk, but it's worth it.'

'What a lovely name.'

'You should visit the church. It stands by the edge of the estuary – twelfth century. Has its own landing stage so that people can arrive by boat.' Her pink-and-white complexion crumpled a little in regret. 'I used to go there quite often. Now, I'm afraid I have to rely on the kindness of others to drive me.'

'I shall certainly go to see it while I'm down here,' Laura told her. 'I'll take you.' There, she silently admonished herself, I am already committing myself.

'I'd better be moving on,' Mrs Shawcross sighed, struggling upright. 'May I take your arm, my dear, as far as your house? What's your name, by the way?'

'Laura Snow.'

They walked slowly, Eleanor Shawcross's grasp on Laura a surprisingly firm one, which did not let up when they came to a halt by the gates.

'Would you like to come in?' Laura asked, capitulating. 'For coffee or a drink?'

Mrs Shawcross said, 'How kind. Another time. I'm a little tired now, and I'd like to get home.' She straightened herself determinedly, her eyes on Laura's face. 'I suppose you wouldn't like to see my little cottage? Not a patch on Gerard's mansion, but we could have a glass of sherry.'

'That would be very nice,' Laura said, saying goodbye to the rest of the morning. 'And how about my driving you?' she added wryly, since Mrs Shawcross was gazing hopefully at the car.

'How thoughtful.'

Her cottage in St Merric's hinterland was reached by an almost perpendicular narrow road, up which the Metro struggled bravely. The interior of the house was cluttered with the accoutrements of a different era, a larger establishment. Tallboys and bureaux huddled beside an inordinate collection of small pie-crust tables; every surface was decorated with delicate pieces of porcelain, silver and china snuff-boxes and photographs in silver frames. Every inch of wall space was taken up by pictures, some of them, Laura guessed with her limited knowledge, rather good watercolours. The room smelt of musty pot pourri until Mrs Shawcross opened a window and let in the salt breeze. The views across the harbour were breathtaking. Laura accepted a cut-glassful of sherry and gingerly edged her way to an upright chair. Mrs Shawcross seated herself on a Victorian velvet sofa, which she shared with the terrier, his head in her lap.

'Tell me about yourself, Laura. Are you convalescing?'

Laura pictured herself draped on a chaise longue, smelling salts at hand. She smiled. 'Not exactly. Just taking a break.'

'I suppose,' said Mrs Shawcross, 'you're one of those hard-working young women executives trying to run a family home and a business? I imagine it's exhausting. You look a little tired, if I may say so.'

'I can't claim to be doing anything so strenuous, I'm afraid.'

'But you have a family?' Mrs Shawcross enquired, eyeing the wedding ring on Laura's finger. 'I feel sure—'

'I have a husband, a daughter and a stepdaughter. We live in Barnes in London. I am not particularly hard-working, but I have left them at home because the children are at school and because I am trying to write poetry. I need to be alone to do that.' Laura hoped this brisk résumé of her affairs would satisfy Mrs Shawcross's curiosity.

'Your husband sounds an understanding man,' she said sweetly. 'And can he cope?'

'No' to the first and 'yes' to the second; the words sprang to Laura's lips, but were left unsaid. 'He's one of those people,' she said flatly, 'who's terribly competent at everything.'

'My dear, how brave!'

'Brave?'

'To leave your husband footloose and fancy-free. You must be very sure of him,' Mrs Shawcross murmured gently. 'I wouldn't have thought it wise with my late husband Alec, but then the young these days—' Her voice trailed away.

'We trust each other,' Laura said, shocked into laughter. 'Is this your husband?' she asked to change the subject, peering at the photograph of a man in ceremonial uniform, his face obscured beneath a bristling moustache and a plumed helmet.

'Dear Alec, yes.' Mrs Shawcross did not elaborate. 'Help yourself to sherry, Laura, to save me getting up.

So you write poetry, do you? You should meet Mark Wainwright. He was a don at Oxford. Now he teaches, crams boys for exams. A literary man. Lives by himself about a mile away on the upper road.'

Laura said firmly, 'I don't really want to meet people, Mrs Shawcross. The idea is for me to be alone.'

'Like Greta Garbo,' said Mrs Shawcross with a little trilling laugh. 'And call me Eleanor. You don't get lonely in Gerard's house, then? It is quite isolated. I hope you lock up properly at night.'

'I'm not lonely, I love it; and I don't suppose St Merric is overrun with crime, is it?'

'No. But times change. There have been incidents that wouldn't have happened ten years ago. But I don't mean to frighten you—' Mrs Shawcross smiled at Laura, her blue eyes innocent.

Laura swallowed the last of her drink. 'I must be going,' she said, carefully avoiding the *objets d'art* while she shook hands. 'Thank you so much for the sherry. Your cottage is lovely.'

'My pleasure, my dear. Forgive me for not seeing you off.' Mrs Shawcross hesitated. 'I have a favour to ask.'

'Yes?'

'When you go for a walk, I wonder if you'd take Tigger with you occasionally. I can't give him much exercise, and he does love a run.'

This is the thin end of the wedge, Laura thought. The dog thumped his tail. 'Of course. I'd be delighted,' she said.

'I shall take you up on your offer of a coffee one of these mornings,' Mrs Shawcross assured her.

'Do.'

The old witch, Laura thought as she put the car into gear and drove slowly down the steep incline. There was a manipulator if ever she saw one. If she did not watch out, her precious solitude would be relentlessly invaded. She supposed it was one of the hazards of living in a village.

She let herself into Gerard's house with a sense of relief and space. There would be no intrusion this afternoon. The sun streamed through the kitchen windows, belying the cold wind, inviting her outside to the terrace. She made a huge sandwich packed with ham and lettuce, and carried it out with a glass of wine to sit at the wooden table. There she ate in a gloriously slovenly manner, licking her fingers while the sun warmed her face and the gulls soared above the rippling water.

The young man walked slowly down the lower road to St Merric, the same route Laura had taken three days previously. He had travelled a long way, hitch-hiking and walking, and he was limping slightly from a blister on one heel. A keen wind from the sea penetrated his shapeless navy blue sweater, but he was not aware of it. He seldom noticed heat or cold. He did not stop to untie the grubby anorak looped round his waist. Under one arm he carried an artist's portfolio, and two carrier bags full of his worldly possessions dangled from his other hand.

He wandered lopsidedly by the harbour wall, his eyes skimming the line of shingle for seabirds. Drawing and painting birds was what he did for money; not that it brought much in, but it was the only thing he could do reasonably well. There was a group of strutting sandpipers, plenty of seagulls and a bird he could not identify which might have been a curlew. He knew he would have to get cleaned up before trying to flog anything. His own nostrils could detect a faintly sour smell which he supposed could only be coming from himself. He had been sleeping rough for three nights now; last night the long-distance lorry driver who had given him his final lift, had let him sleep in the cab. It had made a nice change from ditches and woods. The one or two inhabitants passing by on the harbour road were giving him sharp looks of suspicion. It was not going to be easy to find somewhere to wash. The neat white hotel on the bend was out of the question; it was too smart, they would almost certainly turn him away.

Halfway up the winding main street he saw the Ship and Anchor pub. He hesitated at the entrance, walked on a few paces. To the side was an alleyway; 'Gents' and 'Ladies' were written side by side above two latched wooden doors. He tried the Gents tentatively; there was no-one there. It was less primitive than it appeared from the outside; there were wash-basins with soap and a towel on a hook. The water ran hot. He searched in one of the carrier bags and found a throw-away razor and a small towel of his own. In the mirror over the basins he stared at his reflection: a thin face with a dark growth of stubble, dark troubled eyes, dark brown hair in need of shampoo. He did not possess shampoo, or shaving-soap. He washed all he could of himself with the block of Palmolive, scraping away at the worst of the stubble until there was only a blue shadow left around his jaw. A man came in from an inner door, whistling, said 'Afternoon' and showed no more interest. When he had gone, the young man combed his hair, the mirror showing up a less disreputable presentation of himself.

Before leaving, he counted the money in his purse; a five pound note and some loose change. He found the public bar and bought a glass of cider and a ham roll. Then he went to sit on the harbour wall to eat and drink, watching the gulls riding the choppy water. He had not set out to reach St Merric; he had not even known it was called St Merric until the lorry driver had told him. When he had started his journey, it was with the vague idea of heading west, that was all. Now he was here, it seemed a good place to be: it had the right vibes.

Remembering something, he pulled a bottle of pills from the pocket of his anorak and poured the contents into the palm of one hand, counting the small blue capsules with a finger. He swallowed one with the last of the cider, frowning into the sun; only a dozen left. Besides money, this was his chief worry, running out of pills. This was how the trouble usually started. He put the bottle back in the pocket and tried to forget about them. His eyes travelled up the village street, judging where he should begin his door to door attempt at selling a drawing. He did not feel like facing this hopeless endeavour; he longed to curl up and go to sleep somewhere, preferably in a bed. It seemed a long time since he had slept in a proper bed.

'Time for lunch, I think,' Rick said at one o'clock on Sunday. 'I've made a kedgeree. Pop it in the oven, would you, darling?'

He was in the garden, doing some autumn pruning, and Annabelle was raking up for him. It was not the best time to have chosen; it had rained the night before, and the shrubs had brought down a constant shower of water on his head and shoulders. But outdoor activity was preferable to skulking indoors with the Sunday papers, his mind elsewhere. It was the only antidote to a gnawing sense of failure.

'You and Hannah have the kedgeree,' Annabelle said. 'I'm not very hungry.'

'You must eat something.'

'I'll have a salad.'

She disappeared inside the house, leaving him feeling unwarrantably irritated. What was the point of bothering to cook for them if nobody ate? From an upstairs window came the sound of Hannah's flute, a sweeter sound than the cacophony of pop music, but nevertheless oddly plaintive. A Sunday gloom hung over the house and garden. Earlier in the day Hannah had tackled him about going to some concert or other, and he had turned down her demand, knowing perfectly well this was what Laura would have done in his place. Quite likely Hannah had already asked her, and was trying it out on him as being a soft touch. Now she was making a statement with her soulful music.

He rammed the last of the prunings into a plastic sack and turned his thoughts to Sarah Pemberton. She was coming to London early in the week and they were to have dinner together; the one bright spot in the near future. The idea of unburdening himself to a close friend was overwhelmingly appealing. Strangely enough, she had not seemed particularly surprised to hear of Laura's defection over the telephone. Doubtless she would elaborate on this when they met; he knew he could rely on her for an unbiased opinion.

Annabelle opened the oven door and slipped the kedgeree inside without looking. Her stomach rumbled faintly. Presumably, if you stuck to a diet, your stomach shrank and you no longer had hunger pangs. The problem was that Rick would eventually notice she was slimming, and disapprove. She would face that one when she came to it. It was quite possible to live on salads and fruit; look at all the people who were vegetarian. Low fat cottage cheese could supply the protein. She would try it for a week and see how many pounds she lost at the end of it.

Nothing had gone really wrong the previous evening, and yet she felt deflated, as if it had not come up to her expectations. After the film, she and Ben had had a pizza, and then he suggested coffee at his place. This was how they usually ended an evening, in his house or hers, talking and playing tapes softly so as not to wake their parents. His parents were away for the weekend, he told her, and her hopes had soared ridiculously. But it had been the same as any other time, except they played the tapes slightly louder. He did not turn the lights down. She had sat curled up, invitingly she hoped, on the sofa, and he on the floor, his long legs hunched, expounding his theories on life. There was nothing new about this, but they had just watched a film full of explicit sex. It had embarrassed her in the cinema; now she could not get her mind off it. At about one o'clock he had yawned, and said he supposed it was time he walked her home.

She was not sure what her reaction would have been if he had kissed her and put his hand up her jersey to undo her bra. She only knew she wished he had tried. Discussions on abortion and Proust and the greater meaning of life were all very well, but she yearned to know more about the other side of life, the basics. The mental imagery of Jodie Foster and Richard Gere panting naked amongst the bedclothes was imprinted tantalisingly on her memory. She knew she could not accuse him of being just a cold-blooded intellectual because she had observed him at parties, dancing and chatting up other girls. It would have been better if she had not. It all pointed to the fact that he did not see her in that light: she did not attract him. She had uncurled herself from the sofa feeling lumpish and awkward, and they parted outside her house with a peck on the cheek. His inaccessibility made him infinitely desirable. In her bedroom, she had taken a long, hard look at herself in the mirror, and come to a decision. She would lose weight, enough to discard the full, sloppy clothes; slim or bust.

She rinsed lettuce under the tap and started to

make herself a salad, trying to ignore the smell of the kedgeree. Laura would understand, even if her father did not. She thought of Laura's enviably slim lines and small bones, and pressed her lips together in determination, wondering how long it would be before she could wear a tight skirt.

Laura wrote at the kitchen table. The limb of land on the other side of the water was the shape of a dragon. *Let sleeping dragons lie, dormant let them be,* so her poem began. She was thinking of the dragons in her life, rather than the peninsula opposite; potentially dangerous dragons that were best left undisturbed. She was aware of her poetry having a rhythm to it that was unfashionable, but it came naturally to her, she could not write in any other form.

She drew a thin line beneath the completed poem and put the pen down, surprised to see from the kitchen clock that it was 4 p.m. Feeling cautiously satisfied with this first achievement, she switched on the kettle to make tea. The wind had dropped, and the sea had calmed to a gentle swell streaked with bands of deep blue and pale silver. It was going to be a beautiful evening. She lifted one of Gerard's bone china mugs, decorated with roses, from its hook and thought about how she would spend the time from now until supper. The wonderful thing was that it did not matter, nothing had to be planned. An unexpected wave of the guilt that hit her periodically chose this moment to do so, casting up its pictures of pining children and a depressed husband. Commonsense told her that none of this was true, that they were getting on with their own lives quite successfully without her. Nevertheless, the idea of something having gone wrong made her take the receiver from the telephone and ring the number without waiting.

Hannah answered, with only a cursory enquiry about Laura before crashing on with a list of complaints. It did not take Laura long to sort out the root cause, which was Rick's sudden and unexpected parental firmness.

'It's no use going on about the concert,' she said. 'I've already told you "no", and Rick is confirming it, quite rightly.'

'It's not fair. All my friends are going. I'm treated like a child.'

'You still are one,' Laura pointed out. 'I hope you aren't going to make everyone's life a misery because of it.' There was silence at Hannah's end of the line. 'Put me on to Rick, please, Hannah.' A long pause, then Rick's voice sounding taut.

'Hello.' There was muttering in the background. 'D'you mind going away, Hannah? I want to speak to Laura alone,' Laura heard him shout, most unlike Rick. A door slammed.

'I'm sorry she's being difficult,' she said placatingly.

'Yes, well, what can you expect?' he replied. 'Listen, Laura, how long are you planning to stay – wherever it is you're staying?'

'Why?' she said, alarmed. 'Is there a real crisis?'

'Only the everyday ones which you have run away from.' He sounded harassed rather than bitter. 'Unless you count you and me.'

'Rick darling, there is no crisis for us,' she said. 'It's all in your mind.'

'How can you say that when you refuse to tell me where you are, either by address or telephone number?'

'I'm in Cornwall,' she said, after a slight hesitation, 'in a cottage I've borrowed. And I'm alone, before you get the wrong idea.'

'It hadn't occurred to me you weren't,' he answered untruthfully.

'I am only doing what hundreds of people do at some point: taking a break. There is no drama, no more to it than that.'

'It's not what you've done, it's the way in which you've gone about it; secretively. The drama is of your own making,' he said.

'Over two weeks holiday?'

'Can't you *see* how hurtful it is for me?'

'I'm sorry,' she said quietly. 'But if I'd given you warning, you'd have tried to stop me. Be honest, Rick.'

He was silent for a moment. 'So you'll be away for two weeks?' he asked eventually.

'Probably. About that.' She added, 'Please try to understand. I love you all, you know.'

'I'm having dinner with Sarah this week, Sarah Pemberton,' he said suddenly.

'Oh. I'm glad,' she told him genuinely. 'You'll be able to discuss my misdemeanours.'

'That isn't the purpose,' he said. 'Look, perhaps it's better we don't talk on the phone. It only makes things worse.'

'Is that what you want?'

'No,' he said heavily, 'it isn't. Goodbye, Laura.'

She replaced the receiver slowly, her sense of peace momentarily shattered. Her hand shook a little as she reboiled the kettle and made the tea. She had not in truth expected her escape to have such repercussions. It had caused the divide between herself and Rick, which had been mentally plaguing her, to become a chasm. Now she was afraid of never being able to bridge it. She had not wished to wound him deliberately; she had imagined that, when she explained the *fait accompli*, he would come to accept her reasons for it. It had been, she supposed, a naïve assumption on her part. She tried to envisage Patrick's reactions had she bolted from him into the blue; it would probably have taken him a week to realize she was not there. She would not, in fact, have done so: he was too unreliable to be left in charge of two children. She had traded on Rick's goodness; that was the basic truth, and her growing awareness of it made her miserable.

'Hell!' she muttered to herself, clasping her hands round the warmth of the mug.

The sun had been temporarily eclipsed by cloud, and the sea had changed to a uniform grey. The day had lost its sparkle in conjunction with her spirits. If this mood persisted, she thought, she could see herself packing up and going home, ignominiously shrinking back with her tail between her legs, putting the folder of poetry in the bottom drawer, once more to be ignored.

The moment demanded action. She no longer felt able to let the evening drift pleasantly, taking its own course. A walk with a purpose was what she needed, and the local church was the answer. Widespread country parishes sometimes dispensed with evensong; if there was a service going on, it would do her no harm to join in. If not, she rather liked the idea of sitting quietly in an empty pew and meditating.

While she was rinsing the mug the doorbell rang, so unexpected and alien a sound that she nearly dropped the mug in the sink. It was a tentative ring, as if whoever was pressing the bell was doubtful of a friendly reception, or of any reception at all. Mrs Shawcross sprang to mind, and alternately the Jehovah's Witnesses. Laura very nearly did not answer it, irritated by this invasion of privacy. Only the thought of some kind of an emergency drove her to the front door to open it, forgetting as she did so to hook the chain across.

Chapter Three

Laura led the young man through to the terrace and told him to sit down, which he did immediately like an obedient dog. It seemed the safest place to put him.

'Would you like some tea?' she asked.

'D'you have coffee, by any chance?' He looked up at her anxiously. 'If it's no bother.'

She had found him on the doorstep with his finger poised over the bell, about to press it a second time. He started as she opened the door, as if caught in some nefarious act, dark, nervous eyes in a pale, inexpertly shaven face staring at her. It did not take her long to sum him up as one of the three million unemployed: there were enough of them in London alone, slumped on the pavements, begging. The portfolio under his arm reassured her slightly. Artists were unlikely to have criminal tendencies, was her unfounded belief, and at least he had something of his own to sell.

'I w-wondered whether you'd care to look at my drawings,' he said, hopefully easing the portfolio to lean it against long, thin legs.

She had hesitated, torn by commonsense and compassion. It was not her house and there were quite a lot of Gerard's valuables lying around. She took another look at the emaciated figure and the holey sweater, and compassion won.

He could not do much harm on the terrace. She could see him, sideways on from the kitchen as she filled the mugs, undoing the tapes of the portfolio: a good-looking boy with accentuated cheek-bones. She reached for a tin, piled a plate with chocolate biscuits and carried everything outside to put it on the table.

'Why don't you give me the drawings,' she said, 'while you have your coffee?'

She settled herself in a chair with the portfolio open on her lap. Out of the corner of her eye she watched him take a biscuit, put its entirety into his mouth and reach for another before he had stopped chewing. His hand shook as he lifted the mug; she turned her full attention to the first of his drawings. It was of a falcon, and he had used pen and ink and wash. The detail and the colour were lovingly portrayed, from the bird's soft breast feathers to its angry, predatory eye. She put it carefully to one side and turned over the second, a cormorant, and then another and another until she came to the end of the collection. They were all executed in the same medium, and all with the same competence. Surprised, she raised her head and looked at him.

'They're very good. You've been to art school?'

He shook his head. 'I learnt a bit at school. There was quite a good teacher there. After I left, I just carried on, on my own.' He studied her face intently. 'You really mean it? You really like them?'

'Yes, I do.' She peered at the initialled signature. 'I can't read this. What's your name?'

'Joe,' he said. 'Joe Blythe.'

'How much are you asking for them?'

'Six pounds each,' he said tentatively. 'Mind if I have another biscuit?'

'Help yourself,' she said. 'Do you manage to sell many?'

'No. Most people won't even look, they don't want to know.' He added, 'I've been up the main street this

63

afternoon and only one person came to the door. An old man who told me to get lost.'

'Well, I'll take two,' Laura told him. 'One for myself and the other as a present. I'd like the falcon, and the seagull in flight, if that's all right.'

His face showed incredulity, then lit up. 'That's great! Wonderful.'

She left him alone to fetch her bag from the kitchen, wondering, as she searched her wallet for the money, where he came from and where he was going. Very likely he did not know himself. She decided she must be kind but firm in showing him out before long. He did not irritate her in the same way as Mrs Shawcross, but with too much encouragement he might stick like a burr.

She placed the twelve pounds on the table when she returned. He was standing in the middle of the terrace looking out to sea, a tall, lanky figure with hands in jeans pockets.

'D'you live here?' he asked. He did not seem to notice the cash.

'No. I'm only staying for a week or two. I live in London.' She started to put the mugs and plate purposefully on the tray. 'And where are you from, Joe? You're not local either, are you?'

'From Birmingham. That's where we were when I was a child.' He was watching her without moving.

'But not now?'

'My mother went to Surbiton. I don't live with her, though, not since my dad left. She says I'm trouble.'

'That's sad,' Laura said inadequately.

'I don't want to, anyway. I don't get on with the bloke she's moved in with. I'm old enough to make my own way, aren't I?'

'How old are you?' she asked, not sure whether or not he wanted to answer.

'Twenty-one.'

'Is this your only source of income?' she said, sounding to herself like a social worker. 'Trying to sell your drawings?'

'I couldn't find a job,' he said simply. 'I don't think the Jobcentres like the look of me. I just move around now, picking up what I can.'

'What about Social Security?'

'You can't claim any benefits without an address. No home address, no money.' He stared at a gull swooping low across the cliff face. 'I claimed when I was in hospital,' he said. 'That was home for a bit, you see. They signed on for me then.'

Laura fiddled with the mugs, divided between pity over the hopelessness of his existence, and the secret worry of how to send him on his way. 'I'm sorry,' she said. 'It's all so unfair.'

'It's not so bad,' he said. 'I quite like going where I want to. Hospital made me feel shut in.'

'Are you better now?'

He nodded. 'I'm fine. Just have to take some pills, that's all.' He jerked his head towards the sea. 'Nice place, this, isn't it?' he said, as if he wanted the subject changed.

'Come and look,' she said, crossing to the parapet. 'There's a garden built down the side of the cliff.'

He came unwillingly, peered and backed away. 'Jeez! Can't take heights, they give me vertigo.'

She said, 'Me, too. But I've found a little path that winds in and out between the rockery, so you can garden. Once you're there, it doesn't seem so bad.' She straightened up, glancing at her watch. 'There are things I have to do now,' she told him. 'It's been nice talking to you, and I shall enjoy the drawings.'

'Thanks,' he said, 'for the coffee and all.' He tied the tapes of the portfolio slowly and in silence, as though reluctant to go. 'D'you know anywhere round here where I could get a bed in return for work?' he asked her. 'I can do quite a few things: decorating, washing-up and so on.'

Her heart turned over for him as she pictured him going from door to door on another pointless quest. 'I don't know the village well, I'm afraid,' she said. 'The pub is your best bet, I should think.' She picked up the money and handed it to him. 'Don't forget this. I hope it helps a little.' I should have made it more, she thought; at least he could have rented a room for the night.

He stood the portfolio on the table, balancing it with a bony, long-fingered hand. 'I s'pose I couldn't stay here for a bit?' he said. 'Just until I find somewhere. I'd make myself useful.' He lifted his eyes to her face; intense, troubled eyes that spoke of rejection, expecting it before it had happened.

She had a swift longing to show him to one of the pretty bedrooms, let him run a huge hot bath, supply him with fluffy towels and supper. Sanity prevailed.

'I'm afraid I can't do that, Joe,' she said gently. 'It's not my house, you see, I'm not able to ask whom I like to stay.'

'Yeah,' he said tonelessly. 'OK. Thought it was worth asking.'

'I really should try the pub,' she repeated as she led him back through the house to the front door. Delving once more into her bag, she found a ten pound note and handed it to him.

'I can't take that,' he said, staring down at it. 'You've paid me already.'

'Your drawings are worth more than you're asking.'

'Not much use asking more when I can't sell them anyway.'

'You've sold some to me. Please take it.' She pressed it into his hand. 'Good luck, Joe.'

'Thanks very much,' he said, pocketing the note and tucking the portfolio under his arm once more.

At the gate, he retrieved the two carrier bags he had left there, lifting his hand in salute. 'Thanks again. See you,' he said.

She watched him walk away down the hill, destination unknown, his head and shoulders visible above the harbour wall until a twist in the road hid him from view. Sighing, she went back into the house and closed the door, depressed by his unexpected intrusion. There was something dreadfully wrong about a system that left so many people helpless to help themselves, allowing them to become no more than human detritus. She ran hot water fiercely on the mugs in the sink, knowing it was not merely the system that was bugging her, but her inability to do something about the Joe Blythes of life. There but for sheer luck and the grace of God went the Annabelles and the Hannahs as well. The hopelessness of his situation made her own problems seem like so much self-indulgence, an egotistical figment of her imagination. A husband who irritated her with his lack of insight, and an ambition to have a collection of poetry published, appeared suddenly unforgivable reasons for running away: almost obscene in their triviality. The boy Joe had achieved more with his talent than she deserved to with hers, and managed it in the face of impossible odds. Where, for instance, did he find the money for his drawing materials?

When she had dried her hands, she took the two drawings through to the living-room and stood them up between a bronze figure and a pile of coffee-table books. They looked even better in these surroundings, and she was struck once more by their delicate accuracy. The boy should be in art school, she thought, or at very least have a job as a draughtsman and go to evening classes. 'What a bloody waste,' she muttered out loud. Back in the kitchen she opened her folder of poems and read through the most recent one. She liked to do this: leave it for a while and creep up unexpectedly on what she had written, her critical faculties freshened. Surprisingly, she was quite pleased with the result; to a small degree it seemed to vindicate her being there in Gerard's house.

Remembering church, she went upstairs to change her jeans for the one skirt she had brought with her. If there was a service, it seemed politer not to turn up in trousers. She rather hoped the church would be empty and silent. Joe Blythe's plight had set her thinking about the girls, worrying about the various pitfalls which inevitably they would have to contend with before long. She thought of Joe's mother, living in Surbiton with a 'bloke' he detested, having washed her hands of her son. Although it was only for a fortnight, Laura was made uncomfortably conscious of having defected. A prayer was definitely needed, she felt, to ensure she did not become a replica of the dreaded Mrs Blythe.

Mark Wainwright saw his Sunday pupil to the door and on his way by bicycle, a battered copy of Ovid sticking out of his jacket pocket. Then he wandered into the garden which reminded him so forcibly of his late wife, and along the herbaceous border. Michaelmas daisies and Japanese anemones grew in healthy clumps, and a few late roses were still in bloom, bravely pretending it was high summer. Behind him waddled his elderly labrador, Brutus, nose to the ground in search of any bones he might have left lying about. The cold wind had dropped and a gang of gnats danced above the lawn in the last of the sun. It was a beautiful evening. Mark sat himself down on a wooden seat by the copper beech and lit a cigarette, wondering why on earth he was bothering about evensong when this place was riddled with memories of Alice. But it was the anniversary of her death, and it had become a habit with him to go to church on that day, although he had no strong beliefs and in fact carried a grudge against a deity callous enough to let her die. He had no idea why he persisted, knowing merely that, having knelt there without addressing a word to God, he came away feeling calmer. There was not a logical explanation.

He finished the cigarette and rose reluctantly to walk back to the house, limping slightly from the leg damaged in the same car crash in which Alice was killed. They had bought the farmhouse fifteen years ago and lived there ever since, high above the estuary. It was a mutual decision to leave the academic world of Oxford, she to join a local practice of GPs and he to cram the Classics into those children who were remotely interested. Neither of them had regretted it. It had been suggested to him by friends that he should move from somewhere that held constant reminders of her. He had never once considered it seriously. He was aware that he was regarded as something of a recluse, but then he was not, and never had been, a social animal. He enjoyed teaching, enjoyed for the most part the company of the young whom he taught. There was a handful of friends he liked and trusted, and that was enough. The rest, the fringe acquaintances, he tolerated, except in the case of spare women who eyed him with a view to marriage; there were one or two of those who found his manner astringent.

The time was twenty minutes to six. He put on a tie, and gathered up the car keys from the hall table. Brutus, knowing he was not to be included on this trip, regarded him balefully from his basket. Then he set out to drive the mile and a half to St Merric Church, where there would doubtless be the usual half-dozen pensioners, amongst them the lethal Eleanor Shawcross, trouble-maker *par excellence.* He wondered as he drove, when, if ever, one stopped missing someone as badly as he did.

In her bedroom Hannah was occupied with strategy. She had finished her homework: French translation and an essay which she had written in record time, satisfactorily for one planning to be the future Julie Burchill.

She sat back in her chair with her feet on the desk, in a suitable journalistic pose, thinking. The day had not been in the least satisfactory. She had lost out on the Michael Jackson concert through the sheer stupidity of her parents and their outdated attitudes. Worse, she had lost face; all her friends were going and they would make bitchy remarks about her absence. She had misjudged Rick; she had always thought of him as an old softy. It was disastrous when parents got together to form an opposition. After this setback, something had to happen to reinstate her with her 'in-crowd', and it must be soon. She had already figured out what: a party of her own, a disco, here in the house. Now it was just a matter of persuading Rick that this would be an OK thing. There would have to be dreary promises that the music would not be too loud, no-one would go into the bedrooms, it would end when he said so and she would clear up afterwards, and so on. She also hoped to persuade him to go out for most of the evening: it would be a complete downer if he hung around. Annie could be relied on to make herself scarce without prompting: she had nothing in common with Hannah's crowd. She took her feet off the desk, tied her hair back demurely in a ponytail and ventured downstairs, prepared to start with an apology for the day's behaviour.

She found Rick in the drawing-room, hidden behind *The Sunday Times*. It was odd to discover him being inactive; he was normally busy doing things. She gave the paper a little tap.

'Hi there,' he said, lowering it.

She sat down beside him on the sofa. 'I've come to say sorry; about today, I mean, for getting in a miff.'

'Apology accepted.'

She gave him a kiss on the cheek, and curled her legs under her. 'Would you like me to do supper tonight? I expect I can manage if it's easy.'

He eyed her speculatively, suspecting an ulterior motive. 'I imagine you could. It's cold beef and baked potatoes.'

'I'll do a salad, shall I? I like making salad.'

'Good idea, I'll remember that. D'you know how to make the dressing? All right, I'll show you.'

Hannah could be uncommonly good company, he decided as they messed about in the kitchen. She still threw her tantrums, as she had as a small child, but at least nowadays one got the occasional apology.

'Large teaspoonful of French mustard, plenty of sugar, crushed garlic, a little vinegar, the best olive oil.'

'Do I stir or shake?'

'Stir first, shake before using.'

'D'you think Mum sounded all right?' she asked as she laid the table.

'You spoke to her,' Rick said, his head buried in the fridge. 'I thought so, didn't you?'

'We were arguing, so it was difficult to tell.'

When Laura had announced her departure, Hannah had had a secret and rather shameful sense of freedom. She foresaw at least two weeks of everything going her way: manipulating Rick, she considered, would

71

be comparatively easy. It was not that Laura was particularly strict, but the rules she made, she stuck to, and no amount of wheedling would shift her. Hannah was not certain how she was going to make the most of the imagined freedom, but it lay ahead of her temptingly, waiting to be used. The concert plan had fallen through, admittedly: things did not always work out the way they were meant to, and she had not thought of her mother wielding her influence from long distance. The party idea would have to be put over with more diplomacy.

Rick might not seem all that worried about Laura's going away, but Hannah knew better. After slamming out of the room during their telephone conversation, she had listened at the door. She thought the talk would concern her and how impossible she was being. She was wrong; it was about themselves, and any fool could have grasped the fact they were having a sort of row. Her first intuition had been that Laura had a boyfriend. Everything she had heard since served to convince her of this. Hannah did not like it in the least. Supposing this was to be the cause of her mother and Rick splitting up? She did not want to lose Rick, he was the best kind of stepfather for lots of reasons, and besides, the other man might be perfectly dreadful. Anything would be preferable to that happening. It began to dawn on her that an attempt should be made to get Laura home, even at the cost of Hannah's so-called freedom.

She opened the oven door to test the potatoes. 'I thought she sounded a bit funny; you know, not like she usually is, quite sparky,' she said.

'Really? Well, that was probably because you were arguing with her,' Rick answered, refusing to be drawn.

'Oh! Shit!'

'Hannah!'

'Sorry. Burnt myself.'

72

'Run it under the cold tap, and don't swear. It's unattractive.'

'Where's Annie?' she asked, her thumb under water.

'She's jogging.'

'Jogging?' Hannah said. 'Heavens!'

'Rather what I thought,' agreed Rick. 'But I'm quite pleased. It'll do her good to get some exercise instead of slogging at that desk.'

Hannah considered telling him what she suspected, that Annabelle was in love and wanted to get her weight down. She decided not to, however. She needed his full concentration on what she was about to ask, not on Annabelle's emotional problems. Judging that he had mellowed enough to be receptive in the companionable atmosphere of the last half hour, she took a breath and put the question to him, casually, as if it did not matter much.

'If you say "no", I promise I won't bang on about it,' she assured him.

'No,' Rick said promptly. 'Sorry, but it's not on.'

She stirred the salad dressing thoughtfully. 'Are you sure about that, or does it mean perhaps?'

'I'm fairly sure I don't want to cope alone with a whole lot of your mates bebopping the night away, and getting complaints about the noise from the neighbours.'

'We wouldn't have the music that loud—'

'Hannah—'

'All right,' she said sadly. 'It's just that I didn't have a party last birthday because I wasn't well, if you remember.'

Rick sighed inwardly. He wished very much at that moment that Laura would suddenly materialize. He was beginning to discover with a certain amount of surprise, just how many domestic decisions had been taken out of his hands and quickly resolved by her.

Always susceptible to Hannah's emotional blackmail, he recognized the game she was playing right now, and knew that if he was half a man, he should take a firm stand. But it had been a depressing Sunday, and once again he found himself lacking the drive which apparently Laura instilled in him. He felt suddenly that he would be the better for a dose of Sarah Pemberton's no-nonsense wisdom. Until then, compromise was the only answer.

'I'll think about it,' he said.

Hannah's eyes sprang open in triumph. 'For how long?' she asked.

'Until Tuesday.'

'Why Tuesday?'

'There are reasons,' he said firmly, 'and that's that.'

'I rather wanted it to be next Saturday,' she said cautiously.

'And I'd rather Laura was home first. You may have to wait.'

'Thank you, Rick,' she said meekly, an idea taking shape in her mind. After a pause, 'Of course, if we told Mum I was having a party next Saturday, she might decide to come back – in case I wreck the house,' she added with a grin to show she was joking.

'And pigs might fly,' Rick replied, relieved to notice it was now the legitimate time for pouring himself a whisky. 'She'd merely veto the whole thing by telephone.'

Annabelle came in by the backdoor, her fringe flattened damply to her forehead, strangely sack-like in her tracksuit.

'You've done everything,' she said breathily, taking in the preparations for supper. 'Sorry, didn't know it was so late. What are we having?'

Rick told her. 'Go and have a bath,' he said, 'there's plenty of time. You look exhausted.'

'Not to mention sweaty,' Hannah said unnecessarily.

'No potato for me, thanks,' Annabelle said as she started up the stairs. 'I'm not very hungry.'

'That's what she said at lunchtime,' Rick muttered.

'I can eat another half if you can,' said Hannah.

Annabelle stood under the shower and let the cold rivulets splash over her flushed face. Her stomach rumbled from emptiness; actual hunger had left her quite abruptly for different reasons.

When she had set out, it was with the intention of following the path on the Hammersmith side of the river. She liked the river with its brown, muddy smell, its dilapidated barges anchored by the shore and topped by seagulls, and people sculling down the middle reaches. But once out of the house, her feet had turned left instead of right, as if of their own volition, leading her in the direction of Ben's street. Jogging had looked so easy, but she was surprised at the amount of energy it entailed. She trotted rather heavily, uncomfortably aware of her breasts bobbing up and down, and crushing the first fall of leaves underfoot as she wound her way along the intersecting roads. Ben's family house stood on a corner behind a laurel hedge. The garden ran round the two sides, with trees and a lawn at the back. She could hear voices and laughter as she approached it, slowing down to a walk. If the family had been there alone, she would not have minded dropping in uninvited. She knew the parents quite well; Ben's father was a thin, ascetic-looking man who taught physics, and his mother a benevolent, cushiony woman absorbed in charitable works. But judging by the noise, there were other people. Annabelle wandered along the hedge and peeked over. A badminton net had been put up on the lawn, and four people were playing. A girl with long brown legs and a lot of blonde hair was leaping around beside Ben and shrieking every time she missed the shuttlecock. As Annabelle watched, the girl slipped and clung to him as he fell to the ground beside her. They were both laughing and did not seem in a hurry to get to their feet. Annabelle felt her face redden a deeper shade than it already was; she turned away with a sick feeling in the pit of her stomach, and headed leaden-footed for home.

She tried to argue logically with herself. Ben had masses of friends, girls amongst them. He obviously had different ones for different activities. She, Annabelle, was reserved for intellectual pursuits, being unsuitable for anything frivolous like hitting moving objects with a racquet, and flirting. Neither of these sports came naturally to her: it was going to be hard going if she were to change her image as well as her shape. She knew this should not be necessary; she should have enough confidence to be happy with what she was, and if he didn't like it, then tough luck. That would be Laura's advice. But Annabelle's self-esteem was at a low ebb, lowered still further by peering over the hedge. All she wanted was to take the place of the giggling girl with tanned legs rolling about on the grass. Nearing home, she broke into a half-hearted trot, weighed down by the heavy despair of being left out.

'And this is Mark Wainwright,' said Mrs Shawcross outside the church. 'Laura Snow. I've been hoping to get you two together.'

Besides the three of them, evensong had been attended by a scattering of the elderly, all huddled in the front pews to make the most of a poor congregation. Laura sat further back, a stranger not wishing to break into their close community. Across the aisle she had noticed the only male under seventy-five, tall with beaky features rather like Joe Blythe's drawing of the falcon. When she knelt, the worn hassock gave off a musty smell redolent somehow of childhood, bringing her own children to mind. She wondered why she found it harder to concentrate when two or three were gathered together than when she was alone. They had risen, sung 'Abide With Me' at a snail's pace, and filed out into the beginnings of dusk to shake the Rector's firm, ex-naval hand.

'Good to see you here. Staying with us long?'

'A fleeting visit, I'm afraid,' Laura had smiled at him, to take care of further church appearances. And now she was holding out her hand to Mark Wainwright, hoping he had overheard her. She disliked being told whom she should meet.

'You should have a lot in common,' Mrs Shawcross was saying. 'Laura writes poetry.'

'Really?' Mark Wainwright said with a hint of boredom that irritated Laura. She wished Mrs Shawcross had not mentioned it. Poetry was not like any other form of writing; there was a feyness about it that was open to mockery.

'I try. And you teach Classics to small boys, I believe?' she said, attempting the same off-hand manner.

'To quite large boys,' he corrected her, 'and a few girls as well. Do you read Ovid?'

'No,' she said.

'Well, as a poet you should do. I have a spare translation if you care to borrow it.'

'Thank you,' she replied, quietly furious, 'but I shan't be here long enough to get stuck into it.' She imagined for a moment there was a glimmer of humour at the back of his eyes. He was laughing at her.

'Laura has a family in London to get back to,' Mrs Shawcross commented sweetly. 'Don't you, my dear?'

'Right; I think I'll get back to my temporary home now,' Laura said calmly. 'I'm rather cold.'

'Good night then, dear. Oh, would you be an angel and walk Tigger for me tomorrow morning?'

'Of course.'

'And if it's no bother, could you pick up my wholemeal loaf from the baker on the way?'

'No problem.' Laura walked away with a vague wave of her hand, a 'good night' casual enough to include both of them.

'Such a nice girl,' Eleanor Shawcross was confiding to Mark Wainwright, who was taking a purely aesthetic interest in Laura's disappearing legs. 'So helpful. Can't help feeling something's wrong with her marriage. Poetry isn't the only reason for her coming down here on her own, I'm sure.'

'I'll see you to your front door,' Mark said by way of an answer.

'My dear boy, it's only two yards. You might offer Laura a lift, though, since it's on your way.'

Laura stumped down the hill in a worse frame of mind than on walking up it. She was not certain of the cause; an accumulation of small incidents, she supposed. It had been a day crammed with people; a large dose of Eleanor Shawcross, followed by Joe Blythe and finally the brief but irksome introduction to Mark Wainwright. She had taken one of those illogical dislikes to him based on nothing but his faintly supercilious attitude and the fact she did not find men with hawkish features attractive. He had been less than forthcoming; this, however, should have been a point in his favour, the only thing marking him out as a kindred spirit, since the whole purpose of her being there was solitude. Damn Mrs Shawcross with her interference, Laura muttered to herself, she did not want to have to fight for peace and quiet.

Mark Wainwright's car drew alongside and he lowered the passenger window. 'Like a lift?' he asked. 'I'm told you're going in my direction.'

'Thanks, but I like the walk,' she said, stooping unwillingly to answer him.

'You look tired,' he remarked unflatteringly, 'as if you could do with a drink. Hop in.' Without being downright rude, there was no alternative but to open the door and slide herself onto the seat beside him. 'I've no idea where you're living,' he pointed out.

'Cliff House, the white one on its own at the top of the hill.

'Gerard Wyatt's place,' he murmured, moving off slowly. 'Very nice, too.'

'Does everyone know everyone in St Merric?' she said sarcastically.

'Of course. It's a village,' he replied. 'A beehive existence, virtually impossible to find privacy, although I do my best. But I forgot: you are used to the glorious anonymity of London, aren't you?'

'I should think Oxford is pretty gossipy, isn't it, in an intellectual sort of way?' she suggested.

'It has a series of cliques, each with its own grapevine, yes.' He glanced at her. 'How do you know about my connections with Oxford?' he asked.

'Mrs Shawcross gave me a run-down.'

'Dear Eleanor, who else?' he sighed, manoeuvring into the narrow main street.

A young man was leaning against the harbour wall, a lock of dark hair flopping over his forehead. Laura waved, but he did not appear to notice.

'Who's your friend?' Mark asked

'Someone you *wouldn't* know,' she said. 'He came to the house selling his drawings and I bought two.

'You mean you let him in?'

'Yes,' she said.

79

'Taking a bit of a risk, weren't you? He might have banged you over the head and absconded with Gerard's paintings.'

'He obviously wasn't the sort,' she said defensively. 'He's a rather sad boy trying to eke out a living, and the drawings are really very good.'

'Ah. All that would account for his unsavoury appearance.'

'How bigoted can you get?' she demanded angrily as they stopped outside Gerard's gates, opening her door at the first jerk of the brakes.

'Your bag,' he said, handing it to her and ignoring her remark.

'Thanks for the lift,' she said coldly.

His grey eyes smiled at her briefly. 'My pleasure,' he answered, and then the car shot away, turning the sharp corner to the upper road and disappearing behind the rise of the hillside.

What an insufferable man, she told herself, slamming the front door behind her without meaning to. He was right about one thing, however. She went straight to the kitchen, poured herself a whisky and sat with her feet up on Gerard's squashy white sofa to savour it slowly.

Joe Blythe had been thinking of walking up the hill to Laura's house. He had found a room and a job at the pub, and he wanted to thank her; not to stop for long, just ring the doorbell and have a quick word. Then she had passed him in a car driven by a man, and now he did not like to. She had waved to him which was nice of her, but he did not wave back; it seemed a bit too, well, friendly with someone else there, so he pretended not to have seen her. He wondered who the man was; perhaps the owner of the house, although he had got the feeling she was there alone. He could try again the next day, in the afternoon when they would not need him for work.

The landlord of the Ship and Anchor was large and middle-aged, with a stomach that bulged over the belt of his trousers. It had taken Joe a long time to screw up courage to tackle him in the bar before opening hours. Samuel Grimond, Proprietor, it said over the front entrance. He had been polishing glasses when Joe appeared; he eyed him up and down, but he had listened. Joe had propped the portfolio and the carrier bags against the bar, knowing the stammer would come back, and the tremor in his hands. He managed to get the words out, though, somehow. Sam Grimond came from the Midlands and perhaps that had persuaded him to bother with Joe at all; the sound of a familiar accent.

'As it happens, my son's broken an ankle,' he said, working his way through the beer mugs, 'rolling a barrel across the yard.' He looked at Joe. 'That's the sort of work you'd be doing, if I took you on. That, and what I'm doing now, and quite a lot more.'

'I don't mind what I do.'

'You'll have to clean yourself up a bit,' Sam Grimond said. 'Been sleeping rough, have you?'

'Some of the time.'

'I don't know. This bloody government.' The landlord shook his head in disgust.

His wife had come in at that moment, and they had gone into another room to discuss it. Snatches of conversation drifted back to Joe. She thought her husband was mad to take on casual labour with no references, when he could have his pick of trained applicants from the Jobcentre. Joe guessed it was getting someone on the cheap that made up their minds for them, because Sam Grimond came back to say he would try Joe out for a couple of days in return for bed and half-board, and what amounted to pocket money. Joe did not mind much about the money. His afternoons would be free; he might be able to pick up other odd jobs in the village, and he would have time to draw.

He felt suddenly exhausted. It seemed to him days ago that he had walked down the road into St Merric. He pushed himself off the harbour wall, taking a last look at the sea, almost black now in the semi-darkness and glinting in the lights from windows. Gulls rode the ripples in white blobs. The pasty, peas and chips which the landlord's wife had doled out to him at six o'clock lay heavily on a stomach unused to full meals. Mrs Grimond reminded him of his mother's best friend, Sharon. She had the same expression in her eyes when she looked at him; a kind of wariness as if expecting him to rape or knife her or something. He could not think why: no-one would bother with either of them. Of course Sharon had known about hospital and why he had been there, and could not believe he was not violent; Mrs Grimond knew nothing. It was as though he was carrying a stigma around with him.

Work started the next day; Sam Grimond had let him off this evening, said he'd be more use when he had had a bath and a night's sleep. The thought of lying in hot water and sleeping in a bed seemed incredibly wonderful, making him quicken his steps as he walked towards the pool of light spilling over the pavement from the public bar.

Late that night Rick decided to go through Laura's desk to see if it yielded up any clues – letters, an address, anything – as to her whereabouts. He had never done such a thing before; he despised underhand tactics as a rule. But he could not sleep and the current book on the American Civil War failed to hold his attention.

Laura's desk had pigeon-holes crammed with every-thing from paper clips to sticky labels and neat packets of letters. He took the packets out carefully and went through them one by one before replacing them. They were mostly communications from old girl-friends, chatty and of no particular interest, some of them dated six months previously. Laura was a hoarder of such things. He did not read them, there was no point. There were two piles of receipts, quotations from decorators, matters to do with admin, lying below the pigeon-holes – a pending file, he presumed. Amongst none of these did he find a lead to where she might have gone. He left everything tidy and closed the lid of her desk with a sigh.

If he had found any information, he was not at all certain how he would have acted upon it. To have gone roaring off to try and persuade her home would not have been a clever move. In her present frame of mind it would only increase her determination to stay. But to have an address would make her seem less elusive; a solid fact would have been a comfort. He imagined her wandering by herself – it was to be hoped – on some remote beach, if such a thing still existed in Cornwall, trying to sort out whatever was bothering her. His failure to understand precisely what that was filled him with frustration. Perhaps it was simply that she had fallen out of love with him, and the so-called searching for an identity was merely an excuse, or perhaps they amounted to the same thing. He was beginning to doubt himself, wondering if he were not terribly dull; peering in mirrors for a deterioration of his even-featured face and reasonably trim figure. Comparing his looks rather childishly with those of the darkly piratical Patrick, he realized she could hardly have married a more disparate couple of men, in every way.

He climbed the stairs reluctantly to the bedroom

which smelt of Laura, and where the various bottles and face lotions she had left behind on the dressing-table gave an encouraging intimation of her return. The other consolation, he remembered as he lay down to sleep, was dinner with Sarah Pemberton the following night. He found the idea of some feminine insight very consoling indeed.

Laura woke jerkily in the middle of the night from a weird and vaguely disturbing dream. It was gone in an instant, only the foggy edges of it clinging round her memory. She lay there in the darkness, listening to the sound of the sea washing the rocks and subsiding again endlessly with a sigh: a soothing sound. She wished she could transport it to London.

Something at the back of her mind bothered her, something she had meant to do and had not. Then she remembered Joe Blythe, and how she had planned to call in at the pub on the way home from church, to see if he had struck lucky. Mark Wainwright insisting on giving her a lift had prevented her. There was a vulnerability about Joe which worried her. Turning on her side in the soft bed, she hoped very much that he was not having to spend another night in the open.

Chapter Four

'They're nice,' April August remarked of the bird drawings as she dusted the living-room next morning. 'Life-like, aren't they?'

'Aren't they?' Laura agreed. Propped where she had left them, she studied them afresh with satisfaction. 'I bought them from a young man who came to the door.' Then she realized that April would not approve of her inviting strangers into Gerard's house, any more than Mark had done. 'I had a quick look,' she added, 'and I was so impressed I took two.'

'That'll be the lad that's been taken on at the Ship and Anchor,' April said, moving her upholstered figure to the tallboy. 'They say he's something of an artist. Looks a bit rough, according to Dolly Grimond, but that's nothing to go by. She's a one for thinking the worst of people.'

'He's been out of work for a long time,' Laura said. 'He told me. I don't imagine it helps one's looks.'

'He'll be cleaner now, anyway.' April polished vigorously. 'Dolly says it took a half hour to get the black line off the bath after he'd used it.'

News travelled fast in St Merric, Laura thought, pleased to know that Joe Blythe had found a base, however uncertain. 'I must go,' she said. 'I'm supposed to be taking Mrs Shawcross's dog for a walk.'

'That's kind of you, but don't let her run you round in circles,' April warned. 'That Mrs Shawcross trades on good nature, and you've got your writing to think of. See you Friday.'

It was an Indian summer of a day with a softness in the air, as Laura walked down the village street to the bakery. The sun sparkled and glittered on flat, calm sea in the harbour, and the moored boats were motionless in the water. She bought a loaf for Eleanor Shawcross and one for herself, feeling the warmth of them through her tracksuit as she climbed the hill behind the houses. Pausing for breath, she looked down on the back courtyard of the Ship and Anchor; there was no sign of Joe. She wondered if he had already started his duties, and whether they would be patient with him.

'That' Mrs Shawcross, to quote April, was ready and waiting, full of instructions about her dog. 'He doesn't chase sheep, so it's safe to let him off the lead. He is a teeny bit aggressive with other dogs, I'm afraid, aren't you, you naughty thing? Best to keep him with you if you see one coming. And don't let him near the water, he'll swim for miles. Thank you so much, my dear, it'll be a great treat for him.'

Laura finally extricated herself, leaving her loaf to be collected later, and allowed the terrier to pull her, tugging at the leash the whole way to the estuary. Safely in open country, she let him go, doubtful of whether he would even obey if she called him. He scudded ahead, zig-zagging to right and left on the scent of rabbits, intoxicated with unaccustomed freedom, and occasionally stopping to glance back at her. She started to relax, taking her eyes off the rough tan coat and watching instead a flotilla of dinghies more or less becalmed on the still water, their rust and white sails flapping. It was reminiscent of the misguided holiday on the Isle of Wight, where Rick had yelled instructions from the shore while Hannah, bored, and Annabelle, frightened, got their ropes hopelessly entangled. It had not been funny at the time, but Laura smiled at the memory.

There had been no rain for days, and the turf was dry and crisp beneath her feet. Wild flowers were clustered along the hedge above the estuary, blooming in the only part of England which would allow them such unseasonal behaviour. Yellow splashes of gorse dotted the humps and hollows of the fields as far as the eye could see. She had one of those swift surges of happiness that come so seldom and for no particular reason, and thought involuntarily of Annabelle, because she was the kind of person who would love this place. But even a sense of guilt at being alone to enjoy it did not dispel the euphoria, part of which was aloneness itself.

After the second field, she stopped at the stone wall and sat on a stile in the sun. Tigger's rump stuck out of a thicket of brambles as he investigated what was within. To the right the close-cropped land rose, gradually at first and then steeply, to an escarpment running as far as the distant woods, and disappearing into their autumn foliage. High above her, perched some way back from the brow of the hill, stood a solitary grey stone house with a path ribboning downwards from a wicket gate. A man in a blue anorak and with a golden labrador at his heels had reached the bottom, where the land flattened out and became grass, and turned in her direction. She gave the terrier an experimental shout, moving towards the bramble bush with the lead at the ready.

'Tigger!'

The dog, half-buried, pretended not to hear. A rabbit burst from the far side of the thicket and bounced away, swerving across the field with Tigger in wild pursuit, oblivious to Laura's whistles. He gave up when the chase became hopeless, trotting back to her, his tongue lolling as the man drew close enough for her to identify him as Mark Wainwright. The terrier's behaviour changed dramatically at the sight of the elderly labrador; hackles rising, he stiffened like a pointer, crouched for attack. Too late, Laura made a grab for his collar; he shot forward like a bullet from a gun across the space between him and the other dog. The peace of the morning was shattered by a sudden mêlée of yelping, snarling animals, in the middle of which Mark stood grim-faced, wielding a walking-stick. She ran forward to hover uselessly on the periphery, yelling at the terrier and making ineffectual snatches at any available bits of him she could see.

'Don't!' he shouted at her. 'D'you want to get bitten?' Raising his stick, he brought it down sharply, twice, on the terrier's backside. The dog howled and fled between Laura's legs, where she pinioned him and secured the lead with fumbling fingers.

'Are you in charge of that bloody little pooch?' he asked, examining his own dog for injuries.

She nodded, her face burning.

'It's Eleanor Shawcross's, isn't it? In which case you shouldn't have let it off the leash.'

'The whole point was to give it some exercise,' she answered defensively. 'There wasn't a soul around and then you appeared from nowhere. I'm sorry,' she added, brushing dishevelled hair out of her eyes. 'Is your dog hurt?'

'A nip on the leg, that's all.'

'I really am sorry,' she repeated.

He said grudgingly, 'Not your fault, you weren't to know.'

'I did, actually. Mrs Shawcross warned me, but I didn't realize he was *that* aggressive. Shut up, you beastly thing,' she admonished a still growling Tigger. Mark lifted his stick an inch or two, and the dog cowered. 'I think I'd better get him home,' she said. 'I'll walk on ahead.'

'I'll walk with you as far as the next wall,' he replied.

'The little bugger can't do any more harm. Let's go by the side of the estuary; I like watching the boats.'

The dinghies had scarcely moved since she first passed them. They stood on the bank, gazing in silence. He took a packet of cigarettes from his anorak pocket and offered it to her. She shook her head.

Lighting one without looking at her, he said abruptly, 'We seem to have got off on the wrong foot, one way or another. I wonder why?'

She shrugged. 'No reason, I expect. It just happens between people, don't you think?'

'I put you down as rather prickly.'

'And I thought you were decidedly condescending,' she retorted.

'So there you are: a natural antipathy.'

'In fact,' she said, 'I resent being flung at people with the automatic assumption you're going to get along just fine.'

'And I resent people being flung *at me*. So we've got one thing in common after all: we're both loners.'

'I'm not, by nature,' she said. 'Only for the short time I'm down here. That's why I came, to be alone.'

'To write your poetry?' he asked. 'And please note I am not patronizing you now.'

'That, mainly,' she agreed, with the slightest hesitation.

'I suppose I was marginally less anti-social when my wife Alice was alive,' he remarked matter-of-factly. 'She didn't allow me to be.'

'How long ago was that?'

'Eighteen months.' He paused. 'She died in a car accident.'

She did not say how sorry she was; it was impossible to make it sincere. 'It must be very difficult for you,' she said. 'Coming to terms with it.'

'I'm beginning to understand that one probably never does.'

She glanced up at him, at the beaky profile turned seawards. 'Are your pupils frightened of you?' she asked suddenly.

He looked at her and smiled, and the whole granite aspect of his face changed. 'What a curious question,' he said, 'and the answer is no, certainly not. I'm as gentle as a lamb where they're concerned. I suspect they regard me as something of an oddity, but since most of them are interested in learning, it doesn't really matter.'

Mrs Shawcross's dog, fed up with being tethered, gave a little whine. 'I must go,' she said. 'Eleanor will think I've drowned him.'

'I shan't come any further,' Mark said. 'This is as far as Brutus and I can manage.'

'Whereabouts do you live?'

He pointed with his stick to the grey-walled house at the top of the hill. 'Up there.'

'How fantastic.' She gazed at it. 'The views must be quite something.'

'They are, when you reach it. I'd ask you to come back for a drink if you didn't have to push on.' He smiled at her once more. 'D'you think we can call a truce now?'

She nodded. 'Of course. Dogfights obviously have their uses.'

She stroked the labrador's blond head. 'He's lovely. We had one like this when I was a child.'

'How about coming this evening?' Mark said casually.

She looked at him, trying to decide whether it was wise to accept. 'I'd like that, thank you. How do I find you?'

'The gates are about a mile along the upper road; Stonewall Farm, on the left. It's the only house around,

90

you can't miss it. About six-thirty.' He added, 'Whatever you may think, I am interested in poetry. Seriously, there may be something you'd like to borrow.' Turning on his heel, he started back the way he had come, Brutus ambling slowly in the rear.

'See you later,' she called after him. He raised his stick in reply. She watched his tall, slightly stooped figure crossing the grass to the path and wondered about the limp, before beginning the walk home. Tigger, a lot of the bounce gone out of him, trotted docilely beside her on his lead.

'I don't know whether to feel indebted to you or not,' Laura told him out loud. She felt faintly irritated, now that it was too late to back out, for letting herself be drawn into a social commitment. She tried telling herself it was the lure of a library full of books that had persuaded her, but she had an uneasy feeling the library had little to do with it. By the time she reached Eleanor Shawcross's house, she was in no mood to gloss over her dog's misdemeanours.

'He behaved abominably,' she said bluntly, 'attacking a poor old labrador.'

'Naughty, naughty Tigger. I wonder whose dog that was?'

'It was Mark Wainwright's and he wasn't exactly pleased.'

'Oh dear.' Eleanor's blue eyes had a prurient gleam in them. 'How unfortunate. Never mind, I'm sure he'll forgive you,' she said, handing Laura her loaf of bread. 'And I'm sure Tigger enjoyed himself.'

After school on Monday, Hannah caught the tube to Covent Garden. It was her favourite place; there was always something going on, things to watch or listen to, like acrobats and street musicians. But today the sights came secondary to shopping in her order of priorities; she was banking on Rick giving her party the go-ahead, although for some reason he would not decide until Tuesday, and she was about to use the last of her allowance on something to wear. She suspected his reason for deciding on Tuesday was because he was having dinner tonight with Sarah Pemberton, and he needed the advice of a woman. Hannah did not mind; Sarah was all right if a bit bossy. She would be unlikely to veto a harmless little disco party. Hannah had very nearly asked Samantha to come with her on this expedition because it would have been more fun; but Samantha would have side-tracked her by wanting to stop and look at things, and Hannah had discarded the idea.

She threaded her way between tourists and shoppers, slightly hampered by her flute case in one hand. Music had been the last lesson of the day, and she had been forced to bring it with her. She paused by a hamburger stall, tempted; but the pressing nature of her mission drove her on. There were a couple of shops she wanted to try, ones she had frequented before; it was just a matter of searching for them. She never noticed the names of shops, expecting to find them again by instinct, like a homing pigeon. The secondhand ones were the best value, but they were unlikely to have what she was looking for, a picture of which was clear in her mind. Grunge was out for the evening, it would not do at all.

Three quarters of an hour and three shops later, she was standing in a packed communal fitting-room, dressed in a scarlet mini and black crocheted top under which you were obviously meant to wear nothing. It would have looked better on someone with a larger bust, she decided, as dissatisfied with her small breasts as Annabelle was with her large ones. In fact, it would suit Annabelle, but of course it was not the kind of thing she would dream of wearing. Jostling for a share of the mirror, she eyed herself critically. Rick would not approve, she knew that; he'd ask if she really wanted to dress like a teenage prostitute. He wouldn't like it any more than he liked grunge, but he would give in, in the end, he always did.

Pleased with herself, not only because she had bought what she wanted, but had a bit of her allowance left over as well, she left the shop clutching a plastic carrier and the flute case in either hand. Free now to wander, and thirsty from shopping, she found a table outside a café and treated herself to a can of 'Tango'. Street musicians, two men and a girl, were playing jazzed-up Mozart. Hannah sucked at her straw, engrossed. One of the men played the flute rather well. She tried to imagine herself, if she failed to get into the Royal College of Music, playing for the crowds in the streets, and decided it would be quite fun.

Someone pulled out the chair on the other side of her table and a voice said, 'Mind if I sit 'ere?' It seemed an unnecessary request since, when she turned her head, the boy was already seated, a tin of lager in his hand. He had a round, ingenuous face with baby-blue eyes and very long lashes, and if his hair had not been shaved to a pale shadow it would have been blond. She squinted to right and left, and considered he had a cheek when several tables were unoccupied. She gave a non-committal shrug, and moved the carrier bag from the table-top to her lap, leaving the flute case there where she could see it.

'Not bad, are they?' the young man remarked, waving his lager towards the musicians. They had switched to Tchaikovsky now, and were getting quite a lot of coins in the instrument case at their feet. 'So you play then, do you?' he asked, his eyes on Hannah's flute.

'I'm learning. I play in school concerts,' she said.

A conservative upbringing told her not to strike up

conversations with strangers, but music was different, it knew no barriers.

'I play the piano a bit; picked it up for myself,' he said airily. 'Mind if I take a decko at what you've got in the case? Oboe, is it?'

'Flute,' she said, snapping it open. The instrument lay there, gleaming silver in the last rays of the sun. He put out a hand; she shut the case swiftly. Looking was all right, but she did not like the thought of grubby fingermarks all over it when she next came to play. Not that he looked dirty; his white singlet and black jeans were exceptionally clean, as if he had a mother who took care of him.

'So you're at school still?' he said. 'Thought you'd have left; thought you was older'n that.' She shrugged again, recognizing this as flattery. He had taken out paper and a tin and started to roll a cigarette. 'Couldn't stand school,' he said. 'Left when I was fifteen. Boring. Waste of time. You don't learn to make money that way.'

'Oh? How do you make it?' Hannah asked, yawning.

'A bit o' this and a bit o' that.' He licked the cigarette paper and stuck the sides together. 'Window-cleaning, decorating and so on. Helping me bruvver do up old bangers. 'S not difficult to find the lolly if you know how. Got enough to stand you a drink,' he said. 'Same again, is it?'

'No, thanks, I've got to get home,' Hannah said.

'Back to Mum and Dad, that it?' His wide blue eyes laughed at her.

'Yes. So what?' she answered firmly.

'Was going to ask you down the disco,' he said, lighting the cigarette, and letting forth a pungent whiff of cannabis. 'You being musical an' all, thought you'd fancy a bit of dancing.'

She realized the music had been a blind from the

start, just an excuse for chatting her up. 'Well, I don't,' she said. 'I hate discos, as a matter of fact, and I'm doing something else anyway this evening.' She shuffled the carrier bag as if about to leave.

'Have a drag of that,' he said, holding out the joint. 'Might put you in the mood, like.'

'It's pot, isn't it? No, thanks.' She was beginning to get worried, despite her conviction she could handle situations like this.

'Please yourself.' He looked at her with eyes narrowed by smoke. 'Well, you're just a kid after all, aren't you? Green as the proverbial.'

'Oh, naff off!' she snapped, goaded beyond her limit.

'Ooh! Listen to 'er. Naff off's not a nice expression,' he said, mimicking her accent so that her cheeks burned. 'Lovely hair you got, though,' and he put out a hand to stroke it.

She jerked away. 'If you don't get lost, I'll – I'll blow my rape whistle.' She did not possess such a thing, but as she fumbled in her sling bag, she made a mental note to ask Rick for one. He put his head back and roared with laughter, getting slowly to his feet.

'Rape!' he said. 'That's a good one. Don't suppose you'd know if it happened to you.' He leaned across the table, his face close to hers. 'I can take a hint,' he told her. 'And by the by, you've dropped your money on the ground. Shouldn't be allowed out alone, should you?'

She stopped glaring and bent between her knees to scan the immediate area around her feet; and when that yielded nothing, half-knelt to search beside the chair and under the table. There was not a note or coin in sight. A further delve into the bag delivered a closed purse, which she opened, and counted the contents twice. The money, the remainder of her allowance, was there intact. Only then did she glance up to find the boy had disappeared: and so had the flute. It was no use searching for that; it had lain on the table-top beside her – without her moving it.

For several seconds she stood stock still in sheer disbelief that it was no longer there: it couldn't have gone, it was impossible. The truth of it swept over her in a nasty dull cold wave, leaving her feeling sick and trembling. At first she panicked. Clutching her belongings, she went from table to table, asking if anyone had seen a man leave the café carrying a musical instrument. Nobody had. Her white face drew sympathetic replies, but the people were mostly young and in couples, too engrossed in themselves to notice anything much. A pair of middle-aged American women advised her to go to the cops, but there was not a sign of a policeman, and the nearest police station could be miles away. It was getting late; she had promised Rick she would be back by six o'clock. The musicians, who might well have remembered someone holding a flute case, had packed up and left without her seeing them.

She realized there was nothing more she could do. Slowly she started the walk to the tube station, all the earlier ebullience knocked out of her. It was not the thought of recriminations waiting for her at home that weighed her down. Music was the only thing that mattered to her beyond having a good time; without the flute she felt bereft, it was like losing an arm. There was the loss of pride, too. She, who had thought herself so streetwise, had fallen for the oldest trick in the game and shown herself to be incredibly stupid. She tried to comfort herself with vicious imaginings of what damage she would do if she came face to face again with the boy. Shit, she called him in her mind, because no-one could tell you not to swear if you did it silently. If he had stolen her new clothes she would have been furious but not miserable. The idea of a party had shrivelled in importance.

The train was crowded and she had to stand most of the way. Hanging onto the upright pole by the doors, sandwiched between people larger than herself, she found herself suddenly missing her mother acutely. Rick would be all right about the flute; he was endlessly tolerant, especially if she cried, which she knew she would if anyone were kind to her. Laura would not be if she knew about it; she would be full of biting comments on Hannah's carelessness. Hannah would have preferred this; for some reason it brought a feeling of security. In a curious way, she felt that if Laura had never gone, this afternoon would not have happened. All she wanted now was to get home in time for Laura's evening call, and before the tears aching behind her eyes started to fall, shaming her in front of a lot of strangers.

The room which had been allocated to Joe in the Ship and Anchor faced the hillside at the back. It was small and dark, and caught all the cooking fumes from the kitchen, but to him it was an unbelievable haven. It seemed a long time since he had had a room of his own, back in the Birmingham days. He had hung posters on the wall, and listened to his tapes, and read books. That was when things were normal, when he had a father as well as a mother, and friends from the Grammar; a girlfriend, even. Brenda, her name was. She'd been OK, came to see him in hospital quite often; and then quite suddenly she did not turn up any more. Got bored, most likely; hospital *was* boring, and he probably wasn't making much sense at that stage, before they got him on the right pills. Some medication made you feel weirder than you had before they gave it to you; brought you out in sweats and the shakes, and caused bad dreams. The pills he was on now were all right; he had been on them for a year and then they had sent for him and told him he was fit to leave. The hospital was to be closed down shortly. All the patients who were well enough, and probably some who were not, were supposed to be cared for by the community: an amorphous system that did not seem to exist, so Joe had discovered. As long as he took his medication regularly, he would be able to lead a normal life, they had said.

They said an awful lot of things that turned out not to be true, like there was no reason why he should not do a job, something undemanding. There was every reason why not when the work was not there and you weren't qualified; even council work such as road-sweeping was hard to come by. After hospital he had lived in a hostel for a while, and drawn his Social Security. But the boy he shared a room with had manic attacks and cut some of Joe's drawings into pieces and flushed them down the lavatory, so he left. He had landed up at his mother's place in Surbiton. He couldn't stay there, she said; she couldn't stand the responsibility after what he had done to himself in the past. She let him sleep the night, and gave him some money, and he left the next day. He did not mind much, he did not think of it as home any longer. That was the start of living rough. He tried to sell his drawings on the streets. The entrances to tube stations were the best bet; he made a little there, enough to get a meal and a drink, or buy drawing materials: it had to be one or the other.

It was the man trying to pick him up that had finished him, driven him to hitch-hike as far away as possible. The man's face had loomed like a sweaty moon over Joe where he was dossed down in a doorway. He had hit out wildly, then run, his skin crawling. Remembering, it made him wonder about what was normal and what wasn't. 'He's not *normal*,' he had overheard his mother's friend Sharon say of him. 'You'll be able to live a normal life,' the words of the psychiatrist. How did they know, what yardstick did they use to measure normality?

As long as he took the pills regularly, he was fine. If he did not, he knew what would happen: the Pressure would start. He called it the Pressure because that's what it felt like: a stretching inside his head until he thought it would burst if he did not follow the instructions of the Voice. The Voice went with the Pressure and told you what to do next, and you could not refuse. The Voice was all-powerful, there was no denying it; it was as though you had lost control of your own mind. Afterwards, you could not always remember why you'd done something crazy, like cutting your hair off in chunks, or trying to climb out of a window. The medication put a stop to that; he had not felt the Pressure for some time, nor heard the Voice. But it would not be long before he needed to renew the prescription, and that meant getting to a chemist, or maybe a hospital. There was a chemist in the village, but he did not want it known what drugs he was taking. They would cotton on to his problems and talk about them, and he did not want to lose this job. It suited him, he had been lucky.

He had spent the morning unloading crates of bottles and carrying them either to the cellar or the bar, whichever he was told to do. Later he had been in charge of washing glasses and beer mugs. He had managed not to do anything wrong, had not broken anything. There had been ham sandwiches for lunch, and a glass of cider. His muscles ached from the unaccustomed lifting, but that did not matter. Things had gone well, they were treating him fairly. Mrs Grimond had not said much; she looked as if her mouth was sealed most of the time. On the other hand, she had not found fault. The afternoon was his, he was free to do what he liked. He had decided already to visit

Laura Snow and thank her for helping him. Perhaps she would let him draw at the bottom of her garden if he promised not to disturb her, and if he could find a way down the precipice. He had noticed a lot of birds settled on the rocks down there.

Getting up from the narrow bed where he had been lying, he collected his drawing materials together and took the bottle of pills from the bedside table. It gave him a bit of a shock when he held the bottle to the light and saw how few he had left, two, maybe three days supply. He had not realized how near he was to running out, and for a moment he panicked. Then he remembered Laura Snow; she would probably know what to do, know how to find another chemist or where the nearest hospital was.

He thought about her as he walked up the hill from the village. He liked her; she had been kind to him, and she was pretty with her silky blond hair, although he supposed she was quite old, old enough to be his mother. It would be wonderful to have a mother like her, he reflected; one who would not disown you because you became a problem. He could not imagine her doing that, if she had children. He supposed, thinking about it, that she was the best example of a normal person whom he had ever met.

'You can't tell me it's normal behaviour,' Rick said, 'disappearing into the blue without leaving an address or phone number.'

He lifted the bottle of wine and refilled Sarah Pemberton's glass. They were sitting at a corner table in an Italian restaurant which he had chosen for its widely-spaced seating arrangements as much as for the quality of the food. The subject of Laura embarrased him. He wondered if Sarah suspected it was his own fault that Laura had left home, imagined that he was hiding some sexual perversion such as bondage or transvestism. They had finished their first course of Parma ham and melon and so far her attitude, he felt, had inclined towards an understanding of Laura's actions. He could not help feeling a little disappointed; he had expected an unbiased opinion, of course, but a modicum of sympathy would have been welcome also.

The idea of this meeting with Sarah had kept him going throughout the long, bleak weekend. He had known her for years, from the days when she and her husband Dermot were first married. Dermot he saw every weekday of his life, they worked in the same investment firm. After the divorce Rick had managed to stay friendly with both sides; he was godfather to one of their twins, and Sunday visits to Sarah in the country had become a regular ritual for a while. She was not unattractive in a big-boned, slightly equine way, but not attractive enough for him to think seriously of striking up a relationship with her. There was a time when he suspected that her feelings for him ran deeper than his own; but then Laura had materialized and Sarah had seemed delighted at the outcome, so he was probably mistaken. Her face across the table was thoughtful. It occurred to him that she was looking unusually pretty this evening, her rather high colour toned down by a paler make-up, her wavy brown hair drawn back in combs.

'From what you've told me,' she said eventually, 'she did give you quite a lot of warning about what she *wanted* to do.'

A sense of guilt stabbed at him, bringing him close to bluster. 'Well, I admit she said she needed time to herself, but I didn't understand the urgency of it.'

'You mean, you didn't take her seriously?' Sarah gave him a bland stare, forcing him to look at her.

'Something like that,' he admitted. 'Certainly not to

the extent of expecting her to bolt,' he added, rallying a little.

'What did you expect, then?'

'I thought she really meant she wanted a break, away from the children and domesticity, just the two of us. We haven't done that for a long time.'

'After she had carefully spelt it out to you that that was not what she needed?' She smiled faintly. 'Come off it, Rick.'

He began to wish he had not been quite so open about what had passed between Laura and himself. 'What you're saying is that I've been insensitive, which is more or less what *she* told me.'

'Not so much insensitive,' she said, 'as obtuse.'

'Oh? Stupid, in other words.'

She glanced at him with very clear grey eyes. 'I don't think you honestly want my opinion, do you, Rick?'

'I do. I do.' He touched her wrist placatingly. 'I suppose I'm on the defensive. Sorry. I'll shut up and listen.'

There was a pause while plates of tagliatelle were put in front of them. 'Have you ever stopped to think what Laura is really like as a person?' she asked, winding pasta neatly round her fork.

He raised his eyebrows. 'I've been married to her for seven years.'

'I've known her for much longer,' she continued, 'and I think there are bits of her you've missed. In the Patrick era she was left alone a lot, he was constantly indulging in some sport or other, and it suited her in many ways. She's creative, and creativity demands a certain amount of solitude, and quite a lot of encouragement. It sounds to me,' she said, reflecting, 'as if you either ignored that side, or weren't aware of it.'

He said slowly, 'I knew about her poetry, of course. I have to admit I thought it was no more than a hobby.

Mistake number one?' he queried. She nodded. 'But as for solitude: I'm at work, and the girls are at school except for holidays. She's alone for a large part of the day. She's quite often writing when I come home in the evening,' he said.

'What do you say to her?' Sarah asked.

'Say to her?' He looked puzzled. 'I don't know – some harmless remark like "still at it then", I suppose.'

'You've never asked to read it, or shown a serious interest?'

'I've always felt she'd rather I didn't,' he answered. 'She covers her writing with a hand when I approach.'

'I don't wonder,' Sarah said crisply, 'if you make condescending remarks.'

'Oh, dear.' He took a resigned pull at his wine. 'It seems I've make a cock-up all round.' He looked at her. 'D'you have any ideas as to how I should right my wrongs?' he asked.

'Why don't you encourage her to go back to work?'

'I don't see how it will help,' he said. 'It would hardly provide the solitude you – and she – say is required.'

'No, but she is happy to be involved with books. It would help her to do something for herself alone, find her lost identity.'

'That's what I fail to understand,' he said, knowing he sounded peevish. 'All this talk of "identity" and needing "space". All I've ever tried to do is take care of her.'

'I expect you've mollycoddled her,' Sarah observed. 'Laura would hate that. She'd feel suffocated.'

'I don't appear to have got anything right,' he said.

'I think you've been treating her like Miranda, who thrived on being looked after. Laura is totally different.'

'I have realized that much,' he said drily. He subsided gloomily into momentary silence. 'Perhaps I've bored her,' he said eventually. 'Perhaps that's the real reason for her running away, nothing to do with lost identities or the other psycho-babble.'

'If we're getting into the realm of sex,' she said, 'I can't help. There's a limit to my marriage counselling.'

'I'm not talking about sex; although I'm beginning to doubt every aspect of our lives,' he said.

'Oh, for God's sake, Rick, stop being so negative,' she said with some force. 'You never used to be boring, but you're getting dangerously close to it.'

'Sorry,' he said coldly. 'I shouldn't have dragged you into my problems. It isn't fair.'

'Why on earth not?' she asked cheerfully, refusing to fall out. 'Other people's problems are notoriously easier to solve than one's own. And this one's very easily solved. Leave her alone, and she'll come home, bringing some satisfactory writing with her.'

'I don't know where to go from there,' he admitted. 'I don't know how to pick up the threads. Underneath everything else, I feel angry.'

'So does she, underneath it all. That's why she's gone,' Sarah added firmly. 'Back away, do the same as she's done. Pretend you dont give a damn whether she's in Timbuctoo or Cornwall when you speak to her; everything is just fine and you're busy leading your own life quite happily, thank you. Make her rather less certain of you.'

'Are you suggesting I make her jealous, as well?' he asked, mildly surprised.

'It wouldn't do any harm,' she answered, examining her fingertips. 'You need only pretend.'

He grinned for the first time. 'I'd have to have a genuine name to drop casually into the conversation, to lend credence to my supposed misbehaviour,' he said. 'You'll do nicely, Sarah.'

'Me?' she said, laughing. 'I'm hardly going to cause Laura sleepless nights. Reliable old Sarah.'

'I'm not so sure, if you have dinner with me twice in one week.' He poured the last of the wine into their glasses. 'Will you?'

'I didn't mean my suggestion to be taken so literally,' she said lightly.

'Will you, please?' he repeated. 'I'd like it; and I promise next time not to use you as a counsellor.'

'I'm only in London till Thursday.'

'Wednesday, then.'

'How do you know I don't have a lover around?'

'I don't know. Have you?' he asked.

'I'm not saying. All right, Wednesday. Unless I get a better offer,' she said, smiling. 'But I don't imagine it's going to get Laura running back to you.'

They talked of other things then, of her children and of his.

'How are the girls managing?'

'Oh, fine,' he said. 'They're independent now, busy with their own lives.' Silently she queried this vague male statement. 'Hannah took her flute shopping and had it stolen, careless little thing,' he added. 'It's shaken her, but it'll teach her not to let it happen again.'

While they talked, she tried to keep her mind on the subject and not on the outline of his profile or the close proximity of his leg and shoulder. She was relieved when at last they moved; glad and more than slightly amazed that he was quite unaware, and always had been, of the effect he had on her.

Mark Wainwright's house was square and solid, like a child's drawing, with long sash windows set either side of a white-painted front door and portico. Blue hydrangeas were clustered along the walls. To the right, outhouses huddled behind a further low wall, part of the original farm buildings. It was growing dark as Laura drove her car through the open gateway, and the local grey stone of the house looked vaguely intimidating in the failing light; rather like its owner, Laura decided, knowing a moment of shyness. She imagined a conversation full of stilted pauses, and not usually being afflicted like this, wondered what had come over her.

Inside, Mark led her through the hall to a living-room overlooking the garden where the lawn ran down to the escarpment, bordered by the trees she had seen from the fields below. Logs were burning in a large stone grate, and a tray of drinks was set on a sofa table. She felt immediately better.

'I lit a fire,' he said. 'It gets cold in the evenings. Sit wherever you like. What can I give you to drink?'

This hostmanship was quite unexpected after their previous encounters; perhaps he was happier on home ground. She sank into the corner of a sofa covered in faded cretonne.

'Whisky, please, with water.'

He looked less hawk-like and intimidating in the light of the fire and the lamps. She watched him pour the drinks, a bulky sweater filling out his straggling figure. There was, she saw, a hole in one elbow of blue wool, and found it rather endearing.

'How's the writing going?' he asked, sounding genuinely interested as he settled himself in an armchair opposite her.

'Quite well,' she said cautiously. 'I've done more in a few days than I would have in six months at home.'

'Your escape has been a success, then. I'm glad.'

'Escape?'

'Guesswork on my part.' He took a sip of his drink. 'I imagined you were throwing off the shackles of domesticity.'

'You know nothing about me,' she said, smiling without meaning to.

'I know you have a family, according to that mine of information, Eleanor Shawcross.'

'I don't even know that much about *you*,' she said.

'Where shall we start? You first, I think.'

'I have a husband and two daughters; one each, his and mine. I'm very fond of them, but you're quite right, I've deserted them temporarily.'

'No harm in that, is there?' he asked.

'Oh, but there is.' She leaned forward, cradling her glass in both hands. 'I left without telling them where I was going. You wouldn't do a thing like that, would you?'

'I might, if the occasion arose.' He lit a cigarette. 'May I ask why, or is that prying?'

She shook her head. 'No, but it wouldn't interest you.'

'Go on,' he said. 'Other people's lives are seldom boring, and you obviously want to tell someone. I don't divulge confidences.'

She found herself explaining from the beginning, although where the beginning was she was not certain. Frustration over Rick's attitude had not started at one particular time; rather it was a build-up of numerous small incidents that had gathered momentum like a kettle coming to the boil. She had not intended to confide in anyone, least of all, if she had stopped to think about it, a slightly forbidding solitary man whom she scarcely knew. The mixture of warmth from the fire and the whisky had combined to push her into it and she was surprised at the relief it brought, this confession. It was impossible to guess what he was thinking, sitting there with his shoulders hunched and his elongated legs stretched out against the slumbering form of Brutus. His impassive expression, she reflected, was probably the one he wore when listening to a pupil delivering an inferior Greek or Latin translation.

107

'The trouble is,' she added, 'I've reached the stage where I dread going back. I've made an enormous gap between myself and Rick, and I don't know how to bridge it.'

He heaved himself upright and took the glass from her hand. 'The gap was there already, wasn't it? A whisky?'

'Small, please.' She frowned. 'What do you mean, already there?'

He put the refilled glass on the table before saying, 'I mean, you were never in love with him. That's what it sounds like to me.'

She was about to protest and decided not to. It was a question that had lain hidden at the back of her mind for a long while, without her daring to face it. The two marriages could not be compared, and she did not want to try.

'I wish I knew,' she said. 'That sounds idiotic, but it's true. Rick is kind and competent, and interested in a lot of things, but what I need in life isn't one of them. You'd like him; he's very likeable.'

'I'm sure he is, but that's not the point,' he said. 'In all marriages or relationships or whatnot, there should be an element of fear. The fear of losing whoever you value beyond all else. Without that, something is wrong with the set-up. That's my theory, anyway.' He looked at her and smiled. 'But I'm being didactic and you're looking sad. Shall we go and search out some poetry?'

He got to his feet and held a hand out to her, leading her next door to a room lined with books and piled with papers on every available surface. There were two desks, a large one which was presumably his, and another smaller one at right angles. Again the view was of the garden, dark now beyond the windows.

'You'll have to excuse the mess,' he said. 'This is my

108

work-room and I am hopelessly untidy. It's a mystery how I ever find what I want.'

The books in the shelves were in order, however, properly organized into categories. Anthologies and single volumes of poetry took up an entire shelf. He selected several for her, pulling them out and showing her, giving her little running commentaries on their merits as he did so. As she browsed, turning the pages, he occasionally leant over her, pointing out a passage with a long forefinger. He hummed under his breath as he searched along the shelf, and it struck her that he was enjoying himself as much as she was. Eventually she made a choice of three editions, Dylan Thomas's *Collected Poems*, and two anthologies of nineteenth and twentieth century work respectively, to take away with her.

'Is this where you teach?' she asked, glancing round the room with its two shabby leather armchairs and its air of tutorial chaos.

'Yes, when I'm here.' He was replacing the remainder of the books in their slots. 'I'm not always at home. I teach three times a week at a college on the other side of Truro, and I lecture from time to time at various establishments, besides writing the occasional paper or article. Those are written here, of course, and the school-leavers come to me.' He slipped the last volume into place and took off his reading glasses to look at her, his head on one side. 'So now you know something about me,' he said ironically.

'Hardly a biography,' she answered. 'It's a lovely house. Am I allowed to see round it, or would that be an invasion of privacy?'

'Come on. I'll show you the view from the top rooms. It's dark, but there's a moon.' He started up the broad staircase. 'You must see the sea with the moon on it.'

She followed him into a double bedroom and they

stood by the windows in the unlit darkness. The estuary was ghostly pale in the moonlight, lights from the boats and the far shore yellow dots on silver, Mark's trees black silhouettes against the water.

'It's wonderful,' she said.

'Better than Oxford,' he agreed. 'There's nothing like this in the Ifley Road.'

'Is that why you left?' she asked without thinking.

He moved from her side and switched on a lamp. 'Not exactly. There were other reasons,' he replied without elaborating. She wondered if she had upset him, but he added quite naturally, 'We knocked a wall down to make this a decent-sized bedroom.'

She looked around her at walls and ceiling painted white, old beams, a double bed covered in a patchwork quilt, his late wife's dressing-table standing diagonally across a corner by the window. Any female accoutrements had been cleared away, but an air of femininity remained in the choice of furnishings, in the curtains and the Indian rugs on the scrubbed wood floor. She felt that he was happy to leave it that way. The top of a walnut chest of drawers was crammed with photographs and framed snapshots. There were several of a young woman with dark hair and an attractive rather than a pretty face, and two of the same boy taken at different ages: as a small child and a teenager. In the teenage one his nose had grown into a replica of Mark's, and light brown hair fell into a pair of similar grey eyes. Laura said nothing, it seemed wiser.

Mark stood behind her. 'That's Alice,' he said conversationally, 'and that's my son.'

'Really?' She peered again. 'Alice doesn't look old enough to have a child of that age.'

'Alice and I didn't have children.' He touched the photo of the boy. 'He was what is popularly known as a love-child,' he told her in the same easy manner, 'and the chief reason I left Oxford.' Turning to the door, he added, 'Shall we go downstairs and finish our drinks?'

She followed, unable to think of a suitable reply. The casual tone in which he had delivered his revelation startled her almost as much as the fact of his paternity. He did not seem the type to make sexual blunders, and she was still trying to adjust to this new image of him when they reached the living-room. She picked up her drink while he poked a log into place in the fire, wondering why, all of a sudden, she should see an attraction in his stooping figure.

'I should be going,' she said, 'I have to ring the children.'

He straightened himself, dusting his hands. 'I've embarrassed you,' he said smiling sardonically.

'I don't embarrass that easily,' she answered sharply. 'Although I don't quite know why you told me,' she added, 'a complete stranger.'

'Surely, we're past being strangers by now.' He nudged the dog gently with his foot. 'Come on, old boy, move. You're practically on fire. I don't know why I said anything about it. One does these things without thinking. You gave me your story, and confidences are catching, I suppose.'

'Yours sounds more engrossing than mine,' she said. 'Are you going to leave it at that?'

'For tonight, yes.' He looked down at her. 'It'll give me an excuse to see you again. Although my past doesn't warrant that much interest, I promise you.'

She stood, feeling confused, gathering up the pile of borrowed books from the sofa beside her. 'Thank you for these,' she said, 'and for showing me the house.' On the doorstep she said, out of the blue, 'I meant to ask you. Is there a hospital within driving distance?'

He raised his eyebrows. 'There's Truro General. Do you need one?'

'I don't.' She hesitated. 'It's for Joe, you remember, the boy who does the bird drawings. He's on medication for some problem or other, and needs to renew his prescription.'

'You seem to have got yourself involved,' Mark said with a touch of his original acerbity.

'I mind,' she said simply. 'I knew you wouldn't approve.'

'Besides, he should see a doctor first, who will probably refer him to a hospital. He won't get anywhere just turning up at the hospital reception desk without a general practitioner's referral.'

'How do you know so much about it?' she asked.

'Alice,' he said. 'She was a GP in a local practice here. I can give you a name, if you like. I just feel,' he added, 'you should take care whom you gather under your wing.'

'I'll remember that,' she said, 'when I'm next asked for a drink with a strange man.'

'*Touché.*'

She hovered, uncertain whether to offer her face for a peck on the cheek. She put out her hand. 'Thank you again.'

In the car she glanced at him, tall against the hall light, lifting his own hand in farewell. He looked very much alone. She wound down the window. 'Come and have supper one evening,' she said.

She drove home on the narrow winding road between hedges of fuchsia and low stone walls, the eyes of small animals glowing every so often through the darkness. It crossed her mind that, for someone attempting a simple, solitary interlude, she was in danger of complicating it. It was difficult not to feel sorry for the helpless and the bereft, she told herself; Joe was a genuine case for compassion. When it came to Mark, pretend as she might, her argument did not quite ring true.

Joe had spent the whole of his afternoon at the bottom of Laura's garden, sketching. She had shown him the easiest way to get there: down the long steep row of steps to the little private jetty, onto the flat rocks and into the bottom of the garden itself.

'There's a row of fuchsia bushes,' she told him. 'You'll be able to hide yourself from the birds if you want to.'

She had been as kind as ever. When he asked her about the hospital, she said she would find out for him from someone she was going to meet that evening. A lot of people would have been curious, asked embarrassing questions about why he was on medication; she only said, 'What a nuisance for you, having to remember to take it.' He was not likely to forget, but she wasn't to know that. It had given him a shock to find how few pills were left in the bottle. He found himself instinctively listening for the Voice, without cause; because although he had not missed the necessary dosage as yet, his nerves anticipated it.

He could not see her from the foot of the garden; the rise of the cliff obscured the kitchen window where she sat writing her poetry. He liked to think of her there, her fair hair falling either side of a face lowered in concentration. It gave him a sense of security, as if nothing really bad could happen to him while he was near her. That afternoon he had drawn a heron which perched obligingly on a bollard at the end of the jetty. The first thing he did, when he returned to the pub, was to take out his prescription and look at it carefully. It was covered with stamp marks and the dates each time it had been dispensed; it was difficult to decipher whether or not the repeats had run out.

113

This worried him; it might be awkward, getting a new prescription from a hospital who did not know him or his past history.

He stared out of the window, at the backs of cottages climbing the hill beyond the courtyard, turning purple black in the evening dusk. Perhaps, if he had trouble with the hospital, Laura would help him. (He thought of her as Laura, although he called her Mrs Snow.) She would know what to do. The thought comforted him. He fetched a glass of water from the bathroom, swallowed one of the remaining pills and went down to start his evening stint in the bar, helping Sam Grimond. But his head ached from tension and he broke a glass as he washed up. Luckily Mrs Grimond wasn't there to see.

Chapter Five

Quite late on Tuesday evening, Rick climbed the stairs to Annabelle's room, checked the slit of light under the door and knocked, thinking as he did so how strange it was to have a daughter old enough for such niceties. It was as well that she was, however, for he needed to talk to her as adult to adult about Laura in particular.

He had left work early in order to cook supper, his conscience pricking him slightly over his two evenings of dining out. The girls might not be feeding themselves properly. Only Hannah had rewarded his preparations of perfect roast lamb and its accompaniments by having a second helping. Annabelle refused the crisp potatoes, asked for one slice of meat, and then hid half her cauliflower surreptitiously under her neatly placed knife and fork. To cap it all, Laura had phoned before they had finished eating.

'I'll get it,' Annabelle volunteered, who hoped against hope each call might be Ben's. She had not heard from him since witnessing the badminton incident.

'Fine, thanks, Laura,' Rick heard her say. 'Yes, we're all fine. Do you want to speak to Daddy?'

He took the receiver, mentally bracing himself to be jovial. 'Hi, darling. How are things with you?'

'Wonderful. You sound cheerful.' Laura's voice was surprised. 'Have you been to a drinks party?'

'I *can* be cheerful without a skinful,' he began resentfully. 'No, we're just in the middle of eating dinner cooked by me – rather good, as a matter of fact,' he added casually.

'Well done. I'm having boil-in-bag cod. Delicious,' she said with her mouth full. 'You don't mind me eating while I talk?'

He did mind. He thought it showed a lack of something; manners, for want of another word. 'What have you been doing?' he asked.

'Writing. It's going quite well, especially if I don't look out of the window. It's so beautiful here, the sea changes colour continually. You could watch all day. And I've met one or two of the locals.'

She went on to say something about the loan of some books, but he was only half listening. He was picturing a cottage with a sea-view, a telephone and the shadowy figure of a resident man. Who did they know with holiday houses in Cornwall? 'I thought you wanted to be alone; solitude was the whole point, wasn't it?' he said sourly, his resolution to follow Sarah's advice and stay cool slipping away from him.

'Oh, I'm getting lots of that,' she told him. 'How was Sarah, by the way?'

'Very well, and looking rather pretty. We're meeting for a meal again tomorrow,' he said, glad to have the chance to mention it.

'Oh, good, darling,' she said. 'I'm glad you're not moping.'

Her lack of interest incensed him. He felt like telling her he was actually spending his nights kerb-crawling round King's Cross. Taking a deep breath, he said, 'By the way, I'm letting Hannah have a party in the house on Saturday. Any chance of your being home for it?'

'A party?' For the first time her voice sharpened. 'You don't know what you're letting yourself in for, Rick.'

'I can't see why it should be that bad, if it's kept under control. Besides, I've promised her.'

'Well, you shouldn't have. She knows perfectly well

116

parties are out in term-time. After losing her flute,' Laura added, 'she doesn't deserve one, in any case.'

'You're very tough on her, you know, Laura.'

'I have to be: you spoil her.' There was a short pause. 'I shan't be home for it,' she said. 'I need longer than a week here.'

'Has it struck you that you're being incredibly self-ish?' he said on the edge of losing his temper. 'Not bothering about the children.'

'You wouldn't say that,' she pointed out, 'if you were with me and your mother was looking after them. Are the children suffering?'

'Hannah was very upset about the flute—'

'She was quite all right after I'd talked to her. She needs firmness.'

'And Annabelle isn't eating properly.'

'I expect she's dieting. She's in love, she wants to lose weight.'

'In *love*?'

'Oh, Rick,' she sighed. 'Didn't you know? Shall I speak to her?'

'If you really want to help,' he said, 'you can give me some idea of when you mean to return.'

'Don't tie me down, Rick,' she said quietly.

'Very well.' Anger and frustration mingled painfully inside him. 'Just don't be surprised if you find things have changed somewhat when you do get back,' he said.

'I may have changed also,' she told him. 'Tell the girls I'll speak to them tomorrow, please. Good night, Rick.'

Her receiver clicked into place, cutting them off. He had returned to the supper table, making a supreme effort to be normal in front of the girls, and knowing as usual that he had mishandled the situation. The fact was, he found it impossible to keep his feelings un-voiced. Laura had already changed; he felt as mentally and spiritually far apart from her as he was physically. Communication between them seemed to have packed up. Getting her back took on a new and desperate importance before – and he did not quite know what he meant by this – it was too late.

'They're not getting on,' Hannah observed while she and Annabelle washed up and Rick watched the television news. 'You could tell by what Rick said.'

'You shouldn't listen,' Annabelle said, her mind willing the phone to ring just once more.

'He's taking Sarah out to dinner again tomorrow.' Hannah clattered the lid onto a saucepan.

'So what?'

'Just he's seeing a lot of her, that's all,' Hannah replied, and fell to humming carelessly. Her world had readjusted itself in her favour, and the impact of the terrible Covent Garden incident had already faded. She had cried against Rick's shirt front, and a flute had been loaned her by the school until such time as a new one could be bought with the insurance money. Laura had been condemnatory, but not unduly so; and there was the party on Saturday. Life for Hannah was an eternal roller-coaster, and at present it was on the up.

Rick had not been able to concentrate on the News. Crisis after world crisis passed before his eyes without registering. He was tired with the tiredness that makes one restless and precludes sleep. His mind went round in circles, trying to figure out a positive step to take with Laura; Sarah's advice was all very well in theory, but in practise it was proving impossible for him to remain passive. It occurred to him that Annabelle might know more about Laura than she was prepared to say. Laura had, after all, entrusted her with the going-away letter; it was within the realms of possibility she had also given Annabelle an address, for use only in emergencies. Rick could not really believe Laura to be that devious; nevertheless, at eleven-thirty he found himself sitting on the end of his daughter's bed wondering how to ask her. She had been bowed over her desk in a white towelling dressing-gown when he entered, and swivelled round to face him, reluctantly, it seemed to him. There were dark smudges under her eyes.

'You should be in bed,' he said.

'I was just going. Is this a good night visit, or did you want to say something?' She looked at him warily.

'One question I wanted to put, that's all.' He glanced away from her at the blue-and-white wallpaper so carefully chosen by Laura, afraid that whatever words he used, they would sound like an interrogation. 'About Laura. She didn't leave any clue with you as to her whereabouts, did she?'

'Clue?'

'An address or phone number?'

'Of course not.' Her voice was shocked. 'She'd have told you, wouldn't she, not me.'

'Of course, of course. Silly of me to ask, I suppose,' he said hurriedly, rising from the bed. 'Well, I must let you get some sleep.'

'I shouldn't worry,' she said kindly. 'She's only going to be away for about two weeks, and she does ring every night.'

'You think I'm fussing?' He smiled at her, thinking what a nice person she had turned into. 'I wouldn't be if she wasn't being so secretive.'

Annabelle fiddled with her pen. 'I think she wanted to be anonymous, so we didn't disturb her writing.'

'Can you understand that?' he asked.

'Oh yes, I can,' she said. She gazed at him with dark, earnest eyes. 'Does it matter, about an address, I mean?'

'It matters to me. I'd like to write to her, you see. I hate the telephone, it's such a disembodied form of

119

communication, it distorts what I want to say.'

Annabelle wondered what it was that he wanted to say. She ran her fingers through her fringe and stared down at her bare feet. 'You're not going to separate, are you?' she mumbled anxiously. 'You haven't had a row or something?'

'Now what on earth gave you that idea? I wish I hadn't said anything to you.' He crossed over to her and put his hands on her shoulders, giving them a little squeeze. 'This is nothing to do with partings, or rows. I feel rather left out, that's all, like a piece of luggage Laura decided to leave behind.' He laughed. 'I expect a shrink would explain it as due to some childhood complex.'

She nodded and gave him a weak smile. She knew all about feeling left out. 'She'll come home soon,' she said, 'with piles of poetry, I expect.' She stifled the enormous yawn which nearly overtook her.

It seemed to him her face was drained of colour, but then she had a naturally pale skin. 'You know, you really are going at the work too hard,' he said. 'You're too tired to eat. Don't think I haven't noticed.'

'I had a big lunch,' she lied.

'Nothing else wrong, is there?' he asked, wondering whether she could in fact be pining for someone.

'Nothing at all.'

He kissed her then, said good night and the door closed behind him.

Annabelle expelled a sigh of relief.

Rick was not the only one to notice a change in Annabelle's appetite. It was far more difficult for her to get away with a microscopic midday meal at school. Although the sixth formers were allowed to eat what they pleased, the staff had had the problem of more than one anorexic girl, and signs of this were watched for. That morning Annabelle had felt faint in a political debate, sagging on her chair until a member of staff arrived and took her outside into the fresh air. She had flannelled her way out of the situation by pleading an upset stomach, but there was a gleam of suspicion in the teacher's eye which meant she could not afford to let this happen again.

She had stopped feeling hungry, and had reached the stage where the sight of food made her slightly nauseous. She thought she was eating sensibly: a yoghurt and grapefruit for breakfast, a salad for lunch and as little as possible of whatever was going in the evening. There did not seem much wrong with that. The minus factor was feeling permanently tired; the reward was that her weight was definitely down. When she lay in bed, for the first time she could feel her hip-bones sharp beneath her flesh. After Rick had left her, she went to the bathroom and stood on the scales, watching the arrow point satisfactorily to an ounce or two less than the previous night. Despite having persuaded herself that she wanted to lose weight for her own sake, to improve her morale, she knew that if Ben would only contact her, it would make the effort ten times more worthwhile.

The relief at Rick having said good night and left was twofold. She knew that, at some point, he would mention her appetite, and she did not want to be quizzed on the subject. He would start to worry. Laura was a different matter; she would understand, not condemn out of hand, maybe make helpful suggestions. But Laura was not there, and that was the other reason Annabelle was glad when her father had gone. She did not want to be dragged into discussing the lives of Laura and him; she did not want the responsibility, or to be asked to take sides. Her own problems were all she could manage at the moment.

She prayed to think of an excuse for phoning Ben, and fell asleep as she did so.

Laura was deep in the writing of a poem. The skeletal outline of it had come to her the previous night as she lay awake, listening to the sea; the soft slap as it hit the rocks and the gentle sigh of withdrawal, familiar now and infinitely soothing. With Joe in mind, the poem was about the deprived, the detritus of a non-caring society. Yesterday, she recalled, Rick had accused her of not caring about their own children. The barb had sunk home, riling her in its unfairness, but she felt no guilt. In her view, Annabelle and Hannah lacked very little either in the way of love and affection or of creature comforts. The recollection broke into her concentration; she laid down her pen, stood and stretched before going out onto the terrace and peering over the parapet. Below her she could see Joe's figure crouched by the fuchsia bushes, his dark head bent over a large drawing pad. The sun had been replaced that day with a bank of cloud, draining the colour from sea and land. There was something ineffably lonely about him that caught at her throat. As she watched, he slowly uncurled himself and started to collect his materials together, on the point of moving. She withdrew and went to turn on the kettle.

His occupation of the rocks at the foot of the garden was becoming routine, as was the cup of coffee she gave him before he left. She did not mind, and was certain, knowing Gerard, that he would not object either.

Joe came to the back door and she let him in, handing him his mug and proffering the biscuit tin. His hands were shaking badly today, and he shifted his weight from foot to foot, a habit he had when there was something on his mind, she had noticed.

'How did you get on? May I see?' she asked.

He handed her the pad silently. The drawing of the heron was half-finished, awaiting the colour wash to complete it. On another page there were rapid sketches of cormorants, and another bird she did not recognize.

'The heron wasn't there,' he told her. 'I'll have to finish it from memory.'

'There's always tomorrow,' she said. 'He may come back.'

'I have to get to the doctor tomorrow,' he said, staring at the mug in his hand.

'Their surgery isn't until five o'clock. It's only fifteen minutes away and I'm driving you, remember?' she said.

'You sure? I mean, your writing and everything—'

'I can write any time.'

'Thanks. You're very kind.' He was giving her one of his intense stares, which she tried not to find disconcerting, and she could see the strain in his eyes.

'You're worrying about something,' she said. 'Come on, Joe, what is it?'

'They may make a fuss about giving me a new prescription,' he admitted, 'not knowing about me and that.' He shuffled his feet. 'The medication, the drugs, they're quite strong, you see.'

She wondered whether she was right after all in suspecting epilepsy. 'You can show them the old prescription. At least they'll know what you've been prescribed.'

'Yeah, I guess so.'

'Or they can always check with the hospital where you were an in-patient.'

'I hadn't thought of that.' A lot of the tautness seemed to leave him at the idea.

'It'll be all right, I'm sure,' she said positively.

He rinsed his mug under the tap and put it on the draining board. 'No-one's ever helped me like you

123

have,' he said. 'I'd like you to have a drawing to say thanks; the heron, maybe, if it turns out right.'

'You can't keep giving them away,' she told him, smiling. 'You'll never make a profit. Anyway, I want to help. And now I've got to do some cooking, a friend is coming to supper.'

He said, 'I'll come back and draw, then, tomorrow afternoon, if that's all right. It stops me getting nervous.'

When he had gone, Laura took a small chicken from the fridge and looked at it dubiously. It seemed an age since she had prepared a proper meal; cooking for one was the most boring pastime she could think of, and she had been living happily off deep-frozen food since she arrived. Roast chicken had seemed a safe bet to give someone whose likes and dislikes were unknown. It isn't just Mark's taste in food, she thought as she washed the vegetables; I know nothing about him at all, apart from the fact, that his wife is dead, and he has a son by someone else. I really can't think why I asked him. But behind this piece of self-deception she understood perfectly well. The temptation to talk to someone with shared interests was strong, stronger than her instinct for a solitary and slightly lazy temporary existence.

It made her realize how badly she had been missing this kind of communication, a form of which must have existed once between herself and Rick, otherwise she surely would not have married him. She tried to think what they had talked about in those days before they had been reduced to snapping at each other down the telephone, and found with a shock she could not remember.

By the time she had put the chicken in the oven, laid the table and searched for candles, she felt quite tired from the unaccustomed effort. It would have been a different matter had she happened to be in love with him, she decided; she would be doing all this with great care and expectation. Nevertheless, she recalled the unexpected attraction of his lean figure stooping over the fire; and when she went upstairs to get ready, she bothered to do her face properly, and to choose a reputable pair of rather tight black jeans.

At much the same time as Laura was wriggling into the jeans, Mark was going through his sweater drawer, trying to find one without holes. April August, who cleaned for him and did his laundry, would most likely have mended his clothes also had he asked her, but he had not bothered. There were so few occasions when he had to look presentable, and even fewer people for whom he felt inclined to do so, since Alice died. He was under no illusions as to why now he should be taking the trouble for Laura. He was drawn to her, not only because of her slight and pensive blond looks, but for a certain acerbic quality that showed at odd moments in her conversation. She was not one to be bullied or coerced, and he admired that. The physical attraction was more surprising; it happened seldom in his life that he was struck in this way, and she was unlike either Alice or Francie, the mother of his child. He had no intention of letting his feelings get out of hand, however. He had been the instigator of one disrupted marriage, and once was enough. But it did not prevent him from indulging in a rare moment of vanity. He came at last upon a black sweater given to him by Alice and practically unworn. Black for him had vague connotations of pop stars and media artists, alien to his nature. Pulling it over his head and looking in the mirror, he grinned ironically, unexpectedly pleased with his reflection. It only remained for him to put a bottle each of red and white wine into a carrier bag and call Brutus from his basket. 'Come along, old boy. The nice lady has invited you too.'

He had been in Oxford for three years before the iconoclastic Francie had swept him up and broken his image. Frances and Daniel Burgess were a strangely ill-assorted couple: Daniel, a science boffin wrapped up in his own world of split atoms and black holes, eyes pink-rimmed behind pebble glasses, pale hair thinning on top. And Frances, a fabric designer, concerned with the arts and meditation, and with the face and hair of a gypsy. She wore long full skirts, looked like a drawing by Augustus John and had a sexual magnetism which had been largely wasted until Mark succumbed to it. He had always considered his libido to be somewhat below average strength; it did not worry him to go for long periods of time without a sexual encounter. But then he had not met a woman like Francie before, whose pull affected his body as well as his mind, and more so. The Burgesses and Mark were on an academic social circuit which entailed them meeting at the same cliquey drinks and dinner parties, where, out of politeness, Mark would try to concentrate on the girl designated to him for the evening, while his whole being cried out for Francie. Across a table or a roomful of people, he would watch her in conversation with someone else, speaking in her slow, deliberate way, and wonder at the strength of his longing. There came an evening when her husband was lecturing in Durham and Mark and she were at a dinner party together. Afterwards, he went back with her to the Burgess's rather pokey cottage on the outskirts of the town, and found himself still there when he woke, with Francie beside him.

It was inevitable that the affair should leak out; the academic fraternity gossiped as avidly as any other group. It had its fair share of adultery, and its ear to the ground for the latest piece of scandal. The Burgesses

126

were childless, which had led to the rumour that they no longer bedded each other, and perhaps never had. Despite Daniel's air of indifference towards Francie, this was not true; when he discovered her infidelity, he was extremely angry. By this time she had become pregnant, deliberately so, without telling Mark what she intended. There was no question of a divorce. Between herself and Daniel there existed a bond, unnamed and powerful however nebulous, which was not to be broken. For some extraordinary reason he accepted the child as his own. Feeling hopelessly used and bruised, Mark could not face the close proximity of Francie, the feigned ignorance of friends, or the thought of his child growing up with a substitute father only a mile or so away. He gave up his university career and turned elsewhere, starting as Classics master for the 'A' level form at Westminster. His son he had never seen, except in the photographs Francie sent him; it was part of the agreement that the boy should not be told whence his aquiline nose and deep-set grey eyes had sprung.

All this Mark imparted to Laura after they had eaten and were sitting with the remainder of the wine in front of the fire.

'How cruel for you,' she said when he appeared to have come to a full stop. Privately she thought Francie sounded a bitch.

He shrugged. 'It could be said I asked for it; which is more than can be said for you, left to bring up a child on your own.'

'Oh, but I was glad I had Hannah.' Over dinner she had told him about her first marriage, but only briefly, because the hurt of Patrick preferring another woman to herself remained indelibly planted within. 'I don't know what I'd have done without her. You can't have a breakdown with a small child to look after.' She knelt on the floor and leaned across Brutus to put a log on the fire.

'You still mind about him,' he said, stating a fact rather than asking a question. She did not answer. 'What kind of man was he? Or do you not want to tell me?'

Turning her head towards him she said, 'Charming and restless and selfish. Still is, I expect; I don't suppose he's changed. He arranged life to suit himself, regardless. He was very good at persuading you it was the best thing for everybody, whatever he was planning. That's why he was a success at his job: advertising. When Hannah was born, he wanted me to have a nanny, so that I could give my time to him; watch him power-boat racing or whatever at weekends, and so on. But I wanted to take care of her myself while she was little.'

She settled her back against an armchair. 'It proved to be a grave mistake,' she said. 'There are always plenty of pretty girls around at spectator sports, dispensing admiration. Patrick had a low boredom threshold,' she added with a faint smile. 'He simply grew bored with me.'

The fire had started to smoke. Mark got to his feet and pushed the logs further back with a poker. 'He sounds unbelievably immature,' he said with cutting brevity.

'There are lots of men like him,' she pointed out.

He dusted his hands, looking down at her consideringly. 'I wouldn't have thought physical men were your type,' he commented.

She coloured up. 'There was more to him than that,' she said defensively. 'Anyway, Rick is different, and I married him.'

'And now it's your turn to be bored?'

'That's an abominable remark.' She struggled up from her position on the floor. 'And bloody unfair.'

128

'It was, I apologize.'

She glared at him, turned away sharply, stumbling clumsily on the rug. 'I'm going to make coffee.'

Furiously she banged about the kitchen, clattering cups and spoons into saucers, unable to understand his sudden lapse into the sardonic. What sort of man was he, who invited confidences and then subjected them to sarcasm? It was of course her own fault for hanging out her feelings like so much washing on the line, and blathering on about things which were strictly personal. It was naïve of her, but she had come to think she could trust him. She should never have asked him for supper, given him a foothold in her affairs when she hardly knew him.

'You're going to break something, by the look of it.' He stood watching her from the open doorway. She glanced up at him, her flushed face framed by two curtains of straight pale hair. 'I'm truly sorry I upset you,' he said. 'I was out of order.'

She put the coffee on a tray. 'Why did you? I don't understand. You suddenly revert to how you were when I first met you.'

He took the tray from her. 'How was that?'

'Witheringly unsympathetic. Condescending.'

'Oh dear.' They walked back to their position by the fire and she poured the coffee, waiting for some kind of explanation from him.

'As you were telling me about Patrick, I found that I couldn't be objective about it. I've begun to mind too much about you and what has happened and is happening in your life.' He took his cup from her.

The declaration startled her. Trying to cover her nervousness, she said crisply, 'Then perhaps we'd better stick to your life. It doesn't seem to afflict me in the same way.'

He lifted his eyebrows at her. 'There's little more

to tell you. I've a yen to write a book on the Greek philosophers before I die, but that's hardly interesting for you.'

'Oh, I don't know.' She curled herself in an armchair, anxious to dispel the unease that had crept between them. 'How did you come to live in Cornwall?' she asked, wanting to know something of Alice, and not liking to put a direct question.

'An aunt of mine lived down here, in a house not far from where I live now,' he said. 'I used to stay with her occasionally. That's where I met Alice, at a lunch party. She was a doctor, a GP with the local practice.' He paused, smiling a little as if the memory was a happy one. 'We married. She didn't want to leave her job, I was tired of urban life, so I brought my work to her part of the world and we bought the house you have seen.'

'It's a lovely house.' Laura hesitated. 'She looks so young in her photographs,' she said tentatively.

'Fifteen years younger than me.' He took a cigarette from the packet beside him.

She stared at her hands, at a loss for appropriate words. 'You don't have to tell me about it, Mark.'

'I'd like to, if you don't mind listening, because I killed her.' Laura stared at him in disbelief. 'Indirectly,' he added, 'but none the less my fault.'

'How?'

He drew on his cigarette. She noticed a small tic by the side of one eye.

'We were on the way home from dinner with friends. She insisted on driving because I had been drinking and she hadn't. We came to crossroads; as she edged out onto the main road, a van going like a bat out of hell hit us broadside on: the driver's side.' He looked at her, his face expressionless. 'If I had drunk less, it would have been me in the driver's seat. So you see what I mean.'

Laura sat quietly. 'It might have been worse for her to be without a husband.'

He leaned forward, hitting the arm of his chair with a fist. 'But she'd have been *alive*, with the chance to start again with someone else. Besides,' he sank back against the cushions, 'she was tired; she had had a long day and it was late. If I had been driving, the accident might never have happened.'

She said, suddenly decisive, 'I don't believe that, I'm a fatalist. It would have happened anyway.'

'It's better to face it than to try to run away,' he replied.

'All you're doing,' she said, 'is substituting guilt for misery that she isn't there any more. It's a normal reaction.'

He looked at her in some amusement. 'The words of a psychiatrist; you'll do very well as my own friendly shrink.'

'It's the same with a divorce. I spent months convincing myself it was my fault that Patrick left me. Not any longer, though.'

'How wise.'

They sat for a moment in companionable silence; his face, as he watched the flames through lowered lids, seemed all at once drawn and tired. She had a foolish desire to go to him, put her arms round him in an act of comfort, wondering how he would respond if she did.

'What are you thinking?' he asked without moving his head.

She jumped. 'I was thinking how introspective we've become.'

'Yes,' he agreed lazily. 'Next time we must really try to be more light-hearted.'

Pleased there was to be a next time, she said, 'And you? I suppose you are still torturing yourself with guilt.'

'No.' He rested his feet on Brutus's broad beam. 'I was thinking, it's getting late, time I went, and how nice it would be not to leave at all.'

As if galvanized into action by his words, he rose immediately, picked up the coffee tray and limped with it to the kitchen. 'I should have helped you with all this,' he said, surveying the débris of their dinner. 'Not much of a New Man, am I?'

'You offered.'

Brutus lumbered over slowly in answer to a whistle, stiff from sleep.

'I have a plan to take you to see the church at St Just-in-Roseland,' Mark said as they climbed the stairs to the front door. 'It's twelfth century and on the very edge of the creek. Would you like that?'

'It's a lovely idea,' Laura answered.

'Friday afternoon then. I'll call for you, around three o'clock.'

On the doorstep he kissed her; a very positive kiss on the mouth, setting her free only after several seconds had passed. 'Thank you,' he said formally, not specifying what for – the supper or the kiss. In his usual abrupt manner he turned away towards his car. She stayed by the open door until the tail lights had swung round the steep corner to the upper road and disappeared. She was shivering a little as she moved inside, not only from the night air but also from a sense of being swept along inexorably by events. The plan for Friday, innocent on the face of it, now seemed dangerously like a step through a minefield.

By Thursday the arrangements for Hannah's party were completed, with satisfactory ticks against her list of things to do. Given the necessary incentive, she could be surprisingly organized. Pizzas and hamburgers were to be delivered, and Rick had ordered Coca-Cola and other minerals from the off-licence. Her plea for wine cup had been turned down out of hand. There only remained the question of how to ensure Rick's absence for the larger part of the evening. She tackled Annabelle on the subject as they walked home after school.

'Can't you get him to take you out somewhere, Annie? It'll be a real damper if he's hovering round.'

'I may be seeing Ben.' Annabelle, suffering from the now habitual listlessness, was not inclined to be helpful. 'I shouldn't think he'll want to be there. No-one in their right minds would.'

Hannah peered at her shrewdly. 'I don't think dieting suits you,' she said. 'Never mind; if you won't do it, I'll think of someone else.' She ran up the front steps and put her key in the lock. ' Sarah Pemberton, for instance,' she added.

'You can't just *tell* people to have dinner with each other,' Annabelle protested.

'Why not?' Hannah grinned over her shoulders. 'She'd be exactly right. They were out really late last night.'

Annabelle followed her into the hall and dumped her briefcase on the floor. She too had heard the car return some time well after midnight and had put it out of her mind. Feeling faintly nauseous as well as worn out, she went to the kitchen and took a yoghurt from the fridge. Carrying it to her room, she ate it slowly while she came to a decision. The Saturday date with Ben was a figment of her imagination, thought up on the spur of the moment to cross Hannah. There seemed no reason why she shouldn't phone him and make the idea fact instead of fiction. He could but say no; she had nothing to lose, and he was supposed to be a friend, after all. What were friends for if you couldn't communicate with them? She had been ridiculous in hanging back; it didn't matter who phoned who. She was willing to bet the badminton girl rang him constantly. Settling on this course of action made her feel better immediately. She threw the empty yoghurt carton in the wastepaper basket and went to stand in front of the long mirror on the inside of the cupboard door.

The trouble about dieting was that you lost weight in the wrong places. It was true that the skirt she was wearing felt looser in the waist. But her bust was the same embarrassing size; and she had not yet achieved high cheekbones, so far only apparent by sucking her cheeks in and not smiling. There was something odd about the colour of it, too; she was used to being pale, but now the skin had taken on a cheesy pallor, a distinctly yellowish tinge. Before she became hopelessly dissatisfied with herself, she went downstairs to the telephone in Rick's room which he used as a study.

Ben's mother answered, her voice comfortably maternal. 'Annabelle! We haven't seen anything of you for ages. I'll call Ben.' Annabelle could hear her shouting up the stairwell. She gripped the receiver tightly.

'Hi, how are you?' Ben said suddenly. He sounded normal; surely she was imagining a note of caution?

'Fine, thanks. Working flat out as usual; that's why I haven't been around much. I won't have any friends left by the time my "A"s are over!' She tried a light-hearted laugh, but it came out as a croak.

'Are you sure you're all right, Annie?' he asked.

'Yes. Well, sort of. You know what it's like. Why?'

'You sound funny. You really do take life too seriously. We'll get together soon and do a film or something.'

She rushed on before she lost her nerve. 'Ben, what are you doing on Saturday? Hannah's having a party at home and in no way am I staying in for it.'

'Oh, right.' There was a pause; a minute one, but still a hesitation. 'One or two mates are coming round after supper, Tim and Kate and Sophie and so on. Why don't you turn up too? You know Kate, don't you?'

'I don't think so.'

'I know,' he said, 'come to supper first, then you can leave horrible Hannah really early.'

'If your mother won't mind? All right. That would bo groat.'

She put down the receiver on a wave of gratitude. Afterwards she worried a little that she had more or less forced him into asking her; but the doubt was far outweighed by the advantages. She went upstairs feeling capable at last of working on a half-finished essay. Her thoughts were on the pleasing bagginess of her waistband, and the possibility of wearing jeans on Saturday. Hannah was practising the flute in the next door room; it no longer seemed to matter.

It was raining as Rick reached home on Thursday evening, giving him the excuse to go straight upstairs to change before he could be intercepted by one of the girls. His mood was such that he felt incapable of coherent conversation until he had had at least half-an-hour to himself. Standing in the hall listening, the only sound was that of the flute, drifting down from the upper reaches of the house; which meant that both of them were in their rooms. He poured a whisky to take with him and went to run a bath in the hope that a ruminative soak would help clear his thoughts.

What had happened on the previous night had left him confused, disorientated, so that he could not tell, out of a variety of emotions, which was predominant. Guilt, shame, astonishment and an awful kind of secret satisfaction in what he had done, assaulted him equally. He had gone through the working day mechanically, switched off from private life until he left for home. As he lay in the hot water the events of yesterday seemed like a dream or an extract from a film; nothing to do with him, and quite unbelievable. Sarah had become divorced from reality, no longer the sensible good sort he had known for years. Even he had acted out of character. Soaping himself slowly, he ran through the evening in his mind in order to try to make sense of it.

Whenever Sarah came to London, she stayed with a friend, who on this occasion happened to be in New York. There was nothing unprecedented in her telephoning Rick at the office and suggesting they had dinner at the flat. It was a normal arrangement between old friends who had never been more than that; or so he regarded it. In fact, he had welcomed a suggestion that enabled him to climb out of a suit and into something more relaxed. Because his interest in her was platonic it did not cross his mind that her feelings might differ. Once upon a time, perhaps, but not now there was Laura. He put up the token objection of it all being too much of an effort, and then gave in happily. 'I'll bring the wine,' he insisted.

It was a two-bedroomed flat in a South Kensington square, with a large living-room at the far end of which Sarah had laid a polished oval table. He could tell at a glance she had gone to a great deal of trouble, noting with surprise the central bowl of pinks, the silver and the dark green candles. He had envisaged a kitchen supper, and Sarah in trousers or leggings, but she was wearing a three-quarter length black skirt which wrapped over and parted revealingly when she moved or sat.

'A romantic evening for two,' he said jokingly.

'I rather like doing things properly once in a while,' she said, handing him his whisky in a cut-glass tumbler.

'It all looks very nice, including yourself.'

'Dinner's simple enough.'

Simple was not how he would have described cold cucumber soup, duck *à l'orange* and a sorbet. Sarah's cooking had always been excellent; it brought home to him how bored with his own he had become in Laura's absence. Without her, he did not have the same incentive, conscientious only on behalf of the girls, one of whom did not want to eat anyway. They ate slowly, pausing between courses, while the wine slipped down unnoticed and their conversation flowed easily as it had not done in the restaurant. Laura did not enter into it; enough had been said on the subject. Instead, they reminisced, going far back to the times when Sarah was married to Dermot and he to Miranda; digging up amusing incidents which he had all but forgotten. Several things registered with him as they talked; how laughing suited her, how different she looked in this setting, finer and less raw-boned than Sarah in the country. Her white shirt had ruffles that plunged deeply, showing the tops of her breasts, quite unlike the buttoned-up look with which he associated her. She had always taken herself too seriously in his opinion, and he found himself far more attracted to this new image. It never occurred to him there might be a purpose behind it, merely supposing that most women liked to dress up occasionally, particularly when they seldom had the opportunity.

He could not remember at what point he found himself no longer sober; not drunk, but anaesthetized enough for problems to have miraculously ironed themselves out. They had finished dinner and were drinking brandy with their coffee, and Sarah was sitting on the floor in front of a gas-fuelled log fire. Recalling afterwards, he thought this odd; she was not the kittenish type, but at the time it seemed perfectly natural. Her long legs curled quite gracefully beside her, and showed between the parting of her skirt. The pain of Laura's defection was almost non-existent, hazed over in his mind by a warm and slightly alcoholic glow of well-being. Watching Sarah and cradling his brandy, he felt a tinge of regret, and wondered why one never made the obvious choices in life, especially where women were concerned.

'You're wasted, Sarah,' he said. 'I'm amazed some man hasn't snapped you up long ago.'

She gave him a friendly smile. 'I'm quite happy as I am. Well, reasonably happy.'

'You don't want to marry again?'

'Not at the moment,' she answered calmly.

'You sound very positive. Any particular reason?' She did not reply at once but got slowly to her feet and gazed down at him in his armchair. She took the glass from his hand and put it carefully on a side table.

'You really don't know, do you?' she said. 'All this time and you don't know.' Then she bent over and kissed him long and consideringly on the mouth. 'So now you do,' she told him.

Someone, either Laura or Sarah, had accused him of insensitivity. He remembered that now, searching for words, his confusion the worse for having found the kiss enjoyable.

'I had no idea,' he said not quite truthfully. 'I never realized. Perhaps I'm stupid.'

'Pretty thick,' she agreed amiably.

'I always thought you attractive,' he said in an attempt at gallantry.

'Come off it, Rick. I'm just good old Sarah, supplier of a shoulder to cry on and an ear to listen.'

'Sarah love, that's not so.' He fumbled for his glass and swallowed the rest of his brandy at a gulp. Her accusation was shamefully correct; had he really made it so obvious? 'I rather thought that was how you saw me,' he said lamely.

138

'Just good friends?'

If only, he thought, she would not smile in that disconcerting way. 'We were married to other people,' he pointed out, 'much of the time.'

'And now there's Laura,' she said, fiddling with the ornaments on the mantelpiece.

He was silent with a sense of imminent doom. Whatever he said or did next, it was bound to be disastrous. He knew the correct move was to say good night gently but firmly and go, but it seemed callous to leave her, vulnerable from having given herself away. And to stay for much longer was fraught with alarming difficulties.

She was watching him, her brown eyes amused, as if she knew exactly what he was thinking. 'Don't look so miserable, Rick. I'm not wounded to the quick.' She held out her glass. 'Give me a little more brandy, would you? Help yourself.'

It was a relief to be given something to do, to be on his feet instead of pinioned in a chair by her slightly mocking gaze. He wished she had not kissed him, had chosen some other way of showing her feelings. It had woken in him an urgent need for Laura to be beside him in bed; a need he had been trying hard to forget about for the time being.

He handed her her drink and gave her arm a light squeeze. 'If I look miserable, it's because I've been so obtuse. I don't flatter myself I've blighted your life.'

She took a sip of brandy. In the old days, he remembered, she hardly drank. 'It's my problem, anyway,' she said. 'You've always liked small women, haven't you; not hulks like me.'

'Sarah, I don't have types.' He threw his hands up hopelessly. 'What can I do to convince you that you're a very attractive woman?'

She leaned against the mantelpiece. 'You want to know?'

'Yes, I do.'

'You could take me to bed with you,' she said calmly, as if asking for a lift to the supermarket.

'What, now?' he asked, stunned.

'No time like the present.'

'Sarah, I *can't*. There's Laura. You must see—'

'Just this once,' she said. 'I'm not asking for a repeat. I shan't blackmail you or even mention it again. Laura will never know.'

He took a step back in panic, knocking the coffee tray with a rattle. 'It makes no difference, I wouldn't be able to forget it. It'd weigh on my conscience. Surely,' he added, 'it would weigh on yours?'

'Not in the least,' she said cheerfully. 'I believe it would be a good thing for all of us. Therapeutic.' She put down her glass and lifted the tray. A wave of her scent wafted up his nostrils. 'I take it you don't want to,' she said without resentment as she walked towards the kitchen.

There she was wrong; a hardening in the crotch of his trousers proved it. Irritated by this unwelcome manifestation, he followed her purposefully, determined to put an end to a farcical situation by leaving. They met in the kitchen doorway, practically collided, and her long arms went round his neck, entwining him. It was impossible for him to pull away without being brutal, and after a split second he did not wish to, as he buried his face in her hair and neck. She led him next door to the bedroom and there she made love with all the competence she gave to gardening, cooking and the controlling of her children. It was a surprisingly passionate encounter, and when Rick finally left her sleeping he could feel nothing but a relaxed complacency. Only now had guilt rushed in, as he had known it would, obliterating any other emotions. It was the first time he had been unfaithful to Laura.

Sitting on the side of the bath and drying his toes, he tried childishly to persuade himself it was more her fault than his. Before she took leave of him and of her senses, he would have found the act impossible. In any case, it had meant nothing; was merely three-quarters of an hour of physical relief. It did not work, this self-deception. By the time he shrugged himself wearily into a bathrobe, the stark facts had presented themselves relentlessly. He had allowed himself to become semi-pissed in a moment of weakness and loneliness, bedded an old friend; not only his friend but Laura's as well. He had no idea whether or not Sarah had enjoyed it, and it made no odds. Either way, he would never feel at ease with her again, and the thought of all three of them getting together in the future brought him out in a nervous sweat. No more complacency; the whole futile episode had left him wretched and missing Laura so acutely that he felt inclined to go to any lengths to get her back.

Chapter Six

In the gloom of his small bedroom, Joe swallowed the last but one of his pills and held the bottle up to the light. The remaining one slid about unrestrained. Something worse than panic, a kind of despair, gripped him. All his fears had been realized; the refusal of instant help, the withdrawal of his lifeline. Behind him on the bed lay a packet of tranquillizers prescribed by the doctor, no better than a useless placebo as he knew by experience. For the first time since leaving London, he wished he had stayed. You were meant to remain in contact with your social worker, and the hospital where you collected your drugs, so they could keep tabs on you, not to scarper without telling them. He had broken the rules, the urge to get away from the squalor of the city so strong in him he hadn't stopped to think. He had got into trouble this way before, by not stopping to think things through, he remembered bitterly. And now he was five hundred miles away from anyone who knew what to do about him, facing all the old horrors. He threw himself on the bed and turned his face to the wall.

Laura Snow had done her best; she had driven him to the surgery and waited while he was with the doctor. Afterwards, she had seen the expression on his face, and tried to get in to see the doctor herself. But the receptionist, a misleadingly comfortable-looking woman, had been adamant. The doctor could only see people on appointment. Was Laura a relative? No. A friend? In that case – the receptionist's mouth set into an indomitable line – she would have to wait until next week. All three doctors were busy before then. Laura considered having a stand-up row, decided it would achieve nothing and swept Joe out of the room.

'I'm sorry,' she told him as they climbed back in the car. 'I haven't been much use, I'm afraid.' She glanced at the packet in his lap. 'It's not the right medication, is it?' she said. He shook his head, wordlessly. She sensed he was close to weeping. 'Are they no good at all?' she asked.

'Fuck all,' he mumbled, covering his face with a hand. His shoulders started to shake. A woman leaving the house peered at them curiously through the window of the parked car. Laura glared at her. She searched her handbag for tissues and put an arm round Joe.

'Tell me exactly what happened,' she said.

She waited while he gulped and swallowed and blew his nose. When he finally turned his head, she was horrified by the look in his eyes of stark fear.

The doctor he had seen had been elderly; at least he seemed old as God to Joe. He was due to retire at Christmas and looked forward to the enforced leisure; no more midnight call-outs to heart attacks and pregnant women. His experience of mental illness was limited and did not go much further than the isolated case of post-natal depression. Anything more complicated he referred to the psychiatric department of the local hospital, which was what he proposed to do in Joe's case within the first five minutes of seeing him. He was not unsympathetic towards the mentally disturbed, but he prided himself on being a careful doctor who was not prepared to hand out lethal drugs on the strength of an outdated prescription and the word of an unknown young man. A scruffy young man whose hair could do with a cut and whose jeans were worn through at the knees, which he suspected was to do with fashion rather than age. He tried hard not to be biased, not to regard all the jobless young as drop-outs, but serving in the Forces throughout a World War had given him a biased outlook, and the suspicion remained. He had scribbled on two separate pads, and then directed his gaze at Joe over the top of his spectacles.

'You do understand I am unable to prescribe this medication without your being assessed by the experts? I'm referring you to the psychiatric unit of Truro Hospital; a Dr MacBride. You'll get on with him, I'm sure, most do. Just take this letter with you when you go.'

His mouth dry with apprehension, Joe asked, 'When will that be?'

'They'll write to you giving you an appointment. In the next week, I should say.'

Joe stared at the envelope being placed before him on the desk. 'It'll be too late,' he muttered.

'What's that you say?'

He raised desperate eyes. 'I've run out. Don't you see? I – I'll screw up without the drug. I'll do something crazy and not remember about it afterwards.'

'Such as?'

Joe was silent. He gazed down at his hands, knotted shakily together between his knees. He knew that nothing he said would make this man change his mind. What was the point of telling him about finding himself on a window ledge sickeningly far above the ground, or the reason they wouldn't allow him razor blades or nail scissors in the hospital, or any of the other things that had happened?

The doctor said, 'Well, your only alternative is to return to the London hospital where you are registered. Let me know if that's what you decide.' He rose to his feet, unlocked a cupboard on the wall of the surgery and extracted a cardboard packet from among its contents. He added, not unkindly, 'Fear breeds fear, you know. Whatever you have experienced in the past need not necessarily repeat itself. Meanwhile,' he put the packet beside the letter, 'I've given you enough mild tranquillizers to last you a week. By which time you should have seen the experts. Don't exceed the stated dose.' He glanced at his watch, held out his hand, his mind already on the next patient. 'Chin up,' he said. 'Everything will work out for you, you'll see.'

Joe looked at him with loathing in his heart.

'Would it help,' asked Laura, switching on the car engine, 'to tell me what's really wrong?'

Joe hesitated. 'I suppose so,' he mumbled. 'I'm schizophrenic.'

'I rather thought so.' She manoeuvred out of the driveway and onto the road home. 'Stupid bloody doctor,' she said, thinking rapidly. 'Perhaps the best thing would be to go back to London where they know you.'

'Haven't got the fare, have I?'

'I'll give you the money,' she told him firmly.

'I couldn't take it,' he said, 'couldn't ever pay you back.'

'I don't want you to.'

He did not answer.

'There's something else worrying you,' she said, negotiating a cyclist, 'isn't there?'

He said, 'I'm scared of travelling. I threw myself out of a moving train once.'

She glanced at him, privately horrified, beginning to wonder how much she had taken on by making herself responsible for him. If the train incident was a typical example of what happened to him in extremis, then the sooner he had help the better. She considered the possibility of escorting him to London herself and foresaw the impossibility of dumping him at the Charing Cross Hospital without waiting to hear the outcome. With very little difficulty she pictured herself getting caught up in his life, becoming entirely committed to his uncertain future, and was not at all sure this was what she wanted. Already she was starting to act like a surrogate parent.

'If you do go back to London, would you want to stay there, Joe?' she asked.

'No,' he said positively. 'No . . . I like it here; there's space. Where'd I live in manky London? Have to sleep rough like before. Anyway—'

He paused.

'Anyway?' she prompted.

A sudden wave of colour swept up his neck and face. 'You're here, aren't you?' he said. 'I feel safe when you're around, and I can talk to you. I've never had anyone I could talk to before, except psychiatrists, and they're no sodding use.'

'Joe—' she said.

'Don't worry,' he told her, 'I won't be a nuisance, won't interrupt your writing. It's just knowing you're there.'

'Joe,' she repeated gently, 'that's just the point. I'll have to go back to my family eventually. Quite soon. I shan't always be here.'

There was a moment's silence. 'Yeah. Well,' he said at last, 'they're lucky.' He glanced at her. 'How soon? A week or two?'

'Something of the sort,' she said, her eyes on the road.

'I'll stay, then,' he said. 'I'll have been to the hospital before that. I'll be OK when I get the right drug.'

'What about the gap without it?' she asked.

'I'll manage. I'll get through that OK too.' He did not say it, did not repeat the fact that he had come to rely on her. But the inference was there, and she was filled with trepidation, doubting her ability to cope. She, too, needed someone to talk to, and Mark, despite the fact he would disapprove of her increasing involvement with Joe, was the obvious, the only, answer.

On the Friday, Rick left work at lunchtime and spent the afternoon at home. The night before he had not been allowed to indulge his introspection for long. The washing-machine into which Annabelle had piled a load of clothes, including her favourite white shirt, had stuck between rinses, refusing to empty itself. Annabelle, whom Rick thought of as normally phlegmatic, had taken it singularly badly.

'Bloody machine,' she wailed. 'I'll have nothing to wear on Saturday.'

'Does it have to be that particular one?' he asked.

Judging by the way she gazed at him with brimming eyes, it did.

Now, waiting for the engineer to arrive at an unspecified time, he had the house to himself. A night's sleep, for he had slept from sheer tiredness, had not altered his self-disgust, merely tempered it down a little. Inevitably he had begun to think more clearly and the afternoon's vigil presented him with an opportunity for positive action. He fetched the address book that he and Laura shared, and settled himself in a chair to go carefully and steadily through the contents. It was a long shot, searching for a forgotten acquaintance with a cottage in Cornwall; and of course there was no guarantee that Laura had borrowed rather than rented the property. But he thought the latter unlikely, and besides, this gave him something to do. He worked his way through to the S's before being interrupted by the arrival of the engineer. Rick showed him the washing-machine with the clothes floating forlornly behind the glass porthole, and left him to get on with it while he returned to the addresses. He came eventually to the W's, and Gerard Wyatt's name, London address

147

and telephone number: and underneath, written small, another, country number judging by the amount of digits. It struck a chord in Rick's memory. Gerard was someone whom he knew only slightly as a dinner-or-drinks party guest. But Laura talked about him frequently, and buried amongst that information he seemed to remember a Cornish connection.

He was interrupted a second time, to be told the washing-machine was working once more and to write what he considered an over-inflated cheque for the privilege. Left alone again, he spent some time, address book in hand, sitting by the telephone trying to make up his mind. It was not difficult to imagine Laura's reaction if by a miracle he struck lucky and found her on the other end of the line. She would feel tracked-down, spied-upon, as in a peculiar way he supposed she had a right to do. Her anger would result in an almighty row, driving a wedge between them to join the existing one. He gave up the problem for the moment and went to make himself a mug of tea. There was an assorted collection of crockery, knives and spoons sitting in the sink left over from breakfast; this was not one of the cleaner Carla's thrice-weekly days. Marmalade and honey jars still clustered in the centre of the table. The kitchen had lost its organized look, rubbing in Laura's absence like salt in a wound. The girls arrived home together just as Rick had finished clearing up, and started to dirty everything all over again.

'We'll eat out tonight,' he said decisively. 'Early; seven-thirty, since you've got your binge tomorrow, Han.' Suddenly he could not bear the thought of it.

'Great!' Excitement had an energizing effect on Hannah. She rinsed a mug and plate under the tap, flung cutlery into a drawer and departed upstairs in a rush, muttering about ringing Samantha.

Annabelle said, lolling wearily against the sink, 'I'll cook supper, if you'd like me to.' She did not look well, dark lines under the eyes, her face a study in black and white. Rick put his arms round her. 'You'll have a night off, *and* eat a proper meal,' he told her firmly.

She couldn't, that was the trouble. She leaned against him light headodly, closing her eyes, and the room spun.

'The machine's mended. You'll have your shirt for tomorrow,' he said. 'Serious date, is it?'

She moved away, saying casually, 'Only Ben, and a few others,' as if it did not matter.

Ben, he thought, aesthetic-looking boy with a flop of dark hair. He might well cause chaos in the lives of susceptible girls, but Rick wished he had not done so right now.

At seven o'clock, his courage bolstered by a whisky, he dialled the longer number under Gerard's name.

Hearing Laura's voice answer after three rings was so totally unexpected, the shock threw him off balance. After all, it had been such an outsider's chance of finding her. He listened for a split second before quietly replacing the receiver, feeling immediately guilty at invading her privacy as if there were no bond between them and he was merely a prurient stranger. He hoped very much she would not imagine the call to be burglars casing the joint, but he had not wanted to speak to her; discovery was success enough. Although he did not know quite what to do with it, it made her seem less inaccessible. A telephone number did not provide him with an address, however, and there was far more likelihood of his persuading her home in a letter than over the telephone. Gazing at his London number, Rick wondered just how much Gerard had connived in Laura's plans, and decided that he had never really liked the man. Not that he disliked gays *per se*, but he was perfectly aware that Gerard had tried to woo Laura back to work, which was partly the cause of her disappearance. It was quite likely that he had suggested his house in Cornwall as a bolthole for her. The more he thought about it, the more convinced Rick became that this was how it had happened, and anger mounted inside him. He poured himself another drink and rang Gerard's local number.

'Gerard Wyatt speaking.'

'Gerard, it's Richard Snow here. I gather Laura is at your house in the West Country.'

'Yes, that's so.' Gerard's cultured tones sounded faintly alarmed. 'Why? Is anything wrong?'

Everything was wrong, the stupid bastard, Rick thought. 'I wonder if you would give me the full address,' he said, sidestepping the question. 'I only have the phone number and I need to post something to her.'

There was a short pause the other end of the line. 'I don't believe I can do that,' Gerard said pleasantly, 'if she hasn't told you herself.'

'What do you mean?' Rick demanded.

'Laura wanted a period for time to herself, I gather.' Gerard spoke slowly and kindly as if explaining to a retarded child. 'She expressly asked me not to give away her whereabouts to anyone, and I feel I should stick to my promise.'

'For God's sake!' Rick exploded. 'I'm her husband.'

Gerard was unruffled. 'Why don't you telephone her, and ask for the address yourself?' he said. 'I'm sure she'll give it to you if she wants to.'

'How dare you,' Rick told him, 'play God with other people's marriages.'

'Nothing to do with God. Just sticking to my promise, that's all,' Gerard assured him urbanely. 'If you want my advice, dear boy, I should leave her alone for a while. She'll be so much nicer when she gets back to you.'

Rick was incensed. 'I don't need your fucking advice,' he said, and put down the receiver. He had lost his temper and been abominably rude, neither of which was characteristic of him. It would serve as a black mark against him if Laura were to find out, and Gorard would undoubtedly tell her. But the provocation had been too much; the man was insufferable. The phone rang beside him, and he let it ring serveral times, knowing it would be Laura and steeling himself to sound ordinary, as if nothing of consequence had happened in the last twenty-four hours.

'I've just seen Mrs Snow and Mr Wainwright,' Eleanor Shawcross informed April August in the grocer's, 'setting off for St Just. They've got a lovely afternoon for it.'

April continued to move her solid shape along the shelves. 'That's nice,' she answered non-committally, picking up two tins of Heinz's spaghetti and putting them in her wire basket. She had tried to dodge behind the toilet rolls to avoid Eleanor, but had been too late.

'I knew they'd get on,' Eleanor said, 'when I introduced them. They've got a lot in common. I expect,' she added, 'they'll see quite a lot of each other while she's down here. So good for Mark to be taken out of himself.'

April, who cleaned several people's houses, was quite aware of who visited who. She guessed for instance, that the roast chicken that Laura Snow had cooked earlier in the week was intended for Mark and that the black sweater which he seldom wore had been brought out for a purpose. It was not difficult to put two and two together, but she was not going to encourage Eleanor Shawcross. The old baggage could do her delving elsewhere.

151

'Mrs Snow's got a lovely family,' she said pointedly. 'I've seen the photos. Two girls and a smashing-looking husband.'

'Oh, I know, my dear,' Eleanor selected a packet of rich tea biscuits. 'Although I got the impression when we were having a little chat,' she said, lowering her voice, 'that all was not well on the home front. Just an impression, of course.'

'I must get on. Got Janice and the baby coming to tea.' April started to fill her basket at speed. 'If that's all you're buying, Mrs Shawcross, you better go first, otherwise I'll hold you up at the till.'

But Eleanor's attention had been distracted by the entry into the shop of a dark, gaunt young man. 'Tell me,' she said to April, 'is that the boy who is working at the pub?'

'That's him; Joe Blythe.'

'I've heard he's looking for a spare job. I wonder if he'd walk Tigger for me.'

'Can't say, I'm sure. No harm in asking, is there?'

'Is he *reliable*, d'you know?' Eleanor asked in a whisper.

'Haven't heard nothing to the contrary,' April replied shortly. 'Better hurry if you're to catch him, though. He's only come in for chewing gum, by the looks of it.'

With a sigh of relief she watched Eleanor hobble away surprisingly swiftly, and concentrated on the last items on her list. Out of the corner of her eye she could see Joe being accosted and shifting nervously from foot to foot as if longing to escape. She did not wonder: that Mrs Shawcross had the same effect on a lot of people.

Each time they met, Laura felt she was starting at the beginning again with Mark, as though any rapport built up at the previous encounter had been imagined. While they sat at opposite ends of a wooden seat looking out across the creek at St Just, she thought how she need not have worried about their becoming involved with each other; he was far too detached. She made herself concentrate on what he was telling her in the manner of a friendly but purely informative guide, while she tried to stifle a ridiculous sense of disappointment.

'There has been a church on this site long before the twelfth century, apparently. People used to come by boat to services when the tide was right. I don't know if they still do. The gardens are largely tended by volunteers rather than professionals. An amazing achievement.'

She twisted in her seat to look at the mass of shrubs and climbing plants clinging to the hillside, a backdrop for the ancient church. She could see the steep, winding path down which they had come, leg muscles braced against the gradient, flanked by camellias already in bud. He had not put out a hand to steady her as Rick would have done, his profile inscrutable until he pointed to an out-of-season primrose in flower. It was as though he regretted bringing her, she had decided and, puzzled, turned her attention to the view. That had at least been worthwhile. From above, the church appeared to be floating: tiny and perfect, it sat on the very edge of the creek, its reflection mirrored in the still waters. A rowing-dinghy was moored to the stone jetty, and beyond, a scattering of sailing-boats lay at anchor where the water showed pink in the afternoon sun. It was a romantic and miraculous and unique place, and quite, quite wasted on them, she thought now, listening to his voice feeding her snippets of information, and nodding at suitable intervals.

'We seem to be the only people around,' she said.

'It's late in the season. The holiday crowds have gone, and the locals have it all on their doorstep, to visit whenever they feel like it.'

'I suppose,' she asked, 'you used to come here with Alice?'

He glanced at her. 'Alice brought me here for the first time.'

So there you have it, Laura told herself; the whole venue is littered with memories for him. She stared at some curlews stalking by the water's edge almost at their feet.

'Joe would love this,' she said. 'I must bring him to see it before I leave.'

'Are you about to leave?' he asked, lighting a cigarette.

'I must, before long, obviously.' The longer she left it to go home, the harder it would become to dislodge herself from this solitary way of life, to break the habit of pleasing herself. She refused to admit to herself that the proximity of Mark might make it harder still; as things were going that afternoon, the feeling was on her side entirely.

'I think it would be misguided of you to go driving about the countryside alone with a schizophrenic,' he said in a voice that was distinctly grumpy. 'You shouldn't really be alone with him at all, in my opinion.'

'He's not a criminal, he's unwell!' she cried.

'And unpredictable.'

'If you met him,' she insisted, 'you'd see how gentle he is.'

Mark gave a sardonic lift of his eyebrows. 'And according to our last talk, fast becoming dependent on you. I thought the idea was that you were going to distance yourself from him.' He drew on his cigarette. 'Perhaps you need to go back to your own children if your maternal instincts are being misplaced.'

She glared at him. 'I'm sorry for the Joes of this world, underprivileged and with real problems.' She got up abruptly. 'Why are you being so disagreeable? You really can be bloody when you choose. I'm going to look round the church.'

'I'll come with you.'

'I'd rather go on my own, thanks.'

She stumped away to the entrance on the garden side, fists clenched in her anorak pockets to stop them shaking. The solid oak door with its round handle opened without a squeak on well-oiled hinges, letting her into an interior smelling of musty hassocks and candle wax and age. The nave was surprisingly broad, running between a dozen oak pews on either side, the prayer books neatly laid out in line along the ledges. The remainder of the sun fell in shafts through stained-glass windows, warming the grey stone walls with multi-coloured prisms of light. It was beautifully kept. Laura wandered, lightly trailing fingertips over stone and polished wood, allowing the tranquility of the place to soak in and soothe her angst. She completed her tour by the font and gazed back at the altar, imagining the enchantment of walking the few short steps to be married in front of it. Marriage was an uneasy subject to dwell on, however, so she sank into the nearest pew and asked herself instead why Mark's behaviour should matter to her in any way, although she knew the answer quite well, and that too was unsatisfactory.

She became aware that the church had darkened and the sun had been blotted out. The door opened and shut noiselessly and Mark slipped into the pew beside her.

'It's raining,' he said. 'Am I allowed in, if I promise to stop being bloody?'

'You shouldn't swear in church.' She grinned before she could stop herself.

As they were leaving, she dropped a pound coin into the fund-box and took two pamphlets from a table: a history of St Just-in-Roseland and a copy of the seventeenth century *Nun's Prayer*. They stood in the porch and eyed the drizzle coming from a single black cloud overhead.

'Shall we go and get wet, or wait for it to stop?' she murmured.

'Wait. I want to talk to you.' He drew her down to sit on a bench, keeping her hand in his. 'I can't keep on saying sorry,' he said. 'If you've an ounce of intuition you must know I'm beginning to love you.'

She stared very hard at the worn flagstone between her feet. 'You have an odd way of expressing it. How could I know?'

'It's because you have commitments, and I realize that any moment you'll disappear to fulfil them.' He pressed her hand. 'I'm finding that difficult to take.'

'So am I,' she said sadly.

'The commitments, or not seeing me again?'

'Both.'

They looked at each other, silently admitting the impossible.

'We scarcely know one another,' she said. 'Not long enough to talk about love.'

'I don't know what else to call it, speaking for myself.'

'The right chemistry, mutual attraction, lust?' she suggested with a stab at light-heartedness.

He did not smile. 'All those, probably, but there's more to it than that. Empathy, for want of another word.'

'I'm not certain it's the right one,' she said. 'Quite often I irritate you enormously, and *vice versa.*'

'It's not you,' he told her. 'It's the situation which is frustrating, because I can see no way of reversing it. There isn't, is there?'

She shook her head. 'None.'

The rain had stopped as abruptly as it had begun. She watched a weakened sun creep tentatively across the damp stones of the path outside, and thought how she had set out to find alleviation in solitude, and discovered it was not enough. But then she had not expected to find a Mark tucked away in the depths of the countryside, with a like mind and a willingness to listen. To be taken seriously was seductive in itself. She wondered just how much this factor accounted for his attraction, and whether, if they had met at a party in London, it would have been no more than the pleasant passing of two proverbial ships.

'I suppose we're both looking to fill gaps,' she said. 'The obvious one left by Alice in your case, and a lack of communication in mine.'

'Are you suggesting,' he asked, 'that's all my feelings amount to?'

'No,' she said carefully, 'but it can be misleading, searching for gap-fillers.'

He stood up abruptly, pulling her to her feet with him while his walking stick clattered to the ground. Without saying anything he kissed her, and went on kissing her for an unconscionable length of time, until the sound of a throat being cleared nearby broke their absorption. A small man with thinning hair and an umbrella stood patiently waiting to gain access to the church. Laura felt her face burning, partly from embarrassment because Mark still held her, and partly from the heat of two anoraks pressed tightly together. Mark on the other hand seemed quite unshaken.

'So sorry,' he said cheerfully. 'We're blocking the way, aren't we?'

The small man murmured something about being the verger, and gave them a deeply puzzled look while he sidled past them, as if they were from another planet. The church door closed gently behind him.

Mark picked up his stick and led Laura into the gardens, both of them shaking with silent laughter.

'Poor little man,' she said. 'We've completely ruined his faith in mankind.'

'He ought to be pleased at witnessing a demonstration of true affection.'

'Is that what it was?' she asked.

'I hope so,' he said seriously. 'What a little cynic you can be.'

'Sorry. But I didn't know affection could make you go wobbly at the knees.'

The stiff climb uphill put a stop to any conversation apart from the occasional breathless comment. But it was unlike the walk downwards when they had been separated in every context. Halfway up she stopped and turned to look back, committing the place and the whole afternoon to memory, unsure of experiencing it again.

Reading her thoughts, he said, 'I suppose the only thing for me to do now is make myself scarce. If I go on seeing you, I shall probably try to take you to bed with me and I have an idea you wouldn't be happy with that.'

She smiled. 'Happy at the time, and miserable afterwards, I expect.'

He put his arms round her, held her close. 'That settles it, then.'

'Does it? We could try being grown-up about it,' she pointed out, 'and settle instead for what we already have.'

'I'm not sure that's possible.'

'I don't think I want to stay here if I can't see you,' she said, lifting her head to look at him.

He sighed. 'We'll try, then; we'll sit miles apart in each other's living-rooms and talk of literature. You shall read me your poetry.'

'I shan't. I'm far too shy.'

'Then I'll read it for myself.'

On the drive home, which he achieved one-handedly, the other one clasping hers, she let contentment seep in. There was no longer a barrier dividing them, although the removal of barriers brought their own complications. She was uncertain about the outcome, whether or not they would be able to stick to the ground rules she had laid down. But for now, she allowed herself a whole-hearted idiotic happiness that had nothing to do with logic. In this frame of mind, she was unprepared, as they parked in Gerard's drive, for the sight of Joe huddled on the doorstep, head buried in his hands. He wore the usual jeans, his torso was naked, and the drawing materials lay spread out beside him, his old navy blue sweater on top of them. Laura bent over him and touched an icy shoulder.

'Joe,' she said gently. 'What is it? What's the matter?'

He raised his head and stared at her with dark, unfocused eyes. 'Headache,' he whispered and went on staring as if trying to remember who she was.

Curled beneath the candlewick bedspread in the semi-darkness Joe felt the pain slowly recede. The remains of it shot behind his closed eyelids in occasional stabs accompanied by brightly coloured shapes like shooting stars. Lights from the pub yard shone through the thin curtains and made weird patterns on the ceiling across his inert embryo shape in the bed where he lay sucking his thumb, reverting to childhood. Some of the confusion had cleared from his memory of the afternoon; bits of it remained a blank. He could not remember, for instance, how he had got from the foot of the cliff garden to Laura's doorstep. Had he climbed through the garden itself, or had he used the usual route up the steps from the jetty? These sorts of gaps in recollection panicked him. They meant the start of the old trouble, together with the headaches; both of them preludes to the Pressure and finally the Voice. He had been drawing when the pain began, he remembered that; a band of pain around his head that tightened steadily, blurring his vision. The heron had returned to pose obligingly in its former resting place, and he was sketching rapidly, putting the final touches to the original drawing. He had had to stop, fumble blindly to collect his drawing gear and stumble to his feet. After that, he could not recall anything until he found himself sitting outside the front door in the rain. That was why he had taken off his sweater, to protect the portfolio from getting wet.

Laura had taken him inside, given him hot sweet tea and aspirin. There was a man there who reminded him of a hawk or an eagle, kind of beaky-looking and fierce. Joe had been intimidated by him at first, but it was Mark Wainwright who drove him back to the pub and explained the situation to the Grimonds, dealing firmly with a grumbling Dolly Grimond.

'I knew there was something queer about the boy,' she said triumphantly. 'He's a liability.'

'Anyone can suffer from migraine.' Mark towered over her. 'If you can heat some soup, I'll take it up to him. You won't have to wait on him,' he added pointedly.

Joe drank the bowl of Heinz's tomato soup reluctantly, slopping it with an unsteady hand, while Mark turned to stare out of the window, careful not to watch. He had not wanted to eat but the taste of food was comforting. Mark had found the tranquillizers, read the instructions and insisted he should take one, overriding Joe's arguments.

'They won't do any good. It's not the right stuff.'

'Never mind that. It'll help you to sleep.' And Joe had swallowed it because he instinctively trusted this man, despite his frighteningly authoritative aspect. Mark saw him settled under the bedcover, switched out the light which had been hurting Joe's eyes and stood over him in the dimness of the room.

'I'll try to get you an early appointment at the hospital,' he told Joe. 'I know quite a few of the staff there. We'll try for Monday.'

'You a doctor then?' Joe asked with his eyes closed.

'I was married to one.'

'Oh. When's Monday? What day is it?'

'Friday. Not long to go. I'll do my best, but I can't promise. Mrs Snow will let you know what happens.'

'Yeah. Thanks,' Joe mumbled into the pillow. 'I don't know if I can last that long,' he added.

'Yes, you will,' Mark said firmly, 'and remember to take those pills. Good night, Joe.'

'Mr Wainwright—' Joe raised his head but the room was empty. Mark had gone. He felt suddenly alone and helpless. Mark Wainwright was all right, though, just like Laura Snow. He was lucky they were around, very lucky. The tranquillizer had begun to work, making him drowsy, but he was not fooled; this was all it did. It did not kill the Pressure, or prevent the Voice whispering its insidious instructions in his ears. Through his haziness a small knot of panic held fast in the pit of his stomach at the thought of living through the next two days; and then the sedative won, and he fell into a dream-ridden sleep.

'If there's any driving to be done,' Mark told Laura, 'I'll do it. I don't want you in a car alone with him.'

'You're working,' she protested, 'and I don't believe he's dangerous.'

'He's potentially a danger to himself and therefore to you, particularly in a moving car.'

'All right, then. You win.'

She sighed, partly from relief at having the matter taken out of her hands, partly from tiredness. The afternoon had been full of unexpected twists and turns, without time for quiet assessment. And here they were standing in Gerard's kitchen, he still in his anorak as though poised for flight, already obeying the rules.

'I must go.'

She knew he would say it.

'There's no rush.'

'I only dropped in on the way home, to give an account of Joe.'

She opened a cupboard and brought out a bottle of whisky. 'Thank you for looking after him. You deserve a drink.'

'I might quite possibly ravish you.'

'That's all right. I wouldn't be able to stop you, would I?' She smiled at him, feeling a lightening of the spirits.

Taking the proferred glass from her, he said, 'There's something endearing about your young man, I must admit. I can see now the urge to tuck him under your wing.'

'It isn't just Joe, it's his predicament,' she said.

'I know, and that's the problem. It isn't likely to change for the better, is it? The pub won't keep him for ever, he'll be without work or a place to live, and you,' he stared at his whisky, 'you will leave to go home. Don't become too much of a prop for him, Laura, only to withdraw it.'

'He knows I have to go,' she said.

'I doubt if he'll remember that when the time comes. I doubt if I will, either.'

'Oh dear!' She sank onto a chair. 'To think I came down here to get away from complications. Perhaps I should leave without further ado.'

'No, you don't,' he said, dropping a kiss on the top of her head. 'You're having supper with me tomorrow night; it will be a well-behaved evening of poetry reading and literary appraisal.'

'Lord! Am I?' she said, laughing. 'I can't wait.'

'There is an alternative way to spend our time, of course, but I don't like to be counted as one of your complications.'

Too late, he already is, she said to herself as she waved to him from the front door.

The morning after Rick had come to dinner and stayed on, Sarah found his gold pen on the bedroom floor. Since she had been about to leave for the country, the obvious move was to put it in an envelope and post it back to him. Instead, she had slipped it in her handbag and carried it back to the cottage, where she did nothing about it until Saturday morning.

Her reasons for keeping it were twofold: the sheer sentiment of having something that belonged to him, and the excuse it provided to contact him. She was under no illusions that the night had been anything more than a one-off interlude of spectacular sex. For her it had been rather more wonderful than she had imagined, which had left her with the kind of nostalgic ache not felt since her early twenties. But there was not a future. The whole episode had been at her instigation, she had promised not to pursue it and she had no intention of deviating. All the same, she had somehow believed he would get in touch, and the fact that he had not worried her. It could only mean that he regretted the whole incident to such an extent that he could not bring himself to telephone her. Possibly he now loathed her. She was in the garden doing some dead-heading when this thought hit her, making her stop snipping abruptly. If there had never been a question of keeping him as a lover, neither had she considered losing him as a friend. Throwing the secateurs into her trug, she marched purposefully back to the house, thinking as she did so that personally she didn't regret a single moment of her carefully arranged night with him. Guilt on behalf of Laura was minimal. Sarah had always harboured the feeling that given time, and without Laura's intervention, Rick would have eventually been hers. To Sarah's scrupulously fair and practical mind this more or less made them even. She bore no trace of a grudge, however, and it was up to her to restore her relationship with Rick to its original amiable and platonic footing.

Dumping the trug outside the front door, she went through to the kitchen to make herself a strong mug of coffee, and to ring Rick's number before she lost the determination.

'Do your best to keep the mob out of the living-room,' Rick told Hannah. 'I don't want stained carpets and marked furniture in there.'

'We're civilized, not vandals,' Hannah said indignantly.

'Civilization is apt to slip at parties, and that goes for all age groups.'

They were rearranging what had once been the play-room and had graduated to its present status of teenage stronghold, pushing the sagging sofa and chairs against the walls to make room for dancing. A boy named Barnaby who suffered from acne, was sorting CDs and tapes in a corner, and moving loudspeakers from one position to another. Spasmodic and nerve-wracking scraps of music burst forth as he tried the system for sound. Rick winced.

'And don't forget, keep the volume down. Otherwise we'll have the whole street complaining.'

'You've told me that six times,' Hannah pointed out.

'Just reminding you.'

164

She collapsed into an armchair. 'Are you going out to dinner, Rick?'

'Yes. I am, but not for long. Come on, you haven't finished. Help me roll the rug back or you'll all be breaking your necks.'

'Who with?' She gave him a sharp, bright blue gaze. 'Dinner, I mean?'

'None of your business,' he replied amiably.

'I hope it's Sarah,' she said, tackling her end of the rug.

'Mrs Pemberton to you. And why do you hope that?'

'Because you always spend a nice long time with her. I know why: you're discussing your ghastly children.'

'How right you are,' Rick agreed, relieved at her misconception. 'I'll give you a hand laying out the drinks now, if you like.'

Sarah's call, coming at nine-thirty, had caught him off-guard. He was quite aware that an attempt should be made to put things back the way they were between them, and that he should be the one to make the first move. Frankly, he found the situation so awkward that he had shied away from doing so, hoping it would prove easier after allowing time to elapse. He had imagined she felt the same, perhaps more so after open seduction. In a wild moment of hope when the telephone rang, he had expected it to be Laura to say she was coming home. Sarah's voice brought trepidation and disappointment rolled into one.

'Hello, Rick. How are you?'

She sounded normal and quite unaffected. He said cautiously, 'Sarah.'

'Listen, I've got your pen, the gold one, and I'm coming up to London today for one night. Any chance of supper, so I can return it?'

He hesitated. 'I'm not sure—'

'Oh, not at the flat,' she said briskly. 'Somewhere

cheap, a plate of spaghetti, and no nonsense.' She laughed, the old uncomplicated Sarah.

'It's not that,' he lied. 'Hannah is having her party tonight, and I really ought—'

'To stick around? You'll be unpopular. We needn't be late.'

'All right,' he agreed with growing optimism. 'Around eight? I'll pick you up.'

'Don't sound so reluctant,' she said cheerfully. 'I meant what I said the other night, and I've no intention of making a fool of myself. See you later.'

He had replaced the receiver with a sigh of relief, grateful for having his sense of guilt halved. He had underestimated Sarah's honesty and common sense. Obviously she had managed to put their ill-advised adventure behind her with comparative ease. A faint twinge of hurt pride that his performance could be so swiftly dismissed attacked him and was immediately overridden by the compensations. They would be able to slip back into the comfortable relationship of just good friends without repercussions or awkward scenes. God bless her for what she is, he thought whole-heartedly, replenishing his cup of cooling breakfast coffee. His nagging conscience over Laura remained, but at least he was no longer worrying over two women at once, and there was no reason for all of them to be miserable.

Sarah sat for several seconds at her end of the now silent telephone before fetching her trug and emptying the dead flowers into the kitchen bin. They seemed to symbolize her own equally dead hour of glory. While she packed a bag for London, two tears trickled down each cheek, surprising her. She seldom cried.

Laura sat in front of the fire reading through the seventeenth century *Nun's Prayer*, and savouring her aloneness. Whatever she felt about Mark or Joe, or perhaps because of them, she still needed time to herself. Her evening call home had produced a subtly different Rick. His anger seemed to have left him and he sounded *piano*, which was not surprising, considering what he had let himself in for with Hannah's party. When she rang at seven o'clock, music could be heard already thumping away in the background, reasonably quietly, admittedly, but that wouldn't last. Laura did not feel in the least sorry for him. He should have stood his ground and refused to give in to Hannah's wheedling. Although one disruptive evening hardly accounted for the pleading note in his voice, and the fact he called her 'darling' instead of 'Laura'.

'I miss you desperately, darling,' he had said in that new, quiet tone, and then, 'Please don't stay away too long.'

For a moment he had her seriously worried. 'Nothing's really wrong, is it? No-one's ill or anything?'

'No,' he said after a pause, 'but Annabelle looks it. I admit I'm anxious about her.'

'The dieting?'

'I suppose so. She's going out tonight with black lines under her eyes and a face like chalk.'

'I'll have a talk with her tomorrow.'

'Yes,' he agreed, 'that would be best.'

The conversation left her feeling the familiar pangs of guilt. Rick in this subdued mood affected her far more deeply than his original salvoes of sarcasm had done, which had only strengthened a determination to remain where she was. In the uninhabited stretches of Gerard's drawing-room, all the good things about Rick came flooding back, bringing her dangerously close to homesickness. In fact, there was no badness in him when she thought about it, only a curious blindness where she was concerned. The last lines of the *Nun's*

Prayer summed him up — '*Give me the ability to see talents in unexpected people. And give me, oh Lord, the grace to tell them so.*' Perhaps, she thought, that applies to both of us. Neither of us spends much time boosting each other's morale.

She opened the window when she went up to bed, and leaned her elbows on the sill, smelling the sea on the cold night air. Far away lights of ships and buoys winked in the darkness. Her mind flicked from Rick to Mark, to Hannah and to Annabelle and to Joe — all those people alone with their own particular problems. She felt mixed-up and uneasy for the first time in the pretty yellow bedroom. Paradise is a double bed to oneself, she remembered deciding at the beginning. Lying now between the sheets with an acre of emptiness beside her, she was not so sure. But when it came to filling the void with an imaginary body, she grabbed her book from the bedside table and started to read.

Chapter Seven

Through the mass of hectic, jiving bodies, Hannah struggled to turn the music down for the second time. Flailing arms and legs caught her a series of painful whacks before she managed to reach the stereo. The sound dropped to a bearable level amid yells of 'Can't hear it! Turn it up, Han!' Pink and hot and bothered, she rushed out to the kitchen to find more food for distraction. The clock read ten past eleven and the party was showing signs of getting out of hand.

The kitchen table was already littered with coke tins and bottles, the straws limp inside them, and half-eaten hamburgers on cardboard plates. She found a space by shoving the débris to one side with the hot pizzas, burning herself in the process. While she cut them rapidly into clumsy slices, she could hear the music thumping back to its previous strength. A large gooey lump of pizza topping dropped from the knife down her scarlet skirt. 'Shit!' she muttered, picking a dishcloth from the crowded sink and scrubbing frantically.

It was all Samantha's boyfriend Jason's fault, he was a pain. He it was who had started messing around with the tapes and the sound, and because he looked about eighteen, everybody followed like sheep. Barnaby, who was so much in love with Hannah he made her sick, was no help whatsoever; and Samantha was too nuts about Jason to be any use, although she was supposed to be Hannah's best mate. She mentally crossed Sam off her list of girlfriends, tore back to shriek

'Food!' at the gyrating figures and wriggled round the edge of the room to deal once more with the music. No-one took the slightest notice of her. At that moment the phone rang. She answered it in the living-room, closing the door to keep out the noise, guessing it meant trouble. A man's voice announced himself as the Environmental Health Officer, and ordered her in firm tones to reduce the sound immediately. There had been complaints from the neighbours.

'Yeah, yeah, at once,' she promised placatingly. 'I'm really sorry.' She put the receiver down, feeling helpless and wishing Rick would walk in at that very instant.

Behind her, someone giggled. She swung round in the dim light from a single lamp. Jason and Samantha were lolling about on the large squashy sofa, a bottle of Rick's vodka on the table in front of them, and two cut glass tumblers. 'I'm *really* sorry,' Jason mimicked her. 'Who was that, Han? Some old fart from down the road?'

Red with fury, she ran at him, grabbing the bottle and jamming the top on. 'You can get out! Go on, naff off! You too, Sam.'

'Oh, Han, come off it,' Sam whined.

Hannah held the door open with a flourish. 'You've spoilt everything. Just go. You make me ill.'

'Cool it.' Jason got languidly to his feet, holding his hands palm outwards in a peace gesture. 'Fill the bottle up with water and your father'll never know.'

'He will because I'll tell him.'

'Stupid little cow,' he observed in passing, dragging an unsteady Samantha behind him by the wrist.

'I can't go, Han,' she pleaded over her shoulder. 'My mother's coming to collect me; she'll flip if I'm not here. And I feel sick,' she added plaintively.

'Whose fault's that?' Hannah snapped without sympathy. 'All right, you stay, but Jason can bloody well push off.'

Samantha fled to the lavatory. Jason hung around in the hall, hands in pockets.

'My stepfather'll be home any minute,' Hannah told him ominously. 'He'll throw you out if you haven't gone.'

He gave her a dark parting glare and left, slamming the door behind him. Hannah was too worried to feel triumphant. The bottle of vodka was still in her hand; she put it in the broom cupboard under the stairs, hidden behind the Hoover. The music from the playroom throbbed and shuddered through the house. Barnaby drifted out, looking for her.

'What are you doing? Come and dance, Han.'

She grabbed him, 'People are ringing up complaining. Go and turn the sound down, pull the plug out, anything, for God's sake. Go *on*!' she said with all the confidence of one who is sure of her man and could not care less about him.

'They'll only turn it up again,' he protested feebly.

She gave him a push. He plunged into the crowd with her in his wake. In moments the music had sunk to a comparative whisper. The mêlée of whirling, stomping bodies slowed as a result; there was a lull while everyone stared at the corner of the room where Barnaby was crouched, before further cries of protest. 'Who's done that? Can't hear it. You nit, Barnaby!'

A scuffle broke out. All Hannah could see was Barnaby disappearing beneath several boys, and re-appearing flat on the floor with his jeans around his ankles. A trickle of blood flowed down his upper lip. Music rose to top volume once more as she pushed her way to his side and yanked at his arm. The boys, satisfied with their debagging, had drifted away except for the smallest who stared earnestly into Hannah's furious face.

'I didn't hit him.'

'No-one hit me,' mumbled Barnaby. 'Not on purpose. It was someone's elbow.'

'I don't care who it was,' Hannah shouted above the din. 'You're all a bunch of morons. Get up before you get stamped on, Barnaby.'

He struggled to his feet, pulled up his jeans and allowed himself to be dragged by her to the kitchen where she flung a roll of paper at him.

'Do mop up. It's dripping down your shirt.'

'Sorry about this, Han,' he said.

'Not your fault,' she said ungraciously. 'This is quite simply the last party I ever give, that's all.'

'It's an ace party—' he started to say as the doorbell rang, a long, loud imperative peal followed by the rap of doorknocker.

'Bloody hell,' Hannah swore. 'Now we've had it.'

Half-an-hour after supper with his parents, Ben's friends started to arrive; a steady stream of them, many more than Annabelle had anticipated. Wine with the meal, and the fact she was able to wear jeans for the first time for years, had given her a new-found confidence. Only the steak-and-kidney pudding produced by Ben's mother daunted her, but she had begged for a small helping on the grounds of a recent stomach bug.

'Well, you've certainly lost weight,' Mrs Ferris observed. 'Wouldn't you say so, Ben?'

And Ben had smiled his particularly sweet smile at Annabelle across the table, and her legs had turned to water, so that she was relieved not to be standing on them.

There was not a lot of space in the room given

over to Ben to do what he liked with; last arrivals sprawled on the floor on cushions, while he handed out glasses of Bulgarian wine, and put Mozart on the CD player. Kate, it transpired, was the blonde girl whom Annabelle had seen frolicking about the badminton court. The long brown legs were covered up by leggings now, but the rest of her seemed to be permanently tanned, face and arms golden and smooth as eggshell. No-one, Annabelle decided, could achieve that effect in England; either the girl was Californian or it came out of a bottle. Halfway through a second glass of wine, she found she did not really mind Kate's looks or her irritating habit of tossing back her mane of silky hair. Even her obvious monopolizing of Ben's attentions appeared to matter less when there was a warm glow in one's stomach. Her head swam a little, but not unpleasantly; just enough to make her feel reckless about what she said or did.

She found herself in a corner on one of the cushions, with an intellectual-looking girl and an incredibly handsome boy.

'I'm Tim. This is Sophie. And you are—?'

'Annabelle.'

'How come I haven't seen you around before, Annabelle?' He had a faint accent, American or Canadian, she wasn't sure which, and white, even teeth that went with it.

'I'm pretty busy,' she said, 'working for my "A"s. I expect that's why.' She wondered, with a sinking sensation, exactly how often she had been excluded from evenings like this.

'You should give yourself a break, hang out more often.' He studied her with lazy blue eyes and an appreciative expression, lolling on one elbow.

'Tim avoids hard work at all costs,' Sophie remarked, pushing her granny spectacles up a minute nose.

'I just get my priorities right, I guess,' he said amiably. 'Are you and Ben an item?' he asked Annabelle.

'An *item*?' she said, puzzled.

'Going around together – you know, more than just mates.'

'Oh.' She stared across the room to where Kate had one arm round Ben's neck. 'Just mates,' she said carelessly, gulping her wine. 'How about you and Sophie?' she added. 'Are you an item?'

This caused them to fall about laughing. Sophie made sick noises of disgust. Annabelle laughed too, so as not to be left out.

'You're amazing, Annabelle. A real star.' He got to his feet. 'What's Ben done with the wine? Stay right where you are, I'll be back.'

Annabelle watched him, broad-shouldered against Ben's slightness, and wondered why he made her feel uncomfortable.

'He's a shit,' Sophie announced as if giving her the answer. 'Oozes charm, but a shit all the same. Don't go falling for him.'

'I wasn't going to.'

'I did for a bit. Not for long though.'

Tim returned, picking his way between bodies and holding a half-full bottle. The music changed from Mozart to something contemporary and throbbing. He refilled their glasses, saying, 'Never seen such manky CDs as Ben's got. Dinosaurs, most of them.'

'Who says?' Sophie said crisply. 'You haven't an ounce of musical appreciation in you.'

'I like this one,' Annabelle said.

'Come and dance.' Tim held out a hand to her.

'Where? There isn't any room.'

'Oh, they'll all do the same if we start.'

Annabelle glanced at Ben only a few feet away, talking his head off amongst a group. Judging by the roar of laughter that went up, he was telling a joke. There were whole aspects of him she knew nothing about. It made her feel suddenly lonely.

'All right,' she told Tim, 'but I'm not much good. Sophie would be better.'

'Yuk,' Sophie said succinctly.

They danced apart from each other, for which Annabelle was thankful. At least her feet did not have to obey any particular rules and it did not matter whether or not she jigged strictly in keeping with the tempo. To her surprise, she did not feel self-conscious, and realized vaguely that the wine must have anaesthetized her inhibitions. She saw Ben and Kate join them, and then others were on their feet until the whole roomful was dancing.

'Having fun?' Ben asked in her ear before Kate jerked him away, wriggling her hips in rhythm. Up until then Annabelle was beginning to enjoy herself. Tim put his arms loosely round her and bent his face towards hers.

'You're cute, you know,' he said.

She could not think of a clever reply. He pulled her closer and she smelt wine and aftershave. Her instinct was to draw back and make an excuse, any excuse to get away from the pressure of muscular thighs. But out of the corner of her eye she caught sight of Ben entwined with Kate, and a stab of anger made her change her mind. She forced herself to link her hands round Tim's neck and grin stupidly, and let herself be moved around like a puppet for what seemed an age, willing Ben to notice.

When at last they returned to their corner, there was no sign of Sophie. They finished the wine, while she vowed to herself not to dance again; she hated the way his hands slid down her bottom.

'You'll come out with me, won't you?' he asked.

'I don't know. I'm really busy.'

'And I can be really persuasive. Give me your phone number.'

She mumbled something unintelligible and left him to find sanctuary in the downstairs cloakroom. Amongst the raincoats and Mr Ferris's hats, she stared at herself in the mirror. Her eyes looked huge and slightly glassy. She supposed she should be flattered by Tim's passes, but they meant nothing. All she could think of was the fact that Ben had hardly spoken a word to her during the entire evening. There was a weird, hollow feeling inside her as if she wanted to eat and would be sick if she did. She glanced at her watch; she was to phone her father when she wanted to be collected. It was tempting to do so now; she did not in the least relish any more of Tim's groping. But the obstinate hope of getting Ben to herself stopped her from making straight for the hall telephone. Instead, she let herself out of the cloakroom and found the kitchen, where she searched for something edible and digestive, like a piece of Ryvita. Tim appeared in the doorway while she was opening cupboards and looking in storage jars.

'There you are,' he said, lounging against the wall. 'You've been the hell of a long time.'

'I'm hungry,' she said with her back to him.

'So am I.' He put a whole lot of meaning into the simple words. Then he switched off the lights and grabbed her from behind. Shocked, she dropped a packet of biscuits and trod on them as he swung her round. She felt the crunch of them underfoot, just as she felt the awful sensation of a hard, questing tongue in her mouth. Pressed painfully against a cupboard, she worked one of her pinioned hands free and, planting it flat on his chest, pushed with all her strength. To her surprise, he staggered backwards and into the kitchen table with a muttered expletive. He glared at her in the dim light from the hall.

'What the hell's got into you?'

She glared back, panting. 'Nothing. I don't like you, that's all.'

His expression was comical with disbelief. 'You repressed or something? You gave me the come-on.'

'I did not.' He made a move.

Annabelle picked up the bread knife and pointed it at him. 'Keep away,' she said.

'Don't worry. I don't waste my time on silly bitches.' He turned and walked away, the set of his shoulders expressing nonchalance.

She put the knife back in its place, and wandered through the hall towards the music. It took courage to go back amongst the others. She felt angry and foolish at the same time. She had mishandled the situation, over-reacted; it had been totally unnecessary to wave bread knives in the air. Tim was closeted with Sophie, undoubtedly making the whole thing into a funny story, but she was not laughing. The sick hunger in the pit of Annabelle's stomach had changed to a kind of clammy coldness and the crowded room seemed out of focus. She blinked, her eyes searching out Ben who was sitting on a sofa with Kate, deep in conversation. Annabelle weaved her way unsteadily towards them with a desperate longing for five minutes of Ben to herself. He looked up as she stood in front of him, and struggled to his feet; the usual warm and gentle Ben, although he wasn't interested in her and never would be. She realized that now.

'Annabelle,' he was saying. 'Come and join us.'

'I—' She tried to say, could she talk to him alone, just for a moment but the words refused to come. His face blurred and grew anxious.

'Are you all right?' she heard him ask, before the wine and the emptiness and the misery overtook her.

Her knees crumpled under her and the blur became a blank as she fainted. The last thing she was conscious of were Kate's wide blue eyes staring in astonishment.

Joe was walking Mrs Shawcross's dog across the grasslands above the estuary, where Laura had told him to go. He wished there were long, golden sands instead of fields, but they did not exist around the estuary apparently. The wind was south-westerly; he was too warm in his anorak, and by the first stone wall he took it off and tied it round his waist by the sleeves. The terrier pulled against the lead, snuffling and choking on its collar in its longing to run. Joe liked dogs. He wanted to undo the lead's clasp and set it free, but he had strict instructions from Mrs Shawcross not to do so. Reluctantly he climbed a stile and walked on towards the next grey stone boundary. He thought all these walls dividing up the grassland into fields were a pity; the country should be wide open and unrestricted. But then he hated any sort of enclosure, ever since the walls of the hospital had imprisoned him.

He had not really wanted to exercise the dog. In fact, he had forgotten all about Mrs Shawcross even asking him about it in the shop. Laura had reminded him when he went to see her that morning, because Mrs Shawcross had spoken to her about it. After the blinding headache of the night before, he had woken more or less normal apart from enormous tiredness, but the tranquillizers were probably the cause; they did that to you. He was taking them because they were better than nothing, and Mark Wainwright had insisted he should. Laura had been as kind as usual, sitting him down with a mug of coffee and asking him how he felt, but she would not come with him on the walk when he asked her. She had to put the afternoons aside for writing, she said, or she would not achieve anything. He got the feeling there was something else on her mind. He did not relish taking the dog on his own, but Laura had said the fresh air and exercise might do him good.

Crossing the third field, he could not stand the dog trying to suffocate itself on the leash any longer: he bent down and set it loose, and watched it bound away, nose to the ground. After all, where was the harm? It probably wouldn't go far, anyway. He looked around him; and it was then that he had the weirdest sensation, that the wall behind him and the one in front were moving slowly inwards to trap him between them. He shut his eyes, shaking his head from side to side, and opened them again, hoping to clear his vision. But the illusion persisted, if illusion it was. Turning quickly this way and that, he saw the distance narrow between him and the advancing lines of grey stone, watched them draw, like two invading armies, inexorably closer. He stood frozen with panic; and then a voice whispered 'You're trapped!' The Voice, echoing in his head, brought all the past nightmares to life. And he started to run wildly, blindly, back the way he had come, his feet slipping on the short dry turf. The wind whipped a flop of dark hair across his eyes and he was gasping painfully for breath, but he kept running, any memory of the dog wiped clean from his mind, until the path to the road was in sight. His sole thought was of Laura, and reaching the benison of her protection.

Jeremy Burgess, Mark's natural son, arrived at Truro with the express purpose of meeting his father for the first time. Since Mark was ignorant of the fact, Jeremy decided to telephone from the station to announce himself, rather than turn up out of the blue. Francie, his mother, had pooh-poohed such niceties. 'If it was me, I'd just ring the doorbell, darling. It'll be a wonderful surprise for him.' But Jeremy had not inherited his mother's insouciant nature. She had only recently told him the truth about his parentage during a moment of slightly drunken confidences over a bottle of wine, and it had thrown him into confusion. Partly angry at having been duped for so long, and partly curious to learn more, it had taken him days to get used to the fact. He had a vague picture in his mind of Mark as an ageing, dusty academic. The sudden appearance of a son whom he probably never gave a thought to could be enough to bring on a heart attack.

It had been Francie's idea that he should introduce himself to Mark, although she did not think to fore-warn him by letter. Like a lot of her ideas, Jeremy was not sure it was a good one. It could prove embarrass-ing. Sheer curiosity made him agree reluctantly. In the telephone booth, he smoothed out the piece of paper with Mark's address and number on it, and inserted his money with a certain amount of apprehension.

Mark was in the garden when the phone rang, cut-ting a large bunch of Michaelmas daisies to brighten the living-room for Laura. His leg ruled out running, and by the time he reached the house the bell had stopped.

'I'm sorry to bring him back to you in this state.'

Laura faced Eleanor Shawcross in her tiny kitchen, an almost unrecognizable terrier by her side, tongue lolling. Muddied and stuck all over with burrs, his bright eyes peered out unrepentantly.

Eleanor twittered with anger. 'Stupid boy. I told him not to let Tigger off the lead. If I'd *known* he was unreliable—' The unfinished sentence hung in the air accusingly.

'I'm afraid I didn't know,' Laura said. 'Would you like me to clean him up for you?' she added soothingly.

'No, no, I'll see to him, thank you.' Eleanor waved the suggestion aside. 'He's been rabbiting, haven't you, you naughty thing? I believe that young man isn't quite right in the head,' she said. 'How can you set out with a dog and forget about him?'

'It wasn't quite as simple as that.' Laura thought of Joe, clinging to her like a frightened child. 'I'd better be getting back, if you're sure I can't help.'

'Won't you have some tea?' Eleanor asked, calming down enough to remember about hospitality.

'Thank you, but I must go. I have to write letters and make some phone calls, and I'm supposed to be going out to—'

Laura stopped abruptly, realizing too late the inadvisability of telling Eleanor Shawcross anything.

'To supper?' Eleanor finished for her. 'How nice. Mark, I suppose?'

'Yes,' Laura agreed neutrally.

'I thought you two would get on together,' Eleanor said as she led the way to the front door. She did not open it at once, standing instead with her hand on the latch. 'It will do him good to be taken out of himself. He's been so withdrawn ever since the terrible business of Alice's death.'

'He told me something about it.' Laura waited to be set free, her mind still on Joe. 'He seems unable to stop blaming himself, I don't know quite why. It was an accident, and he wasn't even driving.'

'There was more to it than that.' Eleanor shook her head regretfully. 'The crossroads where it happened aren't particularly dangerous; there is a clear view either way. Yet she drove straight out under the front of a lorry. It looked,' she sighed, 'distressingly deliberate.'

Laura stared at her. 'You don't mean it was planned?'

'Oh no, no. An impulsive action, while the balance of her mind was disturbed. It all came out at the inquest,

181

which of course was dreadfully upsetting for Mark.'

'Yes,' Laura said slowly, trying to equate the theory with his description of an idyllic marriage. 'She would have had to be desperate—'

Eleanor dropped her voice to an unnecessary whisper. 'Well, there was the affair, you see.'

'Mark's?'

'No, Alice's. She had fallen in love with a doctor in the practice. You can't keep such matters private in a country community, however hard you try. People gossip, rumours spread.'

Laura looked at Eleanor's neat white curls, maroon twinset and pearls, and wondered whether she was one of the chief muckrakers.

'I imagine,' Eleanor continued, 'there had been a violent argument between them that evening, her and Mark. Nothing else would seem to account for her suicidal actions. So sad.'

She opened the front door. 'Sex has a lot to answer for,' she said on a note of foreboding, as Laura escaped past her to the fresh air. 'Goodbye, my dear, and don't let him fall in love with you.'

'That,' Laura muttered under her breath, '*would* be a disaster, wouldn't it?'

She walked home with the sharp, clean smell of the sea in her nostrils, glad of its cathartic effect. It was as if Eleanor had laid a thin layer of slime over Mark's past in betraying it. She stood for a moment in the blue light of dusk, the sea-wall rough and cold under her hands, wishing he had told her the true story. Not that he had lied, merely withheld an integral part of it. She understood, and at the same time was hurt by the understanding. He did not trust her; there was no love without trust, no trust without love. She had been right all along; he should not have talked in terms of loving her. It had been too soon, too much of a rush, a kind of hormonal disturbance exacerbated by their separate situations. Anyway, she reminded herself, none of that should matter now they had made a platonic pact. The question of whether or not he had driven Alice into a suicidal state of mind ought not to be worrying her, standing there in the fading daylight. She had no right to be involved. But the thought of spending the evening with him, covering up her knowledge, daunted her: she did not know how to behave naturally.

She moved on, walking quickly remembering her writing, still scattered over Gerard's kitchen table and the events that had led to its interruption. Joe had sent peal after peal of the front door bell echoing through the house, interchanged with desperate raps of the knocker, making her heart leap up in her throat. He had literally thrown himself through the door when she opened it, gripping her painfully by the arms to steady himself. After guiding him downstairs to the kitchen and pushing him onto a chair, it had taken some time to unravel his garbled explanation of what had happened. He sat there with his elbows on the table, running both hands through his hair so that it stood up in a wild shock, and talking disjointedly of voices and pressure and walls closing in on him. His dark eyes had never left her face, intense and terribly frightened. He was shaking so badly he could not lift his mug of coffee, and she had to hold it for him while he drank. Eventually she poured a small measure of whisky and gave it to him neat, past worrying whether it mixed with tranquillizers, and the trembling grew less. Picking out the gist of what he was saying, she tried logic.

'Walls can't move, Joe,' she told him. 'They are very static and have no life of their own. You know that as well as I.'

'They did. I saw them. You weren't there.'

'I don't have to have been,' she said firmly. 'You're an intelligent person; think about it for a moment. It was an illusion. You were having a waking nightmare.'

He looked confused. 'It was real,' he said obstinately. 'The Voice told me. I had to run.'

'This Voice is imaginary, something you hear in your head when you're unwell,' she began, and then suddenly realizing, asked, 'Joe? Where is the dog?'

'Dog?' he said, uninterested.

'Mrs Shawcross's dog. You remember?' She spoke slowly and clearly. 'What have you done with him, left him there?'

He rubbed a hand against his eyes. 'I suppose so. I've forgotten.'

'And the lead. Where's the lead?'

He peered vaguely round him as if expecting it to materialize. 'I don't know. I suppose I must have dropped it.'

Laura grew suddenly angry. She felt like shaking him, despite the knowledge he was beyond helping himself. She got up abruptly, scraping the chair on the floor.

'I'll have to go and find him. Stay here while I fetch an anorak.'

Upstairs she changed hurriedly into trainers, sick with the possibility of Tigger having wandered onto the road and got run over. When she returned, Joe was sitting in the same position at the table, looking pale but calmer.

'Now this is what you must do, Joe,' she told him, shrugging herself into the anorak. 'I want you to go back to the pub, take one of your pills and try to get some rest before you have to work.'

His face registered fear. 'Can't I stay here?'

'No. You need the tranquillizer.'

'I want to stay,' he said sullenly.

'Come on, Joe!' she snapped, losing patience. 'You've lost the dog and I have to find him; please don't waste my time.'

'You're cross,' he mumbled, getting to his feet. 'I thought you'd understand.'

'I'm *not* cross and I *do* understand, but you've got to do as I say.'

Outside in the road he turned to her. For a moment she thought he was going to cling to her once more, but he only said, 'Can't I see you again, then?'

She sighed. 'Don't be silly. I'll see you tomorrow, Joe, to let you know about the hospital.' She gave him a gentle push in the right direction. 'Don't worry, you're going to be all right,' she called after him softly. The loneliness of his back view as it ambled downhill by the sea-wall left her consumed with guilt at her irritation.

She had found the lead on the path near the road, and the terrier in the first field, tired out and aimlessly sniffing the gorse bushes. He had greeted her rapturously as an old friend. Now, letting herself into the house with a deep sense of relief, she realized she should have gone to the pub to check up on Joe. But the disruptive afternoon had left her exhausted, with a strong inclination towards a hot bath and an hour to unwind. Solitude had become a rare commodity; one obviously had to run a great deal further than the boot of England to find it, she decided as she peeled off clothes. And there was still the daily task of phoning home to be undertaken, and a call to Mark to let him know she would be half-an-hour late.

When she rang him, she could tell by his tone he was not alone.

'I'm running a little late,' she said. 'I'll explain when I see you.'

'Fine.' He hesitated, added, 'As a matter of fact,

there will be someone else for supper. I hope you don't mind.'

'Why should I? Would you rather I dropped out?' she queried, imagining old flames.

'Of course not.' Clearing his throat self-consciously, he said, 'It's Jeremy Burgess. He's turned up out of the blue.'

'Who?'

'I can't really talk now. He's having a shower but he might walk in at any moment.' He gave a short, rather pleased laugh. 'You'll realize who I mean when you see him.'

While she soaped herself in the bath, Laura remembered. The boy in the photograph in Mark's bedroom came clearly to mind, with his eyes and nose and floppy brown hair from the same mould as his father. So it was to be a family evening, she thought drily, which would preclude any broken resolutions or awkward moments. She no longer knew how she felt about Mark; the description of Alice's death had left a question mark which refused to go away. Wondering whether this was a sign to pack up and go home, she wrapped herself in a bath robe and steeled herself to phone Rick. The memory of Joe walking away from her, a picture of hopelessness, nagged her persistently, a far greater deterrent to her leaving than any other.

Rick saw the doctor out of the front door and climbed the stairs to Annabelle's room. Their usual doctor was on weekend leave, and the one on call had been a locum, an Indian woman with pale skin and sympathetic brown eyes.

'I can't find anything physically wrong with your daughter,' she had told him.

'Why should she faint?' he asked.

'Probably the effect of alcohol on an empty stomach. She is suffering this morning from a hangover. You say she has been dieting drastically? A glass or two of wine would be enough to cause it.'

'It's so unlike her. She hardly drinks, doesn't like the taste.'

'I'm sure she doesn't,' the doctor said gently. 'But she is young, and is also suffering from boy-trouble, from what she tells me.'

'A crush?' Rick said dubiously.

'Don't underrate the pain. Young unrequited love can be acute. I'm not prescribing anything,' she said, becoming brisk, 'but you must persuade her to eat properly, otherwise you may have an anorexic on your hands. And encourage her to get up and come downstairs. The longer she lies in bed, the more depressed she will become.'

'She's told you more in half-an-hour than she's told me in a week,' he said. 'I suppose because you're a woman.'

The doctor picked up her case, preparing to leave. 'Your wife's away, you say?'

'A short break, yes.' An indefinite break, Rick amended to himself.

'Then I should let her know what's happening. It would be helpful to have her here, I think.'

My feelings entirely, he reflected bitterly. He tapped at Annabelle's door and entered in answer to an indeterminate grunt. Most of her was hidden under the duvet, a desolate lump topped by wisps of dark brown hair. He sat on the edge of a chair by the bed, trying to find a bit of her with which to communicate. The cup of tea he had brought her earlier had been drunk, but the toast lay untouched on the plate.

'Well,' he said with an attempt at jocularity, 'you'll live, you'll be pleased to hear.'

She mumbled into her pillow.

'Do surface for a moment, darling. I can't talk to you like this.'

She turned on her back reluctantly and peered at him with swollen eyes. 'I said, I don't care if I die.'

'Everyone feels like that with a hangover. You'll feel better after a hot bath and something to eat.'

'No, I won't,' she said defiantly. 'I'll feel exactly the same. You don't understand.'

'What don't I understand? I can't be expected to if you don't explain.'

'It's really feeble to faint.' She closed her eyes and tears trickled out below the lids. 'I can't face Ben or any of them ever again.'

'If it's Ben you mind about, why not say so? The others don't matter. And if Ben is worth his salt, he'll do something in the near future to make you feel all right about it.' She did not answer. 'As for passing out at parties, it happens to most of us at some time in our lives,' he struggled on. 'It's happened to me.'

She stared at him in disbelief, then showed signs of burying herself again. 'None of it matters any more,' she said in sepulchral tones. 'He doesn't care about me. He's got this other girl, Kate someone, and she's got long legs and a smashing figure and – and she would never do anything weird like fainting.' Her voice ended on a wail of misery.

'Want a bet?' asked Rick, taking hold of one of her limp hands. 'Listen,' he said, 'it's no use trying to change yourself into someone you're not. You've got to believe in yourself, as you are, attractive in your own right.'

'Oh, it's easy for you,' she said, 'you've forgotten what it's like. You've got Laura.'

'Have I?' he replied without thinking. 'I wonder.' He rose to his feet. 'It's midday,' he said firmly, 'and you are going to get dressed now, and come downstairs and eat a proper lunch. Sarah's coming.'

'I can't face anyone. I can't face Hannah.'

'Hannah's in the doghouse, clearing up the mess from her party, hardly opening her mouth.'

'You can't make me.' She put her face in the pillow.

'Doctor's orders,' he said. 'I've no intention of dragging out a hard-working doctor on a Sunday morning without your following the rules.' He opened the door. 'See you downstairs in half-an-hour,' he added in a voice which brooked no argument.

'I wish Laura was here,' Annabelle said to the closing door, loud enough for him to hear.

In the kitchen, Hannah was still busy stuffing bin-liners with party débris. Her pale hair, escaping the confines of an inexpertly-tied ponytail, hung in strands around her face. She looked ill-used, a modern-day Cinderella. Rick suppressed a smile and took pity on her.

'I'll give you a hand,' he said. 'Where have you hidden the vodka, by the way?'

'In the cupboard under the stairs. I'll get it, shall I?' she offered, sensing a softening in his attitude.

'Not to bother.'

After he had mixed himself a drink, they moved to the playroom to retrieve the residue of plastic cups and coke tins. Someone had stepped in a slice of pizza and trodden it over the floor. The room had the same forlorn air as last night's hostess.

'How's Annie?' Hannah asked, scraping up the mess with a thumbnail and a damp cloth.

'Better. She's getting up.'

'What's the matter with her?'

'She felt unwell at Ben's place, so I kept her in bed this morning,' he said without elaborating. Hannah was quite capable of doing that for herself.

'Fainting,' she said laconically, 'is a very Annie sort of thing to do.'

'And how do *you* know about it?' he asked.

'I heard you telling Sarah after you'd brought Annie home. You must have been worried about her to call a doctor.'

'You both worry me,' he replied sombrely. 'And there's a bit of pizza over here that you've missed.'

She glanced up at him. 'I've said I'm sorry at least ten times. But you do see, it wasn't *my* fault it ended up like it did.' She sat back on her heels and eyed the floor. 'I think I've cleaned it enough, don't you? I'll go and see how Annie's getting on,' she said unexpectedly.

'No snide remarks or taunting,' he warned.

'Of course not,' she said, looking pious. 'I'll be really consoling. I expect she'll want to tell me about it, though.'

'It was no more than a glass of wine on an empty stomach. Nothing much to tell.'

'There is on the subject of Ben.' She picked up the bin-liner and carried it to the door. 'She's crazy about him. Don't you think she's a bit *repressed*?' she added.

'Don't talk nonsense,' he said crossly.

'Sorry,' she said, disappearing before his anger was rekindled.

He sank into an armchair when she had gone, suddenly exhausted, and took a large mouthful of vodka and tonic. The previous evening had developed into a nightmare of confusion. He had arrived home to find a squad car outside the house, two policemen in the hall and a throng of subdued and mainly silent children in the background. A white-faced Hannah was the only one attempting to explain away the unacceptable volume of noise, her fluency finally reduced to apologizing. In the overcrowded hall, a trickle of parents had struggled to collect their offspring, throwing looks of shocked dismay or amusement at Rick on the way out, depending on their tolerance. Sarah, who had offered to return with him to help close down the party, proved invaluable, using her considerable organizing abilities to shuffle people through the front door and into the night.

The police had left once they were assured someone was in charge, their wooden expressions stating clearly what they felt about a bunch of spoilt, middle-class brats. And then the telephone had rung, summoning Rick to fetch Annabelle and there had not been time to vent much of his spleen on Hannah.

'You'd better get some sleep!' he had snapped at her. 'We'll talk in the morning. And make no mistake: you've had it as far as parties are concerned from now on.'

'It wasn't my *fault*,' Hannah was heard to mutter, lurking dejectedly by the stairs.

'Don't be too hard on her,' Sarah had said to him later, having put a white and silent Annabelle to bed. 'I gave you bad advice; you should have stayed at home to control operations.'

They were sitting in the chaotic kitchen, a whisky each in front of them. He rubbed tired eyes. 'I can't remember when I last felt in control. Laura, Annabelle, Hannah – I've ceased to understand any of them.'

She regarded him pityingly. 'They're human beings, not robots, simply being their respective ages. Teenage rebels and lovesick daughters aren't out of the ordinary.'

'And Laura—?' He let the question hang in the air.

'We've discussed Laura,' she said firmly. 'We've been through all that, and I haven't helped; very much to the contrary.'

He glanced at her and away again, embarrassed. There was nothing seductive about her tonight. She was in the guise of the original Sarah; sensible dark polo-neck sweater, hair in need of a comb falling about an honest, sensible if not unattractive face. They had eaten in an unpretentious little restaurant, and she had taken the tension out of an awkward meeting by her diplomacy. 'You must forget what happened, if you haven't already,' she had told him cheerfully; and he had felt some of the shame and uneasiness lifted from him, so that he was able to visualize their relationship returning to normal. It was difficult to recall the uncontrollable urge that had driven him into her bed; not so difficult to remember the surprising amount of passion and expertise which had ensued. Perhaps the answer was that he did not understand women collectively; but Sarah was the one who had demonstrated affection when he most needed it.

He had swallowed his whisky, covered one of her hands and given it a quick squeeze. 'I don't know how I would have managed without you these past few days,' he said, meaning it.

She turned very slightly pink. 'I must be going,' she said. 'It's late, and you look flaked out.'

'I'll ring you a taxi. Sorry I can't run you home, but I daren't leave the house again.'

He kissed her lightly on the lips as she left, saying, 'Come to lunch tomorrow; that is, if you're not sick of us;' and she had replied, 'I'd like that. See you around one o'clock then.'

The thought cheered him now as he heaved himself out of his armchair and went through to the kitchen to test the baked potatoes. He wondered whether they would have to sit through lunch with Annabelle wilting over a plate of uneaten food. Sarah would in any case alleviate the gloom. Hannah was not really a problem; she had taken the rocket he delivered at breakfast with customary resilience and was already bouncing back on form. Annabelle was a different matter altogether. The word 'anorexia' had alarmed him, giving whatever she was suffering from a new and more serious aspect. He felt the situation slipping out of his hands, becoming chronic and unmanageable. 'Laura must come back,' he said under his breath; and it was then, stabbing a potato with a fork, that he made up his mind to telephone her, and hang the consequences.

'I know about your being my real father, by the way,' Jeremy said calmly.

Mark had carried the tea through to the living-room. He sat in a large armchair on one side of the fire, while Jeremy knelt on the floor holding a slice of bread to the flames on the end of a toasting fork. Making toast this way had been one of Mark's favourite pastimes as a child, and something, perhaps a desire to recreate a particle of his son's childhood that he had missed out on, moved him to suggest it. Jeremy had agreed whole-heartedly, having already proved himself to be uncomplicated. As far as Mark could see, he had inherited neither Francie's vague deviousness nor Mark's self-confessed sardonic introspection. How they had managed to produce such a straightforward human being, he could not imagine. He found it extremely difficult to take his eyes off the boy crouched over the fire, fascinated by their physical likeness. When he had answered the door to Jeremy, he had had the strange sensation of staring at his own reflection. Grey eyes had gazed back into his on an equal level, light brown hair with the same tendency to flop falling across his forehead. The shock had stunned him into temporary silence, and it had been Jeremy who had broken it by announcing himself.

'I'm Jeremy Burgess,' he said. 'I'm sorry about just turning up. I tried to telephone earlier but there was no answer. If you're busy, I can come back another time,' he added cheerfully.

'I'm not, and I'm delighted,' and pulling himself together, he had ushered the boy in. They had divested him of his backpack and anorak, and Brutus had lumbered from his basket and come slipping and slithering on the hall rugs to sniff out the newcomer.

In the large stone-flagged kitchen Mark had piled tea-things on a tray, and Jeremy had wandered about examining objects and talking at the same time. 'Ma told me to bring you up-to-date on all the news, since she hasn't written to you for ages.'

'She used to,' Mark replied. 'The flow has rather dried up recently.'

'She either writes reams or nothing at all,' Jeremy observed. 'Father died, you know.'

'No, I didn't know. I'm sorry.' Mark thought of Daniel Burgess with his obsession for his work and his ambiguous relationship with Francie, and wondered how much she minded his demise.

'Is Francie all right?' he asked, filling the teapot.

'She's fine. She's really into pottery, running her own shop now. Shall I carry that tray? I'm ravenous. I only had a burger for lunch at the station.'

Mark found half a ginger cake in a tin which he had been keeping for his pupils. Jeremy made the toast, and Mark buttered it while Jeremy described life at Exeter University and grumbled about its inadequacies. English was oversubscribed, he said, and he had been forced to combine it with sociology, a waste of time, in his opinion. Mark felt inordinately pleased that his leanings were towards the Arts rather than the Sciences like his adoptive father. He dared not express this too strongly without knowing what had prompted Jeremy's visit; he supposed it was a whim of Francie's, the suggestion to look up an old family friend. That was doubtless how he had been described, how a lot of past lovers were described. The thought made him reticent, inhibiting his side of the conversation, until Jeremy suddenly came out with his knowledge of the truth as if it were just another snippet of home news.

After a pause, Mark said, 'Did you discover for yourself, or did someone tell you?'

'Ma told me,' Jeremy said. 'During a rather hazy session over a bottle of wine, she divulged her dark secret.' He drew the toast off the prongs of the fork and handed it to Mark. 'That's the problem about being an only child. You're apt to be the recipient of secrets.'

Mark smiled. 'You don't sound as if you mind too much. Do you?'

'It took time to get used to the idea. Now, in a way, I'm pleased.' Jeremy threw himself into a chair opposite Mark. 'I've always had this weird feeling of not quite belonging. I'm not really like Ma in character or looks, and I obviously wasn't like Father. It's too soon to say, but perhaps I take after you. What do you think?' he asked, taking a slice of buttered toast.

Mark thought of his own dark secrets. 'For your sake, I hope you don't. I'm hardly the success story of the century.' He looked at Jeremy's face, smooth and as yet unbattered by life. 'If you do, then I reckon I'm the fortunate one,' he said.

'Thanks,' Jeremy said, pleased.

'Was it your idea to search me out?'

'No, it was Ma's. I was rather against it at the beginning,' he admitted. 'I thought it might be – well, you know, embarrassing for both of us.'

'And are you embarrassed?'

Jeremy shook his head. 'I feel kind of at home. It's a funny thing, but it's as if I've been here before.' He reached out and proffered the plate of toast to Mark before taking another piece. 'I also thought it might give you a nasty turn if I came; a bit of your past landing up on your doorstep,' he said.

'I'm not *that* decrepit yet,' Mark said, amused.

'Sorry, I didn't mean it that way.' Jeremy flushed, remembering his idea of Mark as an ageing academic. To change the subject, he asked if there was any Marmite, and while Mark went to look, he roamed the room and peered at photographs on a gate-legged table. There were two of a dark, pretty woman and several of the house from the outside, in various stages of renovation.

'It's a wonderfully rambling sort of house,' he remarked when they were settled by the fire again. 'Do you mind living here on your own?'

'How do you know I do?' Mark teased him. 'I might have a bunch of concubines hidden upstairs.'

'Oh God, I keep putting my foot in it,' Jeremy said. 'The thing is, I don't know much about you, do l?'

Taking pity on him, Mark said, 'You're quite right. My wife Alice died.'

Jeremy nodded. 'Ma said.'

'So she knows?'

'I think she saw it in the papers.'

'A car accident,' Mark said briefly, and went on quickly to talk of other things before Jeremy could commiserate. 'I've got my students,' he added, 'who come to be crammed with the Classics, poor buggers, so I'm not alone that much. Besides, I don't mind my own company.'

This was not strictly true. He used not to mind before he was prey to nightmare attacks of conscience. Now the presence of Jeremy, sitting relaxed with his long legs stretched out in front of him, he found strangely comforting. It stemmed, he supposed, from the discovery of someone who belonged to him, however nebulously; the nearest approach to family that he was ever likely to know. He was infinitely grateful to Jeremy for bothering to search him out, and subconsciously began to dread the moment when he would get up, explaining he had to push on, and disappear into the night. Even the thought of Laura arriving for supper in a short while could not diminish the strength of this feeling. He cut a wedge of ginger cake, wooing the boy's appetite to persuade him to stay longer.

'Marvellous tea,' Jeremy said. 'We never really went in for it at home. Well, you know Ma. All meals are a bit haphazard and full of outlandish recipes she's trying out.' He dusted crumbs off his jeans. 'Talking of food, d'you happen to know any B&B places round here?'

'This place isn't bad,' Mark said, careful not to sound too eager, 'and it has the merit of not costing anything.'

'You mean, stay with you? Are you sure you don't mind?'

'I'd like it. What are your plans for the next few days?'

'To explore a bit, if I can hire a bike. I have to be back at Exeter on Wednesday night.'

'You can borrow my bike, I seldom use it. Come and see where you're to sleep.' Off the wide landing upstairs Mark opened the door of a spare-room and switched on the light. 'It smells a bit damp,' he said. 'The central heating isn't on in here, but that's easily rectified. I'll find some sheets; the duvet should keep you warm.'

Jeremy looked round him. 'It smells nice, like old houses do. Kind of woody.'

As they returned along the landing, Mark led the way into his own bedroom and showed him the snapshots of himself as a child. 'I remember Ma taking those. I didn't realize she sent them to you,' Jeremy said.

'It was a way of keeping in touch,' Mark replied. 'The next best thing to seeing you for real.'

'Do you mind if I ask you something?'

'Go ahead.'

'Would you have married Ma if it had been possible?'

Mark hesitated, uncertain of the right answer. 'I would have, but mainly because of you,' he said eventually. 'I was in love with her, but I suspect the marriage would have been disastrous.'

'I suppose it worked with Father,' Jeremy said thoughtfully. 'He was so remote, it was difficult to tell; he seemed to live in another world while Ma did her own thing. I think he forgot I existed sometimes. Perhaps he wanted to. It's understandable.'

'I doubt that. From what little I know of him, he would have reacted the same way with any child.'

'Mmm.' Jeremy sounded dubious. 'I feel as if I know you better than I knew him. Ridiculous, really. Mind if I have a shower?' he asked.

'Go ahead. I've someone coming to supper. I'd better get started.'

'Will he mind that I'm around?' Jeremy, unable to rid himself of Mark's bachelor image, assumed the male gender.

'It's a "she", and I'm sure she will be happy to see you.'

Jeremy paused at the door. 'By the way, what shall I call you?'

'How does Mark suit you?' asked Mark, smiling.

'Fine,' Jeremy said, and smiled back.

Joe was rinsing glasses behind the bar mechanically. The tranquilliser made him feel as if he was working in slow motion, like a home-movie set at the wrong speed. He was ever mindful of the Voice, which had not quite left him, subdued now to a muttered whisper. The lights shone down on the glasses of the drinkers at the bar, dazzling him and hurting his eyes with their brilliance. Slowly he dried a beer mug and put it back on its shelf. All he could see was the row of glasses, half-full of drink, stretching from one end of the bar to the other. He imagined himself putting out an arm and sweeping the long line of them to the floor in one steady movement; the musical crash of breaking glass sounding in his ears as though it had already happened. 'Go on, do it,' whispered the Voice. Joe's hand lifted and stayed frozen in the air in front of him while Sam Grimond's words cut his compulsion in two.

'What's up with you, lad? You're half asleep tonight. I want two of them tankards, if you please.'

Joe bent to retrieve them, his hands trembling. A trickle of sweat ran down one side of his forehead. The half hour to closing-time seemed to extend for ever.

Chapter Eight

Laura woke on the Monday morning with a feeling of unease, of questions and decisions waiting to be answered or resolved. She pulled back the curtains to find the weather had changed, and the sea under a sullen sky had a dark and oily swell. The outlook reflected her mood. As she pulled on a dressing-gown and went downstairs to make tea, the memory of the telephone call from Rick came flooding back with all its disturbing connotations. Annabelle with potential anorexia could not be ignored, even though Laura doubted the validity of the story. If she had stayed at home, none of this would have happened because she would not have allowed it to. It was just another example, she decided, of an otherwise intelligent man being unable to sort out cause and effect. She would have to return, there was no other way, before she was ready to do so. Despite her love for Annabelle, she felt frustrated, full of a sense of missions incompleted: although what they were exactly, she was not sure; only that once again she was being pulled back from controlling her own destiny.

She found April August in the kitchen cleaning the cooker, a fact which would not normally have bothered her, and this morning irritated her unreasonably. April was off to Truro on a planned shopping trip with her daughter and had arrived early. Laura, edging round her extended backside to switch on the electric kettle, felt obliged to offer her tea, and they sat drinking it at the table by the window.

'Change in the weather,' April said, as they gazed out at the grey, banked clouds. 'There's a storm brewing, most likely.'

'I feel cheated without the sun; I've been spoilt by it, I suppose.'

'I've brought you some candles,' April told her, 'just in case there's a power failure. Wouldn't want you to be left in the dark tonight.'

'Is it *likely* to fail?' Laura asked.

'Has been known during a bad 'un. Best to be on the safe side. Well, must get on.'

April removed herself and her mug to the sink. 'By the way, did you know there's a knife missing from this lot?' She tapped the magnetic holder on the wall by the cooker. 'Mr Gerard's pride and joy, those are.'

Laura glanced at the collection of cooking knives. 'I've hardly used them,' she said, thinking of her lazy plastic suppers. 'Only once when I cooked a chicken, and they were all there then.'

'Could have thrown it away accidental-like with the veg peelings,' April commented. 'It's easily done. Never mind,' she said comfortably. 'If it's lost, you can always get him another as a present.'

Laura got up to peer more closely. 'It's the shortest one, that's missing, isn't it? I don't understand,' she said, frowning. 'I'm certain I never touched it.'

While April moved off to the living-room, Laura went through the garbage bin and found nothing. She also searched the well-ordered drawers to no avail, after which she gave up and went to get dressed, wondering why such a trivial incident should make her anxious. It was as if there was an obvious solution that had so far eluded her.

Later she laid out the folder of poems on the kitchen table and flipped through them rather sadly. One of her chief causes of frustration was the desertion of her muse. In the first days of arrival at the cottage, inspiration had flowed, when her mind was receptive and uncluttered by problems other than the background one of Rick's disapproval. Poetry, she had decided, was different from other forms of creativity; it did not just consist of sitting at a table, pen in hand. There were the preliminaries, what she thought of as the walking-about stage, where the words formed in the head while one was doing something else. The writing of them came later. But none of this worked when the mind was preoccupied, and hers had become full of one preoccupation or another. It was no-one's fault but her own that she had allowed herself to half-fall in love, and to become obsessed by a sick boy's predicament. And now she was being summoned home to deal with Annabelle's troubles, and incidentally those concerning herself and Rick. Possibly all these were a direct result of her absconding, and the loss of inspiration was just retribution.

Rick had rung her before she could call him, startling her into the defensive.

'How did you find my number?' she demanded.

'It's not important.' He did not sound aggressive, merely strained and worried. 'Look, I think it's very necessary you come back. I can't deal with this on my own,' he had said, and explained.

She thought of Joe, quietly getting worse. 'Of course,' she had answered. 'Will a day or so make any difference?'

'Does it make a difference to *you*?' he asked, suspecting God knows what.

'Not in the way you imagine,' she told him with a touch of cynicism. 'But yes, it does. Will Wednesday be all right?'

Annabelle had come on the phone, speaking in the

small tight voice of someone holding back tears. Laura had been inclined to give her Joe's story as a moral example of one a great deal worse off than herself, but instead had poured out anodyne words with the assurance that she would be home before long, and they would sort it out together. Afterwards Laura was disgusted at the toughness of her inclination; it showed how far removed from the family she had become in the last ten days.

She closed the folder and stared out of the window at the limb of land across the harbour which had taken on the same uniform greyness of sea and sky. Remembering her first view of it, the sun picking out its varying shades of green, she thought how much she had come to love the cottage and its setting, and already felt the wrench of leaving. But the morning was full of things to be done: solitude must wait until the afternoon. She moved reluctantly and prepared to walk to the village to find Joe, warning April on the way out of her imminent departure. 'That's a pity,' April said as if she really meant it. 'I'll come up Wednesday then and help load the car, m'dear,' and Laura felt mean about her earlier irritation. Mark had asked himself to a ploughman's lunch and she stopped at the shops to buy rolls and cheese. She was not at all sure she wanted to see him; Alice's death remained an open, niggling question, yet whenever they came into contact, the old attraction was still there, undiminished. What was the point of prolonging the agony when there was no future? Best, she thought, to slip quietly out of his life. But, 'Please,' he had said, telephoning while she was dressing, 'there aren't many more chances to see you alone.'

'Where's Jeremy?'

'Exploring the countryside on my bike.'

She could hardly refuse. The previous evening she

had seen a new aspect of him, taking a quiet pride in his child. She supposed it was new to him too, because he wasn't quite at ease, and endearingly anxious that Jeremy and she should like each other. It was not difficult to achieve; it would be impossible to dislike Jeremy, and for his part, he made it obvious he appreciated women, judging by his surreptitious glances at her legs. They ate Mark's *spaghetti al pesto* and played Scrabble, the men striking up a hilarious rivalry. At quite an early hour, Jeremy had produced a barrage of yawns and taken himself off to bed with exaggerated tact. Laura had left soon afterwards, too tired to cope with the self-erected barrier between herself and Mark, and trying to ignore the shadow of disappointment on his face as he kissed her good night.

She walked on along the village street to the Ship and Anchor and round to the yard at the back where crates of drink were being unloaded. She caught Joe as he was returning to the lorry. He looked thin and ill, altogether too frail to be carrying such weights.

'How are you, Joe?'

'All right, thanks.' He gazed at her with the intense stare that seemed to ask for something she could not give him.

'Mark Wainwright's got you an appointment at the hospital, for tomorrow afternoon, three o'clock. I'll take you in and wait for you.'

'Not today, then?' His eyes changed to fear.

'I'm afraid Tuesday was the earliest they could manage.' She touched his arm reassuringly. 'It's not long to go. Are you taking those pills?'

He nodded. 'They aren't much good, though.' His feet shuffled nervously as if he was unable to control them.

With one eye on Sam Grimond's back, she repeated, 'Not long now, Joe. Why don't you come to the house and paint this afternoon? That'll help the day to pass.'

'Joe!' Sam's voice rang out from across the yard.

'I better go,' Joe said. 'Thanks, anyway.' He turned away, the droop of his shoulders expressing despair more poignantly than any words.

Monday was one of the days when Hannah left school late owing to a flute lesson. There was no sign of Annabelle at the bus stop, and neither did she expect there to be, but her mind was nevertheless unusually taken up by her stepsister. She was secretly appalled by the state into which Annabelle had allowed herself to fall, and, although she could not comprehend anyone being so feeble, it infuriated her that whoever had been the cause should get away with it. It was of course a man. Hannah was beginning to develop a strong feminist streak following her own party, and prior to that, the theft of the flute. It had not taken much coaxing to get the whole story out of Annabelle the previous day, while Hannah sat on her bed and fed her questions.

'What did you do, when this Tim character tried to rape you?'

'He didn't try to rape me,' Annabelle had sighed. 'Just to kiss me. I threatened him with the bread knife.'

'I'd have stuck him with it.'

'You probably would, and got into a lot of trouble. It was childish enough as it was. I only had to shove him and he nearly fell over.'

'Drunk, I suppose,' Hannah sniffed. 'And where was Ben while all this was going on?'

'In the other room.'

'Typical.'

'You don't understand, Han. He's got a girlfriend; he's not interested in me,' Annabelle said bravely.

'So what the hell's he been doing, going out with you, then?'

205

'He goes out with lots of people. This one's special, that's all.'

'Drop him, that's what I'd do,' Hannah recommended.

'He's not around to *be* dropped,' Annabelle said miserably.

'Well, you can't go on moping,' Hannah said. 'Honestly, Annie, you're quite pretty, really, when you haven't been howling. He isn't worth it. Has he been round to find out how you are? Oh no!'

'Don't, Han.' Annabelle closed her eyes. 'You're only making it worse.'

'You really are nuts about him, aren't you?' Hannah asked. 'All men are shits, in my opinion.'

'You don't understand,' was Annabelle's repeated phrase. 'Just go away and leave me alone, will you?'

Hannah went, but she was not prepared to leave it at that. Annabelle and she differed in practically every characteristic known to mankind, and Annabelle's passivity annoyed her in particular. But no-one other than herself was allowed to walk all over her. Hannah reflected on this as the bus crawled over Hammersmith Bridge and pulled up at her stop. She was halfway home when a familiar figure came in sight ahead of her, walking in the same direction, a tall, lanky figure carrying a case bulging with books. She started to run to catch up.

'Hey! Ben!'

He swung round and waited for her. 'Hello, Hannah, how's everything?' he said with a smile.

His cheerfulness doubled her anger. 'Don't ask me, ask Annie,' she retorted, glaring up at him.

He became immediately serious, his eyes worried behind his glasses. 'I was going to ring her this evening,' he said. 'Is she any better?'

'She's bloody miserable, if you really want to know.

It's a pity you didn't do something about her yesterday.'

'I thought she might want to be left alone – you know, if she wasn't feeling too good.'

'I don't suppose,' Hannah said coldly, 'you thought about her at all, which is a bit much, considering it was your tacky party. Did you know,' she added, 'that she was nearly raped?'

He stared at her in disbelief. 'You're joking.'

'I'm not. Some revolting man called Tim tried it on in your kitchen.'

'Tim?'

'He only stopped because Annie threatened him with a bread knife.'

'*Bread* knife?'

'There's no point in talking to you,' she said contemptuously, 'if all you can do is repeat everything like a parrot.' She started to march away up the road.

He caught her up and grabbed her by the arm. 'Hannah, stop! Are you sure you've got the facts straight?' His face was now creased with anxiety.

'Ask Annie, if you don't believe me.'

'I shall. Will you tell her I'll call round later on? Providing she wants to see me.'

'I shouldn't think so, but I'll ask her.' She fixed him with a look like a laser beam. 'And you'd better buy her some flowers or something, if you want my advice.' That would put him on the spot, she thought triumphantly; it was five o'clock and the shops would be shutting. He fell into step beside her. 'You're going the wrong way,' she added. 'The flower shop's in Hammersmith.'

'I'll take my bike,' he said. Glancing at her determined profile, he asked, 'Why so antagonistic, Hannah? I would have rung Annabelle anyway; we were all worried about her fainting.'

'Who's "all"?' she demanded.

'My mother, in particular, and me, of course.'

'And your girlfriend was worried out of her skull, I suppose?' she said.

He was silent for a moment. 'So that's what this is all about,' he said. He seemed to come to a decision, quickening his step. 'I'd better push on. I'll see you later,' he called over his shoulder.

Watching him disappear up the street, Hannah had the uncomfortable feeling she might have said too much.

'Something is wrong,' Mark said in the middle of lunch. 'Please tell me what it is.' He looked across the table at Laura, who was eating bread and cheese with a palpable lack of enthusiasm. Two wings of straight pale hair framed her distracted face, and there were frown marks between her eyes. She glanced up at him quickly and away again to stare out of the window at the sunless day, crumbling a roll between her fingers.

'If it's Jeremy—' He left the sentence unfinished.

'Jeremy is lovely,' she said, turning her head quickly to face him. 'If I were twenty years younger, I'd fall instantly in love with him.'

He smiled faintly. In the short pause that followed, he tried to think of a fault in his behaviour that might be the cause of the change in her; it was not so much a chilliness as a kind of withdrawal. He had felt it first as she said good night the previous evening, and today it was still there, an invisible barrier. There had not been a chance to break their platonic agreement even had he wanted to, owing to Jeremy's presence and her rushed departure. If she had been staying on, an explanation would have probably surfaced automatically in time; but there was not any time, in a day or so she would be gone, and he could not bear a flaw in the parting.

He put out a hand and touched her wrist.

'Tell me. Please,' he repeated.

She stopped attacking the roll and started to heap the crumbs into a neat mountain with one finger. 'There isn't any point,' she said. 'If we were about to have a heavy affair, then I'd have to, because I wouldn't be any use if I didn't.' She raised her eyes to his. 'As it is, it's none of my business.'

'Whatever concerns you, concerns me,' he said. 'Simple as that.'

'Give me one good reason why.'

'Because I love you.'

'We've been through all that, and decided it wasn't possible.'

'Possible to love you, or possible to do something about it?'

'Both.'

'You mean, you decided. There's no law that forbids one to love a person.'

She pushed her chair back. 'Would you like some coffee?' she asked to stall the uselessness of this conversation.

'Please.'

'Love is an overworked word,' she said, switching on the kettle. 'It's used to cover brief flings and lifelong marriages; every relationship under the sun, in fact. You can't really know about it until you've lived with a person day after day under one roof. I feel,' she added, 'I know you less well now than when we met.'

'That sounds remarkably like an accusation.' When she returned with the cups of coffee, his face had taken on the hooded look she had first noticed and had not seen since. He said stiffly, 'You might tell me the reason and stop attacking me with veiled hints.'

'Did you love Alice?' she asked.

She had not meant to say it. The words came out inadvertently because she was unable to face returning to London without an answer.

'Very much,' he said quietly.

'But she didn't love you; is that it?'

'Why do you think that? And what has Alice to do with you and me?' He leaned back in his chair, his eyes on her face. 'You've been obsessed with her from the beginning,' he remarked.

'It was the way you talked about her, as if you were guilty of something. It didn't add up. Why didn't you tell me what really happened before the accident?' Laura said without looking at him. He was silent a moment. 'As I said, it's none of my business,' she added, 'so you can tell me to get lost. But I've heard a version of the story I would rather not have heard.'

'Who's been talking?' he said, sighing. 'Don't bother to say. Christ! This bloody village.'

She said, 'We can stop talking about it, if you like. You asked me what was wrong and I've told you because you banged on at me, and I couldn't hide it any longer.' She took a deep breath and added, 'I don't know quite why it matters, but I wish you'd told me the truth.'

'Why should you choose to believe Eleanor Shaw-cross rather than me?' He sat in thought, while Laura waited. 'I didn't lie to you deliberately, merely withheld some of the facts out of loyalty to Alice,' he said eventually. 'I imagine you know now what they are.'

Laura said nothing, wishing she had never asked for confessions.

'I don't know why I ever gave you my account of my marriage,' he continued. 'Too much to drink, perhaps, and a longing to talk to someone about it. Once having started, I realized I couldn't explain the worst parts. You were already becoming important to me, and they don't show me up in a favourable light.' He paused to take a cigarette from its packet, and held it without lighting it. 'I killed her, you see. But I remember telling you that.'

'You can't have literally,' Laura broke in. 'It was after all an accident, wasn't it?'

'I was responsible for her death, which amounts to the same thing. My attitude, the things I said to her immediately beforehand, made her act as she did. That's what I believe,' he said, 'and it's no fun to live with.'

She stared at her untouched cup of coffee. 'There's no need to tell me any more,' she said. 'I understand now.'

'No, you don't,' he answered, putting a light to his cigarette. 'You asked for a full explanation and you shall have it.' He leaned towards her, his elbows on the table. 'Alice and I were happy; I swear we were happy. We had great fun renovating the house, and collecting items to go in it. She loved the garden as much as I did. And then a certain young doctor joined the practice, and things deteriorated between us. She drew away from me in spirit, and eventually she told me she was having an affair and wanted time to work it out of her system. It was so bloody unlike her, or unlike the kind of woman I thought I had married. It was agonizing to sit back and wait for it to come to an end, but that was what I tried to do. Divorce was never mentioned.' He paused, tapping ash off the cigarette with nervous fingers. 'The evening of the accident, she told me it was over. I can't describe the feeling of relief. Like the end of some dreadful illness. But it was short-lived; almost in the same breath she announced she was pregnant. She swore the child was mine, but I couldn't bring myself to believe her. How could she possibly be certain? I foresaw myself watching the baby grow up, watching and wondering in a state of constant torture.'

'Would you really have minded so much, once it was born?' Laura queried, half to herself.

'I'm not basically as good a man as Daniel Burgess, who brought up my child without a protest,' he said. 'I was frightened of being unable to accept it, and I wasn't ready to take that risk.'

'So what happened?'

'After the dinner party and on the way home I made Alice stop the car, and I asked her to end the pregnancy. She got terribly upset, I had drunk too much and we both lost our tempers. She said she would leave me, and I said maybe that was best. Neither of us really knew what we were saying. I calmed down after a while, tried to retract my words, secretly appalled by the harm I'd done. She was crying and I did my best to comfort her. But it was too late. She started the car quite suddenly, driving fast and barely stopping at the crossroads, and shot into the middle of the road.' He lifted his hands in a gesture of futility and let them drop. 'The rest you know,' he added.

'Blinded by tears,' Laura murmured.

'What did you say?'

'If she was crying hard, she may not have been able to see properly,' she said quickly. 'It need not have been deliberate.'

'I'll never know for sure,' he said heavily. 'One certainty remains: I was the cause.'

She said nothing, sadly unable to find words of comfort, or to refute his statement.

'I'd better go,' he said, getting to his feet. 'What I asked of Alice was unforgivable. You'll understand now why I didn't want you to know. I'm no better than your first husband who demanded the same of you.'

Raising her head, she said, 'They were different circumstances.'

'Unforgivable, nevertheless,' he replied. 'I can see by

your eyes.' Picking up his anorak off the window-seat, he added, 'Perhaps you'd like to say goodbye now rather than prolong the agony?'

'No,' she said. 'No, I don't want that. Do you have to go?'

'I've a pupil arriving at three o'clock, and Jeremy will be returning at some point.'

He gave her a swift kiss on the cheek and walked to the door. It seemed to her that his stoop was more pronounced, as if the strain of his revelations weighed him down. She longed to run after him, put her arms round him, assure him that she still felt the same about him; but the trouble was, she did not.

'It's Joe's appointment tomorrow afternoon,' she said. 'I'll ring you when I've brought him back, shall l?'

He turned, rubbing his eyes between thumb and forefinger. 'Joe. Of course, I'd almost forgotten. I'll take him; I'm not happy about you doing it.'

'I've promised him,' she said. 'He sets great store by promises being kept.'

'Then let me know when you've returned.'

At the front door she said, 'Thank you for talking to me.'

'It hasn't done either of us much good, has it?' he said with a touch of bitterness.

'I'm glad. I'd rather know,' she told him; untruthfully, she thought afterwards, standing at the window of her bedroom. Sea and sky melded together in a general greyness; on the horizon giant purple clouds had gathered, giving a bruised impression. A storm was taking place out to sea, circling, ready to pounce on the mainland. She felt bleak and bereft, like a child who has believed in its security and found it suddenly missing. Reflecting, she began to realize that she had looked on Mark as a kind of insurance policy, someone to run back to if renewal of life with Rick did not work

213

out. It shocked her, the fact that her mind had been working along these lines without her acknowledging it, throwing into relief the whole idea of returning home. There had never been any question of leaving the children, but it hadn't stopped her fantasizing about Mark. She was, she supposed, more in love with him than she had wanted to admit; or had been once. Now, his reaction to Alice's baby had shaken her belief in him. Staring unseeingly at the view, she tried, and failed, to understand.

Down below her by the rocks, a movement caught her eye. Joe was sitting, shoulders hunched, by a fuchsia bush, a drawing pad resting on his lap. He did not appear to be working; the hand holding a pencil was motionless, as if waiting to be motivated. She opened the window and called down to offer him a coffee, but the wind which had risen took away her voice, and he didn't answer. She went slowly downstairs to write, wondering without much hope whether unhappiness would lend her inspiration.

Joe, crouched at the bottom of Laura's garden, was fighting his own personal battle. From the moment he had woken that morning panic had gripped him. Even in confused sleep he had been aware of it, twisting and turning in his gut. The weather did not help; weather affected him now as it never had in those far-distant, longed-for days of peace. He had swallowed two of the tranquillizers and they had dulled his senses, but not the vein of panic that continued to crawl through him like a snake. His skin prickled in a series of tiny electric shocks as he tried to concentrate on what he was doing. But it was not a good day for birds; there was no sign of the heron which had probably taken shelter up the estuary, and only a flock of gulls rode the swell, immobile and uninteresting.

There was silence, apart from the slapping of the sea against the rocks. In his head the Voice whispered insistently, demanding to be heard. There was no blocking it out, he knew that from experience, or refusing to listen. Eventually it would get louder, the words clearer with their instructions as to what he must do. There would come a point where he would have to obey, where there was no option, like yesterday out in the fields with Mrs Shawcross's dog. Later, in Laura's kitchen, he had taken a knife from the rack as he was told to do, a small, sharp one, and hidden it in his pocket while she was out of the room. After he was back in the pub, the Voice had subsided a little, and today he had dug a hole with the knife under the fuchsia bush and buried it. He knew that it was only postponing the use of it, he would be made to retrieve it if those were his orders.

Here at the foot of Laura's garden he felt as safe as he could be. He had gone there as much to be near her as for something to do. The hours to the next day's hospital appointment stretched endlessly in front of him, the minutes passing in slow, inaudible ticks through his brain. When he was reasonably all right and under control, he disliked psychiatrists with their useless delving into your past, suggesting you were in love with your mother and suchlike crap. Now, scared and on a knife-edge, all he could think of was the relief they could bring him in the form of an injection. Twenty-four hours seemed an impossible length of time to wait for that. With an effort, he made himself grip the pencil dangling loosely between his fingers and poised it above the pad. He had started to draw the limb of land on the other side of the harbour without concentration, the shape of which Laura thought looked like a dragon. To him it was a prehistoric monster, the sort that had spikes along its back and a sloping neck, its head resting in the sea. He drew in quick, jerky strokes without his usual meticulous attention to detail; a child's horror picture with the distant rocks like pointed teeth, and the trees on the brow of the hill a bristling spine. In front of him the sea rose and fell, rose and fell, the waves never quite breaking, making him giddy, mesmerizing him. He imagined casting himself off from the rocks, becoming enveloped in it, allowing it to fold itself about him like a comforting duvet. Inside his head, the Voice began to speak to him clearly but softly, matching the undulation of the water. 'Why not do it? It would be easy to step from the rocks. So easy and peaceful; no more panic, no more pain.'

He dropped the pad and pencil on the ground and stood up slowly, his eyes never leaving the water. As he took the first step forward, a low roll of thunder grumbled in the distance and a sudden gust of wind scurried from the south, startling him. It rattled the fuchsia bush and lifted the loose sheet of paper with its primitive drawing, bearing it fluttering out to sea. Like a sleep-walker woken from a trance, he started to sweat and shiver at the same time. From a trickle, panic rose in him to a flood tide. His one coherent thought was to turn his back on the sea and to escape, it didn't matter where, but as far away as possible. Stumbling, he scrambled across the flat rocks, his feet slipping on the seaweed surface, to the jetty steps. He took them two at a time, to the top of the steep flight without stopping, without looking back. Instinct made him swerve involuntarily to Laura's front door and lean against it, panting while he rang the bell. Laura, writing furiously, heard it and ignored it; it did not strike her that it might be Joe. Half-an-hour before, she had seen him drawing at the foot of the cliff garden and was reassured by the thought of him apparently occupied for the afternoon.

Breaking for tea, she went out to the terrace and glanced down to find him missing. The white rectangle of drawing pad lay where he had dropped it, and beside it a crumpled blue anorak. Her heart thudding in fear, she walked swiftly indoors as the first large drops of rain darkened the paving stones.

It was growing dark as Rick crossed over Hammersmith Bridge on his way home from work. He paused and leant his arms on the railings; lights showed in the windows of houses lining the shore, and in the cluster of houseboats. In another week or so the clocks would change and winter would be formally declared. Long before that, the day after tomorrow, there was Laura's homecoming to be faced; an event he had moved heaven and earth to bring about and now viewed with trepidation.

It seemed impossible that she had been gone a bare fortnight. All that had happened in her absence, Hannah's escapades, Annabelle's difficulties, his own stupidity, made it appear like months rather than days. None of it would have happened if she had been there, he realized, and the fact underlined his incompetence and undermined his confidence. Added to that, there was the anxiety of her return. He had a very real fear of finding her changed; one woman having walked out of the house and another completely different one returning in her place. Then he reminded himself that he could not have known her very well in the first place, since he would not have dreamt her capable of running off without warning. However she was, whoever she had become, they would have to start all over again as if from the beginning. The thought daunted him.

He supposed Sarah was right: he had made the mistake of treating Laura as a second Miranda. He had done it with the best of intentions; it was his nature to protect, to cosset and, if he was to admit it, to organize. Nanny knows best, he muttered under his breath with irony. Well, Nanny hadn't come up to expectations over the past days. Thinking of Sarah brought into relief the nub of his anxiety. His inclination was to confess the whole story to Laura, to rely on her understanding and forgiveness and start afresh with no secrets. He had always had a rather naïve belief in no secrets within marriage. But he had enough sense to realize that this course of action would be disastrous, that he only wished to unload the guilt of his infidelity onto her shoulders in order to relieve himself. It had been, he told himself, a very small indiscretion, and the guilt of it would soon wear thin and eventually peter out altogether. But right now it loomed large, a definite stumbling block to peace of mind about their future.

He almost wished that she had found someone down there, and had been unimportantly unfaithful herself, so that the two wrongs would cancel themselves out. It was too much to hope: something was making her loth to leave, but he had a feeling this wasn't the answer. He had tried to imagine her life in Gerard's cottage, picturing the long walks of which she was so fond, and the writing of her poems, seeking the space she claimed to need. He could not believe a backwater of a Cornish village, populated mainly by pensioners, would produce many desirable men. No, it was the solitude that held her there, unwilling to return because she had not as yet had enough of it.

A ground mist lay over the river and the playing fields of St Paul's Boys School. It was now completely dark, and he was growing cold. He walked on slowly, undecided whether to turn Laura's homecoming into a celebration, fill the house with flowers, have champagne on ice; or to welcome her undemonstratively, as if nothing had altered: a hug and a kiss, a casserole in the oven. He was still debating the point as he reached home, to find Ben Ferris on the doorstep, holding a bunch of rather limp chrysanthemums.

'I've brought these for Annabelle. I thought she might need cheering up.'

Rick let him in, uncertain whether to warn him against any further tampering with his daughter's emotions. In the end, he decided to say nothing, and directed the boy to Annabelle's room.

'Thanks, Mr Snow,' said Ben, composed as ever, and took the stairs two at a time. A scatter of yellow and white petals fell in his wake. 'These will be bald by the time I get there,' he added cheerfully over his shoulder.

Rick sighed. He had enough problems without trying to solve those of his child. They must sort it out for themselves.

'You'd better have the chair,' Annabelle said.

Ben looked at the small armchair with its feminine frill round the bottom. 'I'll sit on the floor, if you don't mind.'

She laid the flowers in their paper wrapping on the end of the bed. 'You needn't have brought anything,' she said ungraciously. 'I'll put them in water later.'

'I'm afraid they're on the point of dying, it's hardly worth it. Are you feeling better?'

'Yes, thank you.'

'We were all terribly worried about you.' He leant his back against the chest of drawers and stretched long legs out in front of him. The conversation seemed to have got stuck. 'You must have had a bug or something,' he tried tentatively.

Annabelle was past the stage of pretending. She had even worked herself through the acute misery of the past forty-eight hours, and reached a kind of dumb acceptance of the obvious. She was glad he had come to see her, but only in a remote way.

'I was drunk,' she said. 'I was miserable, and I drank too much wine.'

'Oh, Annabelle!' He looked worried. 'Did you really loathe the party that much?'

'Yes,' she admitted flatly.

'Was it Tim?'

'Partly. Who told you about him, anyway?'

'No-one,' he lied. 'But I know what he can be like.' He eyed her. 'You said "partly". That wouldn't mean Kate, would it?' he added.

She felt the colour rise in her face, a wave of unwanted heat. She longed to say something clever, like 'don't flatter yourself', but the words got lost.

'Why should Kate matter?' she said distantly. 'She's your girlfriend. Why should I be bothered?'

'She's a friend, that's all.'

'She didn't look like it, twining herself round you like a garden weed.' He roared with laughter, annoying her. 'She looked ridiculous,' she said indignantly, knowing she would have done the same given half a chance.

'She's that sort of girl,' he said, 'and you're another sort. Different. It doesn't mean anything.'

He watched her, sitting on the side of the bed with a pink face, glaring at her feet.

'I'm not that different,' she mumbled.

'Well, anyway, I like you the way you are. Listen,' he said, 'I've got masses of friends, and that's the way I want to keep it. No-one special; I'm too busy trying to make it to university. I'm not ready to become an item with anybody.'

'That stupid word.' She threw herself sideways and drummed her fists on the pillow in a fit of frustration.

'It sounds like something off a shopping list.'

'It's just a *word*,' he pointed out mildly, taking off his glasses and gazing at her myopically while he polished them with a tissue.

She sat up with a jerk, her hair dishevelled. 'Have you been to bed with her?' she asked. 'I suppose you have.'

'Hell's bells, Annabelle! Be your age. Where, for God's sake? In the back of a car? I don't own one. Anyway, I wouldn't tell you if I had. Why do you want to know?'

'Because I mind,' she said. It was too late to worry about pride. 'Because whenever you and I do something, it's the same old thing: a film followed by manky old tapes and then home.'

'What do you expect us to do? Ride down the road naked on a tandem?' he suggested.

She gave a reluctant and shaky giggle. 'You've never even kissed me.'

'I've thought about it,' he said truthfully.

'But you've never actually tried. I suppose it's because I haven't got long blond hair and a suntan and all that.'

'You always seem so serious and un-get-atable.' He got to his feet and went and sat on the bed beside her. 'If that's what's worrying you, it's easily rectified.'

He leaned over and kissed her firmly on the lips. It was a pleasant kiss, and lasted several seconds; it wasn't quite what she had expected, but it was a start.

'You don't want to lose any more weight,' he said. 'I could put a fist in between you and your waistband. Look.'

He demonstrated with the top of her skirt. She giggled again, happily this time. 'Stop! You're tickling.'

'It's yourself that needs to loosen up, not your clothes,' he told her, pleased with her reaction.

'I'd better go now, I've a pile of work to do. Like to do something at the weekend? It needn't be a film; we could have a plate of spaghetti somewhere – followed by a necking session.'

'Shut up!' she said. 'You're taking the mickey,' but she was too happy to mind.

'Yes or no?'

'Yes.'

'But remember,' he told her from the open doorway, 'no question of becoming an item. All right?'

'All right, Ben. And thanks.'

'What for?'

'The flowers, for one thing.' She lifted them from the bed and a further shower of petals covered the duvet. 'It was a nice thought,' she said, laughing.

At five o'clock, Mark's pupil left and Jeremy arrived home from his exploration, soaked from the rain. He lit the fire, filled up the log basket from a supply in the shed and then enjoyed another of Mark's teas. Listening to Jeremy's description of his day, Mark felt increasingly grateful for the cheerful, uncomplicated companionship. The hour spent with Laura had left him demoralized, raw with fatigue, so that he had had difficulty in keeping his mind on the Classics. Now, his attention drawn to Jeremy's account of old churches, and hidden coves and creeks, he was able to forget, for the moment, the condemnation in her eyes which she had tried unsuccessfully to hide before he left her. Watching Jeremy's face, flushed from fresh air, his heart lurched fleetingly at the thought that he might have had a similar child, if a few diabolical words had never been uttered.

While they washed up the tea things, Jeremy asked out of the blue, 'What do you think about shacking-up with someone? At my age, I mean?'

Mark dried a plate thoughtfully. 'Shacking-up presumably means living under one roof. Under whose roof do you intend to put her?'

'Most people live in digs at Exeter, but there's a flat going. Between us we could just about afford it.'

'I don't think there's anything wrong in it,' Mark said, 'but don't oxpoct tho rolationship to laet.'

'Because of shacking-up?'

'Because of being young.'

'Oh well,' Jeremy said, 'it's a hazard at any age, isn't it?'

'You're right.' Mark stared through the window at the rain-sodden garden and the approaching dusk. 'I'm no example to you, having made a cock-up every time where women are concerned.'

'I didn't mean that,' Jeremy said quickly.

'I know you didn't, but it happens to be true.'

Jeremy pulled the plug from the sink, letting the water go with a gurgle. 'But you were happily married, weren't you?' he said as if it was an established fact.

For a split second, Mark was tempted to lay the facts before him and let him judge for himself. The urge passed. He could not risk losing the tenuous bond of affection he felt growing between them. He turned the topic by asking, 'What's your girlfriend like?'

'Blonde and thin. Rather like Laura, or like she probably was when she was a girl.' Mark smiled at the dubious compliment. 'I like Laura,' Jeremy added. 'I nearly biked over to see her today, but then I thought you might be going, so I didn't.'

'I had lunch with her,' Mark said evenly.

'I thought you might. Will you be seeing her again before she leaves?'

'I don't know. Probably.' He grinned despite himself. 'Whatever you're hinting at,' he said, 'it isn't possible.

She's married, and I'm not messing up another marriage. Look where it got me with your mother.'

'Don't spare my feelings,' Jeremy said in mock despair.

'*Touché.* You're not such a bad result, after all,' Mark admitted.

While Jeremy went to have a bath, Mark banked up the fire and busied himself in the kitchen. The wind had reached gale force, battering and whining through the eaves and the guttering, and slashing the windows with squalls of rain. It was a night for the lifeboat; he would be surprised if they did not hear the explosion of maroons before long. His plan had been to take Jeremy to a fish restaurant in Roseland, asking Laura to join them. The weather had forced him to rethink that idea, and perhaps it was just as well, considering the layer of unease that now lay over his friendship with Laura. It would have to be another evening in, dining off his limited cooking repertoire. She was on his mind, wondering whether the approaching storm would worry her, alone in the house, while he tried to decide between more pasta or omelettes. Thinking about ringing her anyway made him remember that he had not played back the answerphone for messages. Amongst them was a call she had made earlier in the afternoon asking him to ring her back. Her voice when she answered sounded worried, but not for herself.

'It's Joe,' she told him, and explained about his disappearance from the rocks, and the discarded anorak and drawing pad. 'I went down to bring them into the house, and there's been no sign of him since.'

'You shouldn't have done that,' he said. 'Those rocks are slippery.'

'I didn't have to walk on the rocks. I climbed down through the garden. It's not too bad if you don't look

224

down.' She hesitated. 'He just vanished. Mark, you don't think—'

'That he's drowned himself? I think it's highly unlikely. Have you checked with the pub to see if he's there?'

'Yes, at four o'clock. He wasn't.'

'I'll ring them again,' he said, 'a bit later, to give him time to get back from wherever he is. Then I'll call you to let you know. Like to come over for supper? I'll fetch you and take you back.'

'I'd better not,' she said. 'I feel I should be here, at least for the moment, in case he turns up for his things.'

'You *are* all right?' he asked.

'Of course, why not? Oh I see, the storm. I rather like it,' she said. 'There's a superb display of lightning out to sea, and getting nearer.'

'Then don't stand at the window.'

The first crack of thunder exploded overhead as Jeremy joined him in the kitchen.

'A real corker, isn't it?' he said appreciatively. They had a drink before supper, and Mark told him briefly about Joe.

'Laura has been fostering him,' he added. 'She's got herself involved, and I don't altogether approve.'

Jeremy did not agree. 'It shows she cares,' he said, 'and he probably knows that, which must be helpful. It means he'd never be a threat to her.'

'I hope you're right.'

But Mark was not convinced. His sense of unease increased after telephoning the pub and being told by a disgruntled Mrs Grimond that Joe had not been seen since lunchtime. It began to appear that Laura's fears for the boy's safety were not so far-fetched after all; and yet, some unexplained instinct told Mark that this was not the case, that somewhere Joe was wandering about outside without purpose, impervious to the weather. He wished Laura had agreed to be fetched. Not only did he miss her, but he would have felt illogically happier this evening to know that she was not alone. Not wanting to spoil things for Jeremy, he pushed these misgivings to one side, and they ate mushroom omelettes and a salad, and drank red wine in the warmth of the kitchen.

Laura never quite left his mind, however, and when they had finished, he went through to the living-room to call her. He let the telephone ring for a long time before giving up hope of an answer; replacing the receiver slowly as he tried to think of an explanation.

Laura was cooking a lamb chop when the power failed, leaving her in sudden darkness. She groped her way to the worktop where April August had left an upright torch, matches and candles in an assortment of holders, two of which she lit. Taking the torch, she toured the house, putting the candlesticks in all the rooms she was likely to use. Lightning flickered blue at the uncovered windows, and thunder cracked into prolonged rumbles as she went, first to the drawing-room and then upstairs to her bedroom and bathroom. Finally, she returned to the kitchen to switch off the electric cooker and to stare disconsolately at the half-cooked chop, baked potato and frozen peas. It would have to happen on the one evening when hunger had overtaken her; it might be hours before the power was restored. By the diffused light thrown by the candles, she piled a plate with bread, butter and the remainder of the cheese, poured herself a whisky and wondered what to do with herself to take her mind off Joe. The mild sense of adventure induced by the storm, plus the shadowy candlelight and her aloneness were spoiled by worry. She wandered through to the drawing-room, coaxed the sulking fire into flames with another log and switched on Gerard's transistor radio with the sudden longing for human voices.

She could not concentrate on the murder in progress, it merely served as background noise. A picture of Joe's body sinking beneath the waves had lodged itself firmly in her mind's eye. She ate half the bread and cheese and was no longer hungry. How long did one wait to report a person missing? Most likely she should have done so hours ago. Mark would know; he must have telephoned the pub by now. If Joe was there he would have rung to let her know. She decided to leave it half-an-hour before telephoning him. Perhaps, she thought, he was also in darkness, searching for candles and trying to supply Jeremy with some form of supper. A log on the fire toppled and spluttered, sending up a shower of sparks, startling her.

The knock on the door was unexpected; she had been anticipating the telephone. It broke through the howling of the wind, loud and repeated. She was convinced, as she made her way upstairs by the light of the torch, that it was Mark who had decided to come over rather than call her. There was a further knocking as she fumbled with the catch and threw the door open, the force of the gale nearly dragging it out of her hands. So certain was she of finding Mark on the step that the sight of Joe standing there was foremost a surprise and secondly, deep relief. Very wet, very bedraggled, dark hair plastered to his forehead, he was supporting himself with an arm against the lintel of the door.

'Joe! Come in,' she said.

But he had already stumbled past her as if on the point of collapse, and stood dripping on the landing carpet in the semi-darkness. She closed the door with

227

a bang and turned to him as he held his hands out to her in a curiously pleading gesture. The beam from the torch glinted on what he was holding – a knife, held not menacingly but limply between his fingers, as though extending it to her as an offering.

Chapter Nine

For the first time since she had known Joe, Laura was
frightened. It had never crossed her mind he might hurt
her or in any way pose a threat; he had seemed far
too pathetic and in need of protection. Now, although
nothing about him had outwardly changed, she sensed
rather than observed the control that was missing in
him. With only the pool of light from the torch to break
the darkness pressing in on them, she felt suddenly and
overwhelmingly vulnerable. Willing herself to move
slowly, gently as if faced with a nervous animal, she
put out her hand for the knife.

'It's one from the kitchen, isn't it? Thank you for
bringing it back, Joe.' She spoke casually as though
its disappearance was quite normal. He held the knife
out to her, handle uppermost, dangling it between his
fingers.

'I want you to hide it,' he said, and his voice was
hoarse and urgent. 'Put it somewhere I can't see it, so
I don't have the chance to use it.'

'All right,' she told him soothingly, taking it from
him. 'And now, let's get you out of those clothes.
I'll find you a towel and a bathrobe, and you can
warm up in front of the fire.'

She took him by the arm and guided him across the
landing to her bedroom and into the bathroom beside
it, his shoes squelching at every step. 'Right,' she said,
'you start to take off those wet things while I find
something dry. I'll light the candles.'

He stood docilely, slowly pulling the sweater over his head like an obedient child, saying nothing. Her fear subsided as she groped her way along the passage to the airing cupboard; he was as harmless as ever. It was the knife that had scared her. She buried it under folded pillow cases, and collected a towel and a snowy bathrobe from an assortment, imagining briefly what Gerard would say if he knew, and banishing the thought.

Joe was in his pants when she got back, sitting on the side of the bath, shivering. His skin in the flickering light looked blue with cold.

'The water may still be hot enough for a bath,' she said anxiously, turning on the tap.

'I don't want a bath.' He leapt up and knocked her hard away, twisting the tap to off. The gush of water ceased. She stared at him, shocked by the violence of the gesture, irritation rising in her.

'Why ever not? It's the best way of warming you up, but if you want to catch pneumonia—'

'Sorry. Sorry.' He was immediately contrite, pleading with her. 'I don't mean – I'm sorry, Laura.'

He had never called her 'Laura' before. She had always been 'Mrs Snow'.

'They may come here for me,' he told her. 'I can't run if I'm in the bath.'

'Who are "they", Joe?'

'The people from hospital. I ran away when I was sectioned and they'll try to get me back. Lock me up. D'you see?'

His eyes were on her face, huge and desperate, and she saw that he had gone over the edge into his own world where she could not reach him – only play for time.

'I should be safe here, but you never are anywhere, really,' he explained. 'They've a way of finding you in the end. I'm safe here as anywhere. I can stay, can't I?'

'For the moment,' Laura said. She handed him the towel. 'Give yourself a rub down with that while I put these in the airing cupboard to dry out.'

She had started to scoop the scattered clothes off the floor when he let out a cry of anguish or rage, she could not tell which, and was beside her, gripping her wrists.

'Don't take those!' He grabbed the bundle from her, holding it close to him. 'That's what *they* do, take your clothes away and hide them so you can't escape.' His eyes widened as he looked at her. 'You were going to do that, weren't you?' he said with cunning. 'Hide them, and then ring for *them* to come and fetch me.'

She felt all at once her patience ebb away. 'I wasn't, but I shall if you're going to be impossible,' she said sharply. 'Keep the wretched clothes if it makes you happy.'

He looked suddenly bewildered. 'They're very wet,' he admitted.

'Very. Now get that bathrobe on. I want to go down and see to the fire.'

'Maybe,' he said, 'maybe I could dry them in front of that? Where I can see them.'

They spread his clothes out on the floor by the fire, and she put the guard in front of the burning logs to prevent sparks shooting out. There was no way of making a hot drink without electricity; she gave him a small glass of red wine, judging that it could hardly make him more unstable than he already was. He sat huddled on the sofa beside her, watching the flames, his bare bony feet with uncut toenails somehow bringing out the protective instinct in her once again. The unreality of the situation struck her forcibly, sitting there in semi-darkness with a boy whose problems had gone beyond ordinary assistance like hers. She, in fact, needed help herself, for what was she to do with him, where did she go from here? Pinning her faith on Mark, she willed him to call her so that at least she would not feel so alone in her predicament.

He broke into her thoughts saying, 'It's like Christmas, isn't it? The fire and candles and all.'

She wondered from what deep recesses of his mind he had dredged up this memory. 'Is that what Christmas was like for you?' she asked.

'A long time ago – when I was small, I suppose.'

'Joe, where did you go this afternoon? You must have been out in the rain for hours.'

He looked puzzled. 'Don't remember. Yes, I do, though. The Voice was telling me to walk into the sea – I ran as far away as possible, don't know where I went. There was the road, and then grass and a wood, and another road. That's when I thought *they* would be out looking for me. I came back here to be safe, and dug up the knife in the garden in case I was told to kill myself, cut my wrists. I knew I'd have to give it back to you, it was safer. I tried once, look.'

He held his arms out, wrists uppermost. Faint white lines were etched across each of them. She glanced at them, imagining the nightmarish web of his illness.

'I've got your anorak and drawing pad,' she said. 'I fetched them from the garden where you'd left them.'

'Did I?' he said. 'I can't remember.'

The telephone rang from across the room, clearly and comfortingly, cutting through the battering of the wind against the house. She jumped up to answer it, wondering how to explain to Mark what had happened without alarming Joe.

He caught her before she was halfway there, held her by the arms in a grip which was surprisingly strong.

'Don't answer it,' he whispered as if someone might

be listening. 'It'll be *them*. I told you, didn't I?'

She struggled to jerk herself free. 'Don't be stupid, Joe! It's Mark, I'm expecting him. Let go of me at once.'

'It's them, I tell you!' he said more loudly. Pinioning her arms from behind, he frogmarched her back to the firelight, went on holding her prisoner while the phone rang and rang, and then finally stopped. Fear and despair rose in her throat, leaving a sour taste, and the indignity of being man-handled brought tears to her eyes. She felt like bringing her shoe down hard on one of his bare feet, but fighting him she knew was no use. Her only hope was to talk and cajole.

'The phone has stopped, Joe,' she said quietly. 'Let me go now, please.'

His hands dropped to his sides. He looked stricken. 'I didn't hurt you, did I, Laura? I didn't mean to hurt you.'

'It's all right.' She rubbed her arms, feeling cold. 'I must phone Mark,' she said. 'He'll be worried about me, you see.'

'No,' he replied quickly. 'He'll come round here if you do that.'

'Not if I don't tell him what happened. Just to let him know I'm all right.'

He was on the floor now, gathering up his jeans, shoes and sweater in a frenzy. 'He'll come anyway, then,' he said, 'and he'll make me go back to *them*, I know he will.'

'Joe,' she said hopelessly, 'no-one is trying to put you away. You are living in the past.'

He took no notice. 'He won't understand, not like you do.' Lifting the torch from a side-table, he made for the door, damp clothes clutched under one arm.

'Where are you going?'

'Upstairs. Your bedroom,' he said. 'I must be near the

front door so I can run if anyone comes.' He jerked his head. 'You'd better come too. You'll have to help me when it happens.'

She followed him, both of them stumbling in the shadowy darkness. In the bedroom she lit the candles, her hand moving rapidly, clumsily, and wondered in panic how long it would take Mark to decide to drive over, and whether Joe would let her open the door when he finally arrived. The evening had become like a bad dream, or an extract from some television movie seen many times before without much interest. Except that now it was actually being enacted, it had to be taken seriously. She felt drained by interchanging emotions; sorrow, fear, anger following each other over and over.

He was sitting on the floor, trying unsuccessfully to pull damp socks onto his feet. He began to cry. Wearily she went to kneel beside him.

'What is it, Joe?'

He buried his head in her shoulder. 'I'm so tired.'

She got up, turned back the cover on the bed and folded it. Then she spread the discarded bathrobe over the sheets and the duvet, and pulled Joe to his feet.

'Lie down and rest,' she told him. 'Try to sleep.'

It was almost too much to hope that he would do so. He caught her hand. 'Don't leave me,' he pleaded. 'Please don't leave me.'

Then he crawled onto the bed and curled into the foetal position, and lay there shivering. 'It's cold,' he muttered with his eyes shut.

There was no point in reminding him that his clothes were not yet dry. She covered him with part of the duvet and sat, holding his hand until eventually the silent crying stopped and his heaving shoulders were still. He appeared to sleep. Exhausted, she lay down carefully beside him, not daring to creep to the telephone or even to move, for fear of bringing on another outburst from him. After a while she realized the noise of the storm had died to a few distant rumbles of thunder, and only the wind remained, rattling the window frames. With her ears straining for the welcome sound of a car's engine, and her mind fixed longingly on hot tea and freedom, she stayed where she was and waited.

'I wonder why she's coming back,' Hannah said. 'I suppose she got bored. Being alone is all very well for a bit, but it must get boring in the end. That is,' she added, 'if she really *is* alone.'

'Of course she is,' Annabelle said dismissively. 'Don't start all that again.' She was far more concerned with Laura's real reasons for going in the first place, which had never been properly explained. 'She hasn't phoned this evening,' she remembered suddenly.

'She doesn't need to, now that Rick's got her number,' Hannah replied, an inveterate listener at keyholes.

'How do you know that?'

'I heard him talking to her when the phone hadn't rung, so it stands to reason he must have.'

'Honestly, Han!'

'I couldn't help it, he was talking quite loudly. It sounded,' said Hannah, 'as if they were discussing you. I wouldn't be surprised if you're the reason Mum's decided to come home. Fainting and all that.'

'I don't believe it.' Annabelle looked guilty.

'Actually, you're much better now, aren't you? I mean, since Ben called.'

'I was never really ill,' she said. 'Just miserable.'

'Mmm, I know. I guessed you'd sort it out, though.'

Annabelle eyed her suspiciously. 'Did *you* have anything to do with Ben coming round?'

'Me? Why should I?' Hannah changed the subject hastily. 'I must say, it'll be odd having Mum around again. I felt weird about her going, and now I feel the same about her coming home.'

'I'm pleased,' Annabelle said.

'I hope Rick calms down,' Hannah remarked. 'He's all on edge; you'd think he'd be all sweetness and light, wouldn't you?'

'He's just excited,' Annabelle said, far from certain this was the truth. 'I thought you were supposed to be tidying your room?'

'I've tidied it.'

In Hannah's case, this chore consisted of removing the pile of clothes on the floor to the bottom of the hanging cupboard and shutting the door on them. The best welcome home present she could give Laura, Rick had said, would be a reasonably pristine bedroom. It seemed a pretty dull present to Hannah; why anyone should bother about her room, since only she had to put up with the mess, was beyond her comprehension. Flowers in Laura's bedroom were a better idea, surely. There had been a discussion between the three of them at supper about what they should do on her first evening home. Annabelle thought one of Rick's speciality dinners would be best because Laura would be tired after a long drive. Hannah suggested a surprise party, which was immediately vetoed by the other two, although it would certainly answer the problem of those first awkward vibes that Rick dreaded. For the same reasons, he favoured dinner out, where the atmosphere would be mildly festive and not rub in his superior competence in the kitchen, which he was at pains to avoid. It would have the added advantage of putting off the inevitable moment of confrontation, when he and Laura would be alone together and forced to start bridging gaps.

After supper, when the girls had disappeared ostensibly to finish their homework, he tried to map out in his mind a psychological plan of campaign. It was difficult to achieve since he had no knowledge of where Laura's thought processes had progressed to. At worst she could have decided their marriage was finished, that she could well do without him. He tried not to believe in this scenario; it was too painful to contemplate. Perhaps, rested and relaxed, she would be receptive to talking through the differences that had driven her away in the first place. He preferred to trust in this version, which left only his own stumbling-blocks to deal with: the hurt of her defection that still rankled, and his brief hour of infidelity. He kept picturing them both in bed for the first time for a fortnight, he beginning the manoeuvres of love-making and she turning on her side with her back to him (not tonight, I'm tired). Whichever way he viewed it, he could not see any likelihood of a smooth and easy coming-together. Even the valid excuse for bringing her home for Annabelle's sake was starting to crumble: she was showing very real signs of recovery since Ben's visit, finishing a reasonable plateful of food at supper, and talking again. Although it was a relief in most respects, Laura might well think he had dragged her back under false pretences. There could be no planning ahead, he realized, sighing, and switched on the television. The trouble was, she had had time on her hands to work out her own future strategy, with nothing to do except walk and write; no interruptions, no distractions, no-one demanding attention.

Hannah was lolling on Annabelle's bed, saying, 'Shall we get separate lots of flowers, or from us both?'

'Separately, I think,' Annabelle answered. 'It'll make her feel more wanted.'

'I don't think she needs to,' Hannah said. 'After all, *she* left *us*, not the other way round.'

'Everyone needs to.' Annabelle had come to this

conclusion quite recently. 'And I need to finish this essay, so push off now, Han.'

'Work, work, work.' On her way to the door she said, 'You know, I really envy Mum, a whole two weeks of doing nothing.'

'Not true. She's been writing.'

'Yes, but she hasn't had us to bother her.' Hannah was determined to have the last word. 'Writing must be fairly easy without anything else to think about,' she pointed out, echoing Rick's thoughts.

At some undefined time of the night, Laura half-woke to the awareness of an arm beneath her back, and the warmth of a leg touching hers. For one awful moment she imagined it to be Joe; and then, through her confusion, she remembered that Joe had long since gone and there was someone quite else beside her in bed. She had slipped back into sleep, too drugged with exhaustion to worry about the full implications of either fact, and slept until eight o'clock when sunlight behind the drawn curtains woke her properly. She was alone. There was only a dent in a pillow to show where Mark had lain; that, and a scribbled note on the bedside table confirmed that he had been a reality and not a figment of her imagination. Unwilling to face the realization without the help of coffee, she wrapped herself in a dressing-gown and went downstairs to the kitchen, taking the note with her.

Sun streamed in at the windows and the wind had died; it was as if the storm had never been. There were mugs and glasses in the sink, reminding her of how little she had eaten the previous day, which might or might not account for the hollow feeling in the pit of her stomach. She made toast and a cup of coffee, carried them to the table and sat sipping gratefully while she read Mark's note. 'Gone home before I'm seen leaving and tarnishing your reputation. You are so beautifully asleep, I can't bring myself to wake you. Will ring in the morning. Love, M.' Small, scholarly handwriting, the written words sank into her brain. There was no skirting round the fact any longer that she had spent a good part of the night with him. She buttered the toast thoughtfully and ate a mouthful, staring out on a blue sea choppy and sparkling with little waves, aware that she should be feeling something, elation or shame, to show for it. But all she felt was enormously tired and emotionally drained, and a longing to go back to bed and sleep the day away. Then she remembered about Joe, and the whole of the night before returned to her and slotted into place. She made a second cup of coffee, recalling the vigil beside the sleeping boy that had appeared like hours and was in fact less than thirty minutes.

The sound of a car turning the steep corner on the upper road had been like music. She had slipped from the room on shoeless feet to open the front door before Mark could knock, and stood in the howling wind, waiting and hoping. The relief of seeing him cross the threshold had been overwhelming; she had had time to hush him into silence, and then her knees seemed to buckle under her, and tears started to course down her cheeks. He took the torch from her and they crept downstairs to the drawing-room where the fire had burnt itself out, and it had grown cold. He had wrapped her in his arms while she blew her nose and gave him an explanation of all that had happened.

'I don't know what I would have done if you hadn't decided to come,' she said.

'I was worried stiff about you. I don't know what difference I make, though. We are still faced with the question of what to do about him. You can't keep him here.'

'We haven't a hope of persuading him to keep the hospital appointment.' She spoke from the comforting region of his chest where her head rested. 'As far as he's concerned, men in white coats have become the enemy.'

'I can try to coax him back to his room in the pub for tonight,' he said. 'We'll deal with other problems in the morning.'

'I doubt the Grimonds will let him in,' she pointed out. 'He hasn't worked all day. They're not fools, they'll know by now what he's like.'

'Then I'll take him back with me. I'm not leaving him here, and that's for sure.' He put her away from him gently. 'Let's have a whisky to warm us before we decide. Have you eaten anything?'

'Bread and cheese,' she grimaced. 'The power failed, and then there was Joe.'

He had made her a sandwich with ham he found in the fridge, and sat beside her on the sofa while she ate and drank; and she thought how happily she had relinquished her independence when it came to the point, relishing his support in its place. He had not uttered a word of criticism about the situation, how it was her own fault for involving herself so deeply with an unknown and unbalanced boy, although she knew he had thought it unwise. She could imagine Rick in his place being full of recriminations, kindly put and well-meaning and absolutely infuriating.

The whisky had warmed her. It would have been very pleasant sitting in the fluttering candlelight with Mark's arm round her, if it had not been for the problem of Joe.

'We must come to a decision,' she said.

'I've decided. I'll take him home and keep him for the night, and review the picture tomorrow.'

'Isn't it "tomorrow" already?' she asked.

'It's eleven o'clock.'

'Only that.' Aeons of time seemed to her to have passed since she had been alone, troubled merely by lack of light and heating. 'I'm not sure how he'll react if we wake him,' she said doubtfully. 'For some reason, he's connected you with the mysterious people who are trying to put him away.'

'He's not far wrong,' he said. 'Undoubtedly that's what will happen next.'

'I suppose so,' she agreed sadly.

'He isn't safe to roam, that's obvious; on the brink of doing himself or someone else an injury.'

'It would be himself,' she insisted. 'I've never felt he was a danger to me.'

He turned his head to look at her curiously. 'You mind very much about him, don't you?' he said. 'Why, I wonder?'

She thought for a moment. 'I think,' she replied, 'it's because of my own children. There but for the grace of God go Hannah and Annabelle – and thousands like them. I've never come into contact with tragic problems like Joe before, and it's taken over part of me.'

Too late she had remembered his own tragedy of Alice and the unborn child. She had squeezed his hand in the hope that he would understand this to be wordless sympathy.

'We could leave him asleep,' she added quickly. 'I can sleep in another room.'

'No, no and treble no,' Mark said adamantly. 'I'm not leaving you with him, however harmless. Unless, of course, I stay the night,' he suggested formally. 'There are three bedrooms, aren't there?'

'Yes,' she said in a carefully neutral voice.

'I think the other plan is best. I'll have Jeremy there to help if necessary.' He stood up and took her glass.

241

'A little more of this,' he said, 'and then I'll make a move.'

She followed him by the light of the torch to the kitchen.

'Mark, you won't get tough with him, will you? Persuasion is much better than coercion with Joe.'

'I'll do my best,' he told her. 'He quite liked me, the one time I've had anything to do with him.'

'He's far worse now,' she said, worried.

There was a sudden explosion, like that of a giant rocket. 'What's that?'

'The lifeboat being launched. I thought it was inevitable,' he said.

She peered through the window into the Stygian, rain-streaked night, all at once tired of the unrelieved darkness inside and out; and as if in answer to a silent wish, there was a faint clunk and the kitchen was ablaze with light. They had gone from room to room blowing out candles, talking normally at last, for something about the shadowy dimness had made them whisper. In the drawing-room she switched on a blow heater and stood in front of it, warming her hands and feet, while Mark finished the last of his drink. Above their heads a door slammed; one of the bedroom doors, she decided, caught by a sudden draught.

When they walked upstairs together, she remembered, they had been tensed and ready for all sorts of difficulties in the removal of Joe from the house. All, that was, except the sight of an empty room. The overhead light was on, which she presumed was how she had left it at the beginning of the power failure. The duvet was flung to one side, and wet footprints from his saturated trainers led in a direct line to the front door; the only signs of his brief occupancy. She should have had a sense of relief that the matter had been taken out of their hands. Instead, she felt overwhelmingly defeated, as though in some way she had failed him.

'He can't have gone far,' Mark said. 'I'll take the car and look for him.'

'It's no use,' she answered dully. 'One glimpse of anyone searching for him and he'll hide like a frightened animal. There's nowhere for him to go,' she added. 'He'll stay out all night, in damp clothes, and by the morning—'

Her voice trailed away and she had started to cry again, annoyed with herself but equally unable to stop. The strain of the evening with its extraordinary changes of mood, had finally caught up with her. She had leant against Mark and sobbed into his jersey, and he, who seemed particularly good at dealing with weeping women, had allowed her to cry herself out. The rest of the night was muddled in Laura's memory, a series of cameo scenes in which he played a dominant role and she had acquiesced, too mentally worn out to make decisions. She recalled them drinking mugs of hot tea in the kitchen, she in a dressing-gown into which she could not remember changing; finding herself in bed, and Mark removing the duvet that smelt strangely of damp dog, and covering her with another purloined from one of the other bedrooms. Scraps of conversation returned to her: 'You shouldn't be left alone,' he had said, and she, replying feebly, 'I shall be all right.' He had taken no notice and gone to ring Jeremy, and later stood by her bed: 'I don't have to sleep with you. Is that what you want?' She was not sure how she had answered him, or if she had had enough willpower left to answer at all. She remembered thinking she had never felt less inclined for sex, and that this was the least romantic run-up to an adventure she could imagine; in seconds she would be asleep. But it had not worked out that way; she found she was imbued with a sudden nervous restlessness, the result of over-tiredness that kept her eyes firmly open and her mind spinning.

In the cold light of morning, she knew he could not be blamed. It had not been rape or even seduction, her reciprocation had been far too whole-hearted for either of those two. Everything about him was as she expected, from the bonyness of his body compared to Rick's solid frame, to his own method of love-making. It was tempting to revive memories of it now with nostalgia, but she could not afford to indulge the urge. The next day she would be on her way home, the guilt of her enjoyment locked away inside her, her return made doubly difficult because of it. Presumably the guilt will hit me sooner or later, she reflected; at present her chief feeling was one of lassitude, as if recovering from a drug. Somehow she must pull herself together, have a bath, get dressed. There were things to be done. The thought of Joe, lying low having spent the night in a ditch somewhere, came rushing back to nag her; the problem of finding him seemed insoluble as she washed and pulled on a tracksuit. She decided to begin by taking the car and conducting her own search, hoping that he would recognize the Metro as hers if he caught sight of it, and not panic. She had no idea what she would do if she found him, but sitting around would achieve nothing, and there were more reasons than one for not giving herself time to think.

There seemed to be a commotion going on below her bedroom window: voices, and the chug of an outboard engine. An inflated dinghy which she guessed to be the off-shore lifeboat bobbed a few yards out to sea, and a group of figures in yellow oilskins were clustered round one particular place on the rocks at the foot of the garden. A voice calling from within the house drew her to the head of the stairs, where she gazed down into April August's upturned face.

'They've found someone on the rocks, unconscious.' April was flushed with the excitement of sensational news. 'Thought I'd let you know, Mrs Snow, in case you were worried about the ambulance outside in the road.'

'Who is it?' Laura's voice echoed in her ears, a disembodied whisper.

'Don't know as yet. But they do say the boy from the Ship's gone missing.'

She went slowly back to the bedroom and stood watching the scene below, not out of morbid curiosity but from a need to be certain. The group in yellow parted a little, they were lifting the prostrate form of a man onto a stretcher with infinite care. Before they covered him with blankets she caught a glimpse of the blue jersey which had become a familiar sight at the bottom of the garden by the fuchsia bush, corroborating what in her heart she already knew. She gripped the sill with both hands while the room tipped and swam dangerously around her, and April August's voice spoke from beside her, full of concern. 'Why, m'dear, it's given you a nasty shock. You're white as a sheet, best lie down for a few minutes.'

But Laura had already turned away, and, muttering something incomprehensible, fled to the bathroom where she stayed until the violent spasm of nausea was finally over.

Joe had not gone very far after he left the house. At first he had run in the direction of the upper road where the open countryside began, away from the village. He had climbed a gate into a field and hidden for a while, crouched behind the hedge. It was still raining, not so hard, but enough to wet him through once again, and there was no sheltering from the gale-force wind. He did a lot of thinking while he was squatting there. The light coming on in the bedroom had woken him, breaking into weird and confused dreams; and he had heard their voices downstairs, planning, plotting against him. They were in it together, this conspiracy to get him to hospital, pretending it was to find him the right medication when really they meant to leave him there, safely sectioned and locked away: a prisoner. Even Laura, whom he had thought of as special, a friend and life-line, was not to be trusted, and this hurt him. She had given him away to the Wainwright man when it should have been their secret, Joe's and hers, the hiding of him.

No cars passed while he was in the field, and after about an hour he moved, and started to make his way back cautiously towards Laura's house. He had had this sudden idea that if the garden shed was unlocked, he could stay there for the rest of the night. The last place they would think of looking for him was close by, and he would be dry. He decided it was cunning of him to have thought of it, and shivered, not from the cold, he seldom felt the cold, but from nervous excitement as he crept in at the front gate and round the side of the house. The shed door was fastened only by a latch, and full of garden tools well-oiled and stacked neatly. He curled up on a pile of old newspapers in the darkness and listened to the wind buffeting the wooden walls. The Voice was constant in his ears now, not issuing specific orders but keeping up a muddled droning monologue. The funny thing was, he did not mind it any longer; there always came this time when it changed from being an enemy to a companion, someone who made the plans for you so you did not have to think for yourself. This was just as well right now because he was beginning to feel curiously light-headed; it was a long time since he had eaten, and he could not concentrate on what to do when morning came.

He must have slept; the sound of a car, Mark Wainwright's he supposed, startled him as it warmed up and drove away. The shed seemed suffocatingly hot to him, his skin was burning in spite of the damp clothes, and it was difficult to breathe. He unlatched the door and stepped outside,where the wind had dropped and the air smelt of the sea. There was a lot of débris, twigs and leaves lying around the terrace where they had been blown by the gale. They crackled under his feet as he walked round the back and onto the terrace, making him glance up at the house; but there were no lights at any of the windows. A sliver of moon showed itself between a crack in the clouds without lightening the impenetrable darkness. It stretched out in front of him while he edged his way to the low parapet, so that he could sense, rather than see, the empty drop beyond it. It no longer frightened him. He was suddenly filled with a new-found confidence, and not only his head but the whole of his body felt weightless, as though with the least effort he could float on air. The feeling of freedom made him think of birds, soaring and dipping on wings that scarcely moved, surveying the poor earth-bound creatures on the ground beneath them. Once, a long time ago, he remembered being taken in a party of kids to see Peter Pan. Only the flying had stuck in his memory, and it returned to him now, the glorious swooping through the air above the stage, as if by magic. But you could see the wires attached which had spoilt it; it was like cheating, whereas he felt capable of the real thing, so light and yet in control that he would be borne up to fly of his own volition.

He stepped up on the parapet and spread his arms wide, and the wind, gentler now but with a dying strength to it, ruffled through his hair and lifted him on his toes. 'Launch yourself,' the Voice told him clearly. 'You have only to believe in yourself, and you will be free.' There was a roaring in his ears, but out there over the sea there would be deep silence, and the peace of it beckoned him, and he laughed out loud to think of his prison warders unable to reach him. There was a split second, after he leaped, when he seemed to rest quite still, suspended in space; and even when he plummeted downwards, he felt no dreadful moment of fear, for he knew quite well that he was flying in a straight line across the water and into a world without walls.

'I can't pretend it won't be a relief to be rid of the boy,' Mrs Grimond said, leading the way up the dark staircase of the pub. 'He was a responsibility. Of course, I'm sorry for what's happened to him, anybody would be, but there's no doubt he's a sandwich short of a picnic.'

'Actually,' Laura replied sharply, 'he's quite intelligent and very talented.' She left it at that, not wishing to enter into lengthy explanations of mental illness with Dolly Grimond.

'You'll be taking all his stuff, then, what there is of it?' Mrs Grimond asked hopefully. 'I'll be wanting to use the room for a replacement when I can get one.'

She opened the door wide. 'I'll leave you to it, then,' she added. 'Your good deed for the day, I'd say,' and with a tight-lipped smile at Laura, she went away.

Laura looked round the small room that had been Joe's home for such a brief span; at the thin cotton curtains and the fumed oak chest of drawers listing to one side, and the narrow divan bed with its not-quite-clean candlewick cover. It was as inadequate and sad as its temporary occupant. Evidence of that occupancy was also minimal: a screwed-up T-shirt, two plastic carriers with the rest of his belongings spilling out of them, drawing and painting materials stacked in a corner. On the chest lay the packet of tranquillizers, a tube of toothpaste and a toothbrush, its bristles flattened from longevity. She began to collect these belongings together and put them into more plastic bags which she had brought with her, thinking as she did so how much could be learnt about someone by the contents of their bedroom. In Joe's case, it was the paucity of things he owned that struck her, the lack of identifying objects such as photographs or books, leading to an awful anonymity. She hurried over her work before she became morbid, reminding herself that at least Joe was alive and she was taking his things to the hospital instead of a charity shop. He would have a second chance, however dubious the future seemed for him.

'A fractured leg and ribs, concussion, and severe bruising. No internal injuries that they can detect.' Mark had reported back to her from the college where he was lecturing. That was an hour ago at five o'clock, and still she had not packed, or done many of the chores necessary to leaving the house the next day. The morning, she realized, had been spent in shock. When she had finally emerged from the bathroom, April August had poured her some of Gerard's extremely good brandy and stayed with her until the colour returned to her cheeks and her legs had ceased to shake. She was indebted to April, who had also discovered from the ambulance crew where Joe was to be taken, and answered Mark's first telephone call. Laura reflected how April now had enough food for gossip to last her for days if she cared to use it; although there was a reliability about her that probably meant she would not stoop to it.

Later, unable to concentrate on anything, Laura had walked and walked until her legs ached, over the fields by the estuary, the route she had taken her second day at St Merric. There was bright sun and a brisk, light wind that ruffled the waters and blew her hair away from her face. Everywhere lay evidence of the storm; the turf was littered with twigs and small boughs scattered by the gale. She thought suddenly and inadvertently of James, the son who might have been with her now had he lived; for some reason this particular walk seemed to bring him to mind, and she wondered whether today this could be connected with Joe. It was not that she saw him in the light of a son, she decided, but in some indefinable way she had become emotionally caught up, perhaps more with a situation than a personality. She could not stop wondering what was in his mind as he jumped from her terrace; whether it was a death wish or a confused fantasy. Probably she would never know. Neither had she known, as she tramped across the fields, how badly hurt he was or even whether he would live. She walked on, glad of the ache in her legs. At least it was physical and took her mind off the horror of Joe and the hollow pain which was the start of missing Mark. Glancing up as she passed the footpath leading to his house, she saw one of the beech trees at the end of his garden had fallen in the night and lay sprawled across the fence. It had probably crashed as he was lying in bed with her, and she recalled the warmth of his body, and thought how the agony of going away could have been avoided if she had not allowed it to happen.

He had had to work for most of the day, and his concern for her had shown in his voice over the phone. 'Will you be all *right*?' he kept saying over and over again, and she had assured him she would be, although she felt far from being so. In the evening she was to go over for supper; it was Jeremy's last night before he went back to Exeter, so Mark and she would not be alone. They would never be alone again. He told her he would get what information he could from the hospital and let her know as soon as possible. 'I love you,' he had said before he rang off, and she had wanted to cry, but she had done enough of that the previous night, so she stopped herself.

When she got home from the walk, she had found Eleanor Shawcross on the doorstep, peering through the letter-box, and not at all disconcerted at being discovered.

'My dear,' she had said, 'what a terrible thing to have happened. I've been so worried about you. It must have been a dreadful shock.'

Laura had taken a deep breath and agreed that, yes, it had been both.

'How did it happen? Was it an accident?' Eleanor did not wait for a reply. 'Of course, I always said there was something wrong with that young man, he isn't all there. It's most unfortunate you got involved with him,' she added, 'in that he chose *your* terrace to fall from. I gather from April August you are going home tomorrow, so I thought I'd call to say goodbye.'

'Goodbye, Mrs Shawcross,' she said firmly. She could not bring herself to add, nice to have met you.

'I was hoping,' Eleanor Shawcross patted a stray white curl into place beneath her hat, 'that perhaps I might come in for a few moments. Just to wish you farewell properly.'

All at once Laura felt a wave of anger engulf her at this interfering old woman's presumption. She had denigrated Joe, and done her best to sour the relationship between herself and Mark. Her reasons for getting an entry to Gerard's house were obvious: she wished to view the scene of the accident, see with her own prurient eyes the place where Joe had fallen, licking her lips with voyeuristic relish. Laura would have liked to take hold of the felt hat and rammed it down violently over the woman's eyes and ears. 'I'm sorry,' she said coldly. 'I'm terribly busy, I'm afraid, there's so much to do before tomorrow.'

Jeremy had appeared at that moment on a bicycle, unexpected and unannounced, balancing a potted yellow chrysanthemum on the handlebars. 'I've brought you a flower,' he said, 'to cheer you up, with love from us both.'

'How lovely.'

'Well,' Mrs Shawcross's small blue eyes snapped malevolently, 'since you're obviously fully occupied, I shall leave you in peace,' and she turned and marched away in the direction of the village.

Jeremy watched her go. 'Have I upset her?' he asked. 'She looked positively murderous.'

'No, I have.' Laura took the plant from him. 'She's a wicked old woman who falls back on her arthritis for sympathy, and indulges in muck-raking.'

'She doesn't look very arthritic to me,' he observed. 'I've come to take you out to lunch,' he told Laura. 'Mark says I'm to see you eat enough. Sorry if that sounds impertinent, but I'm only following orders.'

After the initial reaction that this plan was the last thing she wanted, she had given in reluctantly and they went to a pub called The Green Man at the far end of the village. She had half-expected his company to be a strain on this day of all days when her emotions were at sixes and sevens. But after one brief and sympathetic mention of Joe, he left the subject alone and talked about his own life and what he wanted to do with it, interspersed with questions about Hannah and Annabelle out of politeness, or so she guessed. He made her laugh with a skilful word-portrait of his mother, affectionately but no doubt exaggeratedly drawn, and when Mark was mentioned, it was within the context of him as a newly-discovered father. Dodgy topics were avoided, and by the end of lunch, she found that youthful enthusiasm and optimism combined with an omelette were exactly what she had needed to revive her. Alone in the house when Jeremy had gone on his way, she got as far as pulling her suitcase from the cupboard before fatigue caught up with her, and she had lain down and slept for two hours, dreamlessly, to be woken eventually by Mark's call.

'It's a miracle he wasn't killed,' he said, giving her what news he had of Joe. 'Apparently, those little terraced flowerbeds of Gerard's broke his fall to a great extent. They say he must have been amazingly relaxed when he jumped, as if he was drunk or on drugs, but they found no evidence of that.'

'He hadn't taken tranquillizers for some time.'

'Getting information out of them when you are no relation is tricky. He's conscious now, but visiting won't be allowed until tomorrow at the earliest.' He paused, then added, 'You may not be able to see him before you leave.'

'I shall,' Laura said. 'I'll make time.'

They had spoken almost exclusively of Joe, their own concerns obscured by the trauma of his fall. Perhaps this was to be expected since there was no future for herself and Mark; perhaps one night spent together was of no significance, should be treated lightly and eventually forgotten. She wondered whether, as one was led to believe, men found this attitude easier to achieve, for she was finding it impossible, and the ache of imminent parting gnawed at her relentlessly. She had taken a pile of jerseys from the drawers and laid them unenthusiastically on the bed, unable to bring herself to do anything as conclusive as packing them. It would have been comforting to know that he was suffering as she was, even if it were to a lesser degree; and now she was unlikely to discover because this evening was to be a family affair, and time was running out.

In Joe's room at the pub she had a last look round to make sure she had not left anything behind. There had been little enough to collect, but even so the place had a pathetic and deserted appearance. She caught sight of Sam Grimond serving customers in the public bar as she left. She made no attempt to contact him; the Grimonds' interest in Joe went only so far as his usefulness, and that had long since run out. She stowed the plastic bags in the boot of the car and drove home slowly up the steep hill. The sky was shot with pink, denoting a return of the fine weather, and lights from the boats shone on the waters of the harbour; and she was conscious of seeing all this for the last time, for she was unlikely ever to return.

At eight-thirty on Wednesday morning, an hour earlier than they had agreed, Mark was already on his way to Laura. It had been arranged the night before that he would drive her to the hospital, saving her the trouble of finding it for herself, and take her home again to start the journey to London. He had not slept well, had been awake at five o'clock, trying to construct in his mind what he intended to say to her, deciding that he needed peace and quiet in which to say it, not the hassle of traffic in Truro. It was not the best time of day for intense conversation, he reflected, but then he had no choice in the matter. There was nothing noble about his intentions; half the night had been spent searching for a conscience that had disappeared. The ridiculous fact was that he did not know exactly what he wanted, only that which he could not bear; the complete absence of her from his life from now onwards. This realization had taken him quite suddenly, almost as a surprise amounting to panic. He had thought himself immune from such compulsion, safely inoculated by past events of loving that had gone wrong, and resigned to a life monotonous but unassailable. It was a false assumption to have made, and he still was not sure how to put it into words as he rounded the steep bend to Gerard's house.

Her face wore a shiny, early morning pallor when she opened the door to him. She gave him a kiss. 'I thought we said nine-thirty,' she said equably as if it did not matter. 'I'm not ready.'

'Don't worry, I'm early on purpose.'

'Oh?' She raised her eyebrows. 'What sort of purpose?'

'Is there any coffee going?' he asked. 'There's plenty of time.'

'Of course.'

The kitchen had become full of memories; of the night – it seemed an age ago – she had cooked a chicken, and he had told her a little, but not enough, about his marriage; and the ploughman's lunch, un-eaten because of painful confessions, and the night of the storm in the shadowy light of candles, which was the culmination of all the other times. There were signs now of departure: a cardboard box full of various tins and jars and bottles.

'I've been clearing out the fridge,' she said, putting mugs of coffee on the table. 'I'm leaving all these odds and ends for April.'

She sat herself opposite him. He noticed a composure about her which had not been there before, a kind of resignation. 'You want to talk about something,' she said, making it a statement rather than a question.

'Us,' he said.

She raised her eyes to his over the rim of the mug, very blue in her pale face. 'Is there any point? After this morning, there won't be an "us".'

'Need that be so?'

255

'I don't understand what you're saying.'

'I'm saying I can't bear the thought of you going away for good and my never seeing you again.' She opened her mouth to speak but he stopped her. 'Just hear me out, please, Laura, darling, then you can tell me yes or no, and I'll abide by it. There's no reason why I shouldn't come to London every so often. I have friends who would give me a bed for a night or two.' He spoke quietly, trying to keep the desperation out of his voice. 'We could meet, have lunch or dinner, go to a play. What do you think?' he asked as casually as possible, watching her face.

She shook her head. 'I couldn't do that,' she replied. 'I'd be unable to hide it from Rick.'

'Would you have to?' he suggested eagerly. 'Couldn't you be quite open about it?'

'He'd mind.' Two wings of hair fell forwards, shielding her expression. 'He'd know, and he'd be hurt and I don't want that. Besides,' she said sadly, 'I'd find it impossible, myself, to see you on that sort of basis. Three days ago I might have felt differently, but not now.'

He was silent a moment, feeling hope slip away. 'It doesn't have to be on that basis,' he said at last. 'I could rent a room or a small flat.'

She looked at him then, almost in anger, it seemed to him. 'You don't understand, do you?'

'Probably not,' he answered, 'for the simple reason I don't want to. I can only think in terms of not losing you.'

His honesty disarmed her. 'I wouldn't be any good at an affair,' she said more gently. 'If I started one with you, I'd become completely taken over by it, and it would mean the break-up of my marriage. Separation, divorce,' she pushed the hair back from her forehead in a nervous gesture. 'I've been through all that and

I don't want a repeat, not only for my sake but the children's as well.' He said nothing, waiting for her to finish. 'I spent most of last night thinking,' she went on in a rush, 'and I've decided I must go back prepared to make it work. I can't pretend it will be easy, but I've created the gap between myself and Rick and it's up to me to try to close it. Do you see?'

'I see very clearly there is no room for me in your scenario,' he said, but without bitterness.

'How can there be?'

'I also see you returning to square one, giving in on all counts: a job, your poetry, the space you've created for yourself, everything going to waste.'

'No,' she said very positively, 'you're wrong. It won't be like that.' She got up from the table. 'I must give you back the books. I forgot to bring them last night.'

She fetched them for him and he stood, turning them over in his hands. 'I want you to keep one of them, whichever one you'd like. To remind you.'

'Do you really think I need reminding?' She faced him, her eyes filling with tears. 'The difficulty is trying to forget; it's impossible.'

He put down the books and kissed her, first on the lips, then each eyelid and her forehead. She sank her face into his shoulder. 'Oh hell! I'm going to cry.'

'Don't, please.'

'No. I've cried enough in the last few days.'

'Shall I never see you again?' he asked.

She found a tissue in her pocket and sniffed into it. 'It'll take months for me to get myself under control. Perhaps, then.'

'For lunch,' he said. 'Lunch is always permissible, even to jealous husbands.'

'How misguided,' she said, attempting a smile.

'We should be getting ready if you're to see Joe,' he told her.

She moved towards the door. 'I feel sick,' she said. 'The last hours before goodbyes are the worst, aren't they?'

But Mark, left alone in the kitchen, thought of the hours that would follow her leaving, stretching into days and weeks and even years of silent pain, and decided her statement was not accurate.

Chapter Ten

The car seemed a great deal fuller than it had been on Laura's original journey. There were the presents of local pottery for Rick, Annabelle and Hannah, packed in three separate carrier bags; and there was Jeremy's sizeable backpack, and in the passenger seat beside her Jeremy himself.

'It's very kind of you to give me a lift,' he had said.

'No problem,' she assured him, and meant it. She was glad of his company; she found him a restful companion, and the fact of him being there ensured that she did not give way to silent floods of tears. She had not looked back at Mark as she drove away, knowing the sight of his solitary figure, waving, would prove too much for her.

'You'll go to visit him quite often from now on, I suppose?' she said hopefully to Jeremy, and he agreed.

'I reckon I'm lucky to have found him. He's quite a discovery. Great, really.'

'Do you mind if we make a detour?' she asked before they reached the motorway. 'There's a place that reminds me of childhood holidays which I'd like to see again.'

They struck across country to the north, following signposts and a map which he read for her as she drove, taking them miles out of their way in the pursuit of her nostalgic pilgrimage. The land became wilder, more isolated, with outcrops of grey stone sprouting from the barren, heather-covered turf. Glimpses of tall black cliffs could be seen in the distance as the road changed direction. They stopped eventually in open country and pulled into a car park where a notice read: Bedruthen Steps. The grass was short and springy beneath their feet as they crossed the hundred or so yards to the cliff-top. A fence had been erected that prevented the public getting close to the edge, and a stone plaque embedded in the ground turned out to be a memorial for the twelve people who had lost their lives attempting foolhardy descents to the sands below. A second notice warned of prosecution for those who tried it again; the legitimate way to the beach was half-a-mile further on.

'It used not to be like this,' Laura told Jeremy. 'You could go as near to the edge as you dared, and there was a lethal spiral staircase built into the side of the cliff. Even children were allowed down it, and nobody got killed.'

'Perhaps the suicide rate has gone up,' he suggested.

'Perhaps.'

They had to speak loudly because what had been a light wind had become a gale on the headland. Bedruthen Steps themselves, the giant pinnacles of rock fashioned and separated by some quirk of nature, rose to cliff height and stretched along the beach to right and left, awesome in the sunlight. The tide was high, and gulls wheeled and screamed above the surf that creamed around the rock bases. They walked some way beside the fence, taking in the rugged coastline that reached into the distance, before returning to the car.

'It must have been a wonderful place to come as a child,' he remarked. 'Quite frightening, though.'

'More so to an adult, I think,' she replied, starting the engine. 'I can't remember finding it so overpowering as I did today.'

'Just as well the cliffs in the south are small in comparison,' he said, 'from Joe's point of view,' voicing what was going through her own mind. 'Do you think he knew what he was doing?' he added with curiosity.

She took some time to answer, saying at last, 'I believe he knew, but I don't think he was trying to kill himself. He lives in his own world half the time, and I think he was acting out a fantasy. But it's difficult to know for sure.' She handed the map to Jeremy. 'See if you can get us back on the right route,' she said.

Joe had been taken from Intensive Care and put in a small room of his own at the end of the men's surgical ward. He was lying in his white starched bed, very still and on his back from necessity, his leg in a cradle under a light blanket. Only his bandaged hands moved restlessly, plucking at the sheet. His head was turned away from the door, and she had the impression that, had it been possible, the whole of him would have been turned away as well, as if escaping from human contact. She had laid down the flowers and the grapes and sat herself on the hard little upright chair.

'Joe. It's Laura.'

To begin with there was no reaction from him. ('He's very doped at present,' the Sister had said. 'Are you the mother? No, well, I wouldn't stay too long.') Laura had repeated his name several times, softly, and eventually his head had moved on the pillow in her direction, so that she could see the livid bruising down one side of his face, and strips of plaster on his forehead. He stared at her as though he had difficulty in focusing and could not recognize her.

'Why are you here?' he whispered, his voice slurred.

'I've come to see how you are,' she told him. 'You had a fall from the terrace, do you remember?'

'My mouth's dry.'

There was a glass of water with a straw in it on the

bedside table. She held it for him while he drained the glass.

'Thirsty,' he muttered; and then, 'I didn't fall, I jumped.'

'Why, Joe?'

'It was a con. It didn't work, the flying.' He closed his eyes.

'Does it hurt very much?' she asked.

'When I breathe, it does.' He half-opened his eyes to look at her. 'They keep giving me drugs,' he said. 'They always do. I hate it, I can't think properly.'

'They have to for the moment, to stop the pain.' She searched for the right words. 'When the leg gets better, when you start to mend, they'll get you onto the right medication, so that this doesn't happen again.'

He did not seem to have heard her. 'They won't keep me here,' he said, so low she could hardly hear him. 'They think I don't know, but I've heard them talking. They'll send me back to where I was before.'

There were long pauses between his speaking, during which she had waited patiently.

'Prison,' he said at last. 'They'll put me back in prison. I told you, didn't I? They always get you in the end.'

She sat helplessly, unable to think of a way to get through to him, to make a breach in the barrier of confusion that occupied his brain. She wished she could take his hand, communicate by touch, but the bandages hiding goodness knew what injuries precluded that. The worst aspect of his affliction, she thought, was its total isolation, cutting off the possibility of all human help.

'Your last hospital was London,' she said. 'If they take you there, I shall be able to come and see you.'

He twisted his head on the pillow. 'Are you going away from here?'

'I must. I have to go back to my family.'

'When?'

She wished he had not asked. 'Today, when I leave you.'

The whole of him seemed to slump, even though he could not move. 'People say that, say they'll visit, but they don't.'

'I shall. Wherever you are,' she promised. 'I've brought your clothes and the rest of your things,' she added, and fetching the drawing pad, she wrote her address and telephone number on the cover. 'You can phone me when you're better, and let me know where you are going to be. Look, I've written it here so you don't lose it.'

The Sister put her head round the door, and raised her eyebrows as an indication that Laura's time was up. Laura nodded, wondering how she was going to leave the desolate figure in the bed. 'Don't forget you've got great talent,' she said. 'That's more than most people have. There's everything to get well for, Joe.'

He watched her silently while she gathered up her handbag and anorak. Tears rolled from his eyes without his face changing expression. She did not know how to bear it. Bending, she kissed him gently on the cheek.

'I'll see you sooner than you think.'

She left the room clumsily, bumping against the door in her desire not to prolong the parting, and walked away down the long corridor that smelled of antiseptic. The Sister had waylaid her halfway, to enquire about Joe's next-of-kin.

'There is a mother,' Laura said, 'but I've no idea where.'

'Never mind. Perhaps Joe will tell me himself when he's less confused.'

'I doubt it. I think she's the last person he will want to see.'

Outside in the hazy autumn sunshine, she had stood for a moment looking back at row upon row of blank windows, behind one of which Joe was a prisoner of his own making. Then she crossed the car park slowly to where Mark was waiting for her, weighed down with frustration at her inability to help, and the awful sense of having deserted him.

She retailed her visit out loud to Jeremy, which she had not intended to do, but she needed to tell someone about it. Besides, it kept her from thinking about Mark.

'Some people's lives are pretty dreaded, aren't they?' Jeremy remarked. 'Will he ever get better, d'you think?'

She shrugged. 'There's a chance, I suppose, if he stays on the right drugs.'

He unwrapped a packet of chewing gum and offered her a piece.

'No, thanks. I never know what to do with it after the peppermint's worn off.'

He chewed thoughtfully for a few minutes, then said, 'I suppose your stay there wasn't like you thought it would be? I mean, you were expecting peace and quiet and it wasn't a bit like that.'

'Not exactly. But I had my moments of solitude.'

'The night of the storm, and not knowing what to do with Joe, must have been hairy. It's a good thing Mark was around so that you weren't alone.'

She kept her eyes on the road, feeling the flush rise up her neck and face. 'I *was* grateful,' she agreed.

There was one of those pauses which, with Jeremy, never seemed uncomfortable. 'He's going to miss you,' he said eventually.

'He'll miss you too.'

'Not in the same way. Anyway, I can go and see him quite often.' He glanced at her profile. 'Will you ever go back to St Merric?' he asked.

'Not for a long time.' She felt uneasy at the turn the conversation was taking. 'I probably won't get the chance. Families are fairly demanding.'

'It's a pity Mark doesn't have one,' he said. 'His life is pretty empty, when you think about it. The trouble is, he hasn't had much luck with women. I had this vague idea when I came to stay with him that he'd get back together again with Ma. But I can see now it wouldn't work.'

'Are you sure?'

'Certain. They'd be a disaster. Besides—'

He hesitated. She waited. 'Besides?'

'Well, he's fallen in love with you, hasn't he?'

She sighed. 'Is it that obvious?'

'Very. But that won't work either. See what I mean about his having bad luck.'

'I am partly to blame,' she said, 'for not discouraging him. And for being there at the wrong time.'

He considered this. 'Things get incredibly complicated as you get older, don't they? I mean, one moment you're young and about to shack up with someone, and the next you're married with a mortgage and two-point-something kids. It's all a bit scary.'

She smiled. 'Don't get put off. It has its advantages.'

'Do you mind if I ask you a question?' he said.

'You can ask. I may not answer.'

'D'you feel the same way about him?'

The last weeks returned to her uninvited, memories involving Mark darting through her mind with little stabs of pain. 'I can't afford the luxury,' she said simply.

They talked of other things for the rest of the journey, and the subject was not mentioned again until the very end. She pulled up at a bus station somewhere on the outskirts of Exeter, on Jeremy's instructions. It was only a short bus trip to where he wanted to go, he told her, and she thought of the girl who in all likelihood was waiting for him there. He stood by the open door of the car, the backpack resting against his legs as he bent to thank her for the second time.

'I suppose,' he added, 'you couldn't visit Mark just *occasionally*? On a friendly sort of basis?'

She looked at him with a mixture of exasperation and affection. Mark's clone looked back at her, his eyes hopeful. Slowly she shook her head. 'In your own words,' she said, 'that would be a disaster.'

Sarah Pemberton was married shortly before Christmas to a man five years her junior, a rowing Blue with a great deal of money and an interest in landscape gardening. Her engagement came as a surprise to all her friends and a relief to Rick, who felt his peccadillo could once and for all be wiped from his conscience.

The reception was held at a house in Cheyne Walk lent by a friend for the occasion. Laura, Rick, Annabelle and Hannah struggled there in cold, drenching rain that seeped into shoes and dampened the spirits. 'People are mad to have winter weddings,' Laura muttered, stuffing her umbrella into an already packed stand.

'Ours was a winter one,' Rick reminded her, hurt that she should have forgotten. This conversation was typical of the sort they now had, ever since her return two months ago; short brittle sentences exchanged across a barrier of uneasiness. Laura knew it was mainly her fault and was ashamed of it, but equally was unable to stop herself. Rick had tried hard, bent over backwards to smooth out the differences that had driven her away. She came barely halfway to meet him, impeded at the last moment by memories of which she could not rid herself. Sometimes she wished he would smack her, which was no doubt what she deserved and probably needed, or at least show some signs of temperament other than eternal compliance.

The reception was not a large one, about thirty-five people besides themselves. Annabelle and Hannah drifted away to talk to Sarah's twins, tall and gangling in identical dark blue suits, and Rick got caught up in conversation with a City acquaintance. Laura was chatting to Sarah's mother when she caught sight of Mark, his hawklike head visible above the crowd. Dumbfounded, she ducked her own head in an ostrich-like effort to disappear and pretended to be listening to the old lady by her side. Desperately she tried to control her shaking hands and took an unsteady gulp of her champagne as her eyes searched imploringly for Rick. All at once his solid presence seemed infinitely desirable, but he had melted away, hidden from view by people's backs. She forced herself to make bright replies in response to Sarah's mother's queries, while she waited for the tap on the shoulder and wondered feverishly why fate should have been so cruel as to do this to her. She exchanged her empty glass for a full one from a passing tray and felt the alcohol begin to sweep up her face in a wave of colour.

Sarah appeared with Mark close behind her.

'Here's an old friend,' she said. 'Mark doesn't know anyone here, so you can natter together.'

She smiled at Laura who for a moment suspected her of guessing more than she could possibly know. But Sarah's eyes were the usual wells of friendly honesty before she led her mother away to reintroduce her.

'How are you?' Mark and Laura asked in unison.

Dropping formality, she asked, 'Did you realize I would be here?'

'I hadn't the least idea,' he answered, lowering his voice. 'The bridegroom's a friend going back a long way, and I've never met Sarah before.' His eyebrow lifted in its old sardonic manner. 'Just an amazing coincidence. How are you really?' he added gently.

'Thrown off balance, at this minute. What do you expect?'

'I hoped you would feel as I do, enormously happy to see you, even in a crowded room.'

'I *am* happy, too much so.' She made herself smile as if they were having a social conversation in case Rick's attention was caught. 'I'm surrounded by family, I can't make it obvious.'

'Shall I meet them?'

'Only if it can't be avoided.'

'Surely it would be more natural if I did?'

'I can't trust myself to be natural. It's easy for you,' she said with a tinge of bitterness. 'You don't have to pretend to anyone like I do.'

'Are you having to pretend a great deal?' he asked sympathetically.

She looked up at him, forcing herself to meet his eyes. 'Only part of the time. But it's the most important part, and I am not very good at it. In fact,' she said, keeping the smile in place, 'I think I'm behaving badly.'

'Poor darling.'

'Poor Rick, is more like it.'

'Why are you smiling?'

'I'm trying to look as if you are a casual acquaintance whom I hardly know. A ship who passed in the night.'

'I suppose that's quite a good description of me.'

'Can we change the subject? I feel like crying. You know how given to tears I am.'

'Don't drink your champagne like water,' he advised. 'It'll make it worse. Tell me about your children. That should be a safe topic.'

There were no children in the house when she had first arrived home on the Thursday afternoon. They were still at school and Rick had not returned from the office, so the house was empty. She was quite pleased to have the place to herself; she needed to acclimatize herself. Wandering from room to room, she had had the strange sensation of trespassing on someone else's property. Everywhere was unnaturally tidy as if there had been a mammoth clean-up, and the sight of it unnerved her rather than made her grateful. Only Hannah's bedroom remained relatively chaotic, and she found this normal state of affairs unexpectedly comforting. In Annabelle's room, her woolly animals reclined in a serried rank across a pristine white bed-cover; nothing, after all, had changed much. Her own bedroom smelled faintly of scent and face powder, and there were two vases of button chrysanthemums, white and yellow respectively, and a terrible card saying: 'To a dearest Mother. Welcome home.' Underneath the inscription, Hannah had written: 'This was too yucky to resist.'

Rick had walked in while they were unwrapping the Cornish pottery, which meant that the edge was taken off that first awkward moment of reunion. He put down the large bunch of red roses he was carrying and kissed her lightly on the lips, saying, 'Lovely to have you back.' She could feel his nervousness reaching out to meet her own, and she quickly handed him his present to cover their tension. The rest of the evening had been reasonably easy to get through. She had arranged the roses – there were already flowers in the drawing-room, a plethora of them. Were they an expression of affection, or a bribe to ensure her loving reciprocation, she wondered in a mean-spirited moment? Unpacking and bathing had taken up much of the time before supper, and Rick had left her alone, forgoing his usual practice of chatting while she bathed, which left her both thankful and vaguely uneasy. There had been enough questions from the girls over dinner in a Chinese restaurant to smooth over Rick's quietness, and she had described Gerard's house and the countryside, and told them a little about Joe, which interested them into silence.

Rick said, 'And what age was your Joe?'

'Twenty, twenty-one, something like that. Too young for me,' she had answered lightly, unable to resist the dig.

'About right for a toy-boy,' Hannah observed, 'although I suppose he was too ill, poor thing.'

'Was he the reason you found it difficult to leave?' Rick asked.

'Well, after the accident I felt I should at least visit him. There isn't anyone else.'

'A surrogate mother.' He gave her a faint semblance of his charming smile. 'You've always had a leaning towards lame dogs.'

'Did you write reams of poetry?' Annabelle asked tactfully.

'Not reams, but enough to make it all worthwhile.' She had looked at Rick to see if he had taken the point, and he had glanced back at her.

'Good,' he said as if he meant it. 'I'm glad.'

'I want to hear now what's been happening to *you*,' Laura said.

'You've heard about Annie fainting?'

'And I suppose you know,' Annabelle told her calmly, 'how Hannah practically wrecked the house with her party. The police were called.'

'Yes, and I've something to say on both counts, when I'm not so tired. How is Sarah, by the way?' she asked Rick.

'Fine. The same old Sarah.' He poured the last of the wine into their glasses. 'She was in London for most of the week, actually, and we met up twice.'

'Three times,' Hannah said. 'What kind of puddings can you have here?'

It was almost as if she had never been away, if it had not been for an undercurrent of things left unsaid. She had scanned the children's faces surreptitiously, like a dog licking over her puppies to make sure they were the right ones, and found no change in Hannah. Annabelle was thinner and very pale, but then she never had much colour. There was a subtle difference in her, but Laura did not think it was unhappiness, and she seemed to be eating normally. Whatever had been troubling her was probably past history.

When they were saying good night, Annabelle had hugged her. 'I am glad you're home,' she said.

The biggest change was in Rick, as she had discovered when they were alone at last and faced with the choice of talking trivia like strangers or risking a discussion. She chose the first option, gabbling about the first things that came into her head as she undressed, putting off the moment of sliding between the sheets that had become oddly embarrassing. He had answered in monosyllables, wandering about the room in his dressing-gown, winding up his watch, and the alarm on the digital clock. Eventually he had crossed to her and kissed her in a very firm but unsexy way. 'Shut up, darling,' he said gently and rather wearily. 'There are a great many things I have to say, and doubtless you have too, but we're not saying them tonight. We're both too tired.'

Surprised and relieved for once to be dominated, she allowed herself to be propelled into bed. She put out a hand for him, expecting his arms to go round her.

'We're not doing that either,' he said in the darkness, 'for the same reasons.'

She thought of the next night and all the other nights that were to come, deciding that until they had made love, however badly, no amount of talking would be successful.

'Please,' she said.

It was a mistake, for all her feigned enthusiasm, desperately summoning up energy she did not have and eroticism she did not feel. He rolled away from her finally in resignation.

'It won't work,' he said, kissing her on the cheek. 'There's plenty of time.'

There had been plenty of time; two months of it since that first abortive evening, and still the invisible barrier remained. They had talked a lot during the weeks that followed, and Rick had been full of concessions, eager to remove any bones of contention that had driven her away. 'I think you should take up Gerard's offer of a job, if that's what you want,' he said. She was not sure that she did want to; other plans, vague as yet, had been forming in her head. He had left her to write at will, without leaning over her, and careful to avoid any patronizing comments; and she had painted the garden furniture, uninterrupted by advice. Everything he could do to ensure harmony had been done, she recognized that, and had tried to reciprocate with small kindnesses of her own. For much of the time she believed she had achieved this; only in bed did she fail to convince either him or herself, like a horse falling at the last fence: hampered by the single memory of a different body against hers, and incapable of forgetting.

'I can tell which is Hannah,' Mark said, eying the crowd. 'She couldn't be anyone but your daughter. And Annabelle, I suppose, is the dark one with the pensive look. How is she facing up to unrequited love?' he asked.

'Not exactly unrequited,' Laura said. 'It's all been put on the back burner for the moment, which is sensible.'

'Even back burners generate a bit of warmth. That's more than can be said for you and me.'

272

'Mark!' She looked at him reproachfully.

'Sorry,' he said. 'That was unfair.' He glanced around him. 'I wish there was somewhere we could go to get away from the mob.'

'There's that giant plant by the window. What is it?'

'A yucca.'

'It's hideous.'

'But useful for concealment. Come on.'

There was only a scattering of people by the tall windows; facing the room, she could see any of her family approaching, and be prepared. Annabelle, with her back to Laura, was talking to an elderly man, his bald head gleaming under the chandelier. She was wearing a mini-skirt that showed her legs to their best advantage.

It had been several days before she had found the right moment to talk to Annabelle; they were in the kitchen while Hannah was practising upstairs.

'Do you want to tell me what happened while I was away?' she had asked. 'Because if you don't, I'll understand, just so long as you're all right.'

'I'm fine now, honestly,' and the whole story had come pouring out of Annabelle, of slimming and sexual harassment and bread knives and an excess of wine, and her misery over Ben's apparent indifference, until Laura's head reeled.

'The worst thing was you being away,' she said. 'There was no-one to tell. I'd have given anything to have your phone number.'

'Darling, I rang almost every day.'

'I know. But there was always Rick and Hannah hanging around, and I couldn't talk privately.'

Laura had realized, with a stab of guilt, how occupied her mind had become with other problems, and how easily she had dismissed Annabelle's trauma. 'I'm so very sorry,' she had said, hugging her.

'It was all right in the end, after Ben had come round and we'd straightened things out. I can see now I'd been pretty stupid.'

'No, you weren't,' Laura said. 'There's no such thing as an easy relationship,' thinking, as she said it, how trite but true her remark was.

She thought about it again, standing opposite Mark, knowing how much it was going to hurt when they both left the reception – a further turn of the knife in the wound. Under the electric lighting of the rest of the room, she had thought he looked well; now, by the harsh daylight through the windows, he appeared drawn.

'I've never seen you in a suit before,' she commented idiotically.

'And I can't remember you in anything but a tracksuit or jeans,' he said. 'You look very glamorous and even less available.'

'Clothes are deceptive; I feel the same inside.'

'I was hoping you might have changed your mind, that you'd meet me for lunch.'

'I can't. It's too soon, I haven't got myself under control yet.'

'After Christmas, then, in the New Year. I'll come up especially.'

'Don't do that. I can't promise anything.' She looked into his face, poised above her. 'Don't pressurize me, Mark, please.'

He withdrew, his expression wooden with suppressed hope. 'I'm sorry,' he said. 'I shouldn't have asked,' and she could tell she had wounded him. 'And here comes your husband,' he added, 'to claim you. At least, I presume it's Rick: blond, chunky and suspicious?'

She glanced quickly at Rick's figure, weaving his way towards them through the knot of people. 'Talk of something trivial,' she muttered. 'What are you doing for Christmas?'

'I'm going to stay with Francie and Jeremy for a couple of days.'

She felt an irrational pang of jealousy. 'Hello, darling,' she greeted Rick. 'This is Mark Wainwright, whom I told you about.'

'Ah yes, the man with a splendid library.' He held out his hand. 'Laura tells me you were a great help to her over the writing.'

She noted his voice was over-hearty, as it always became when he was ill at ease.

'Hardly,' Mark said. 'I lent her some books; that was my sole contribution.'

'That's not what I heard.' Rick waved a hand in the direction of the crowd. 'Good party,' he remarked. 'Quite a coincidence, your knowing Sarah.'

Mark explained that he didn't.

'Even more of a surprise, then, that Laura should bump into you.' Rick smiled at her. 'Isn't it, darling?'

'A complete surprise.' She felt suddenly hemmed in, as though, if she did not escape soon, she would faint. 'I think it's time we were going. I'll go and gather up the girls,' she said, moving hurriedly away.

Pushing a path blindly between guests, she realized she had not said goodbye to him, that she would see him leave the room, hurt by her rejection, and this God-given chance of being with him for an hour would have been wasted. But then what did she expect would emerge from it anyway, she asked herself? Nothing but a renewal of the anguish, a second bout of being torn apart. She found Sarah to thank her and to say how happy she was for her, and Sarah for some reason blushed. 'Life's one big compromise, isn't it?' she said rather obscurely, before someone else took her attention.

Laura's last glimpse of Mark was from the outdoor steps as they were putting up umbrellas. He was limping in the direction of the Embankment, hatless and coatless in the rain.

'I offered him a lift,' Rick told her, watching her face, 'but he said he needed fresh air. A nice man,' he added as an afterthought.

Two nights before Christmas it snowed, and the lawn in the morning was patterned with the criss-cross tracks of birds. Held by the beauty of the garden encased in white, Laura stood by the window, spellbound; then, remembering that this was the day for food shopping, cursed the weather for its bad timing. By the middle of the morning it had started to thaw, and slush on top of icy patches covered roads and pavements. She took the car to the supermarket, driving with extreme caution, and filled a trolley with the things they needed, overdoing it as usual, worried about running out, as though stocking up for a siege. Rick had offered to do it for her; he would be home by midday on Christmas Eve, he said, there would be plenty of time. But Christmas Eve would be bedlam in the shops, and half the shelves would be empty. Unloading the car outside the house with Annabelle's help, she slipped on the steps, a carrier bag in either hand, and bruised her knee so badly that it swelled up like a balloon. The eggs had broken and run amongst the lettuces. It was an inauspicious start to the festive season.

Rick found himself wishing that they had invited friends to join them on Christmas Day. In previous years, he had never particularly wanted other people around; Christmas had seemed complete with just the four of them, quiet but satisfying. This year was different. The past weeks had been a struggle to renew whatever it was he and Laura appeared to have lost.

He could not define it: love, he supposed, for want of another word. She was perfectly loving, quite amenable, but in a passive way that was almost like a wall of resistance. One of the worst aspects of this change was that they had lost the art of communication, seldom getting furthor than domestic and other mundane topics; and the humour had gone, for he could hardly laugh by himself without appearing mad. Sometimes he wondered whether he was imagining the fact that they had ever been in love. He had done his utmost to stand back and let her get on with her own working life, but she did not seem in a hurry to take up the job that Gerard was offering, and hardly if ever was seen to be writing. He could not think what more to do, but all the efforts that were being made seemed to come from him, and inside him he felt faint stirrings of rebellion as he thought about it. The work load was already slackening off with the approach of the holiday; he decided to pack up, go home and do something positive like making the stuffing for the turkey.

Mark telephoned as Rick let himself in at the front door on a blast of cold air.

'Sorry. Can't talk now,' Laura hissed from the kitchen, and put down the receiver.

'Who was that?'

'Wrong number. You're home early. Tea?'

'No, thanks. I'm going to get changed. We seem to be getting rather a lot of them recently,' he said. 'Wrong numbers, I mean.'

'Burglars, probably,' she answered, returning his kiss with cool lips against his cheek.

She was still in the kitchen when he came downstairs, making brandy butter. He was on the point of telling her that he could have done it for her, remembering just in time that being told what not to do was one of her chief dislikes. Instead he gathered together the ingredients he needed for the stuffing, and got to work chopping and mixing. The recipe came from his mother, another source of irritation to Laura.

'Where are the girls?' he asked.

'Annabelle's gone skating, and Hannah is doing something with Samantha, and staying the night.'

They stirred their wooden spoons in silence for a moment. Out of the blue, he said, 'I thought we might take them skiing at Easter.'

She looked up. 'I don't think it's a very good idea. Annabelle's got her "A"s in the summer, and she'll be revising all holidays. Anyway, suppose she broke a leg or an arm?'

'Just a thought.' He tasted the mixture. 'I've had a better one, however: a long weekend in Paris, you and me, only. We've never been there together.'

'When?'

'May, perhaps. May is a lovely month in Paris.'

'Sounds great,' she replied tonelessly. 'But I don't want to leave Annabelle while she's about to take her exams. You know how uptight she gets.'

He rested his spoon carefully against the rim of the bowl, feeling anger rise in him slowly. 'You didn't think about that when you left her for two weeks, did you?'

'I didn't realize she was having a crisis.' She added a spoonful of brandy to the butter.

'I don't think your lack of enthusiasm has anything to do with Annabelle,' he said quietly. 'What is the matter with you? You're stone-walling everything I suggest. In fact, you've done so for weeks.' He leant his fists on the kitchen table to steady himself. 'What do you want of me, Laura? Or is the answer, nothing at all?'

She stood motionless, staring at him, colouring up from her own temper. 'Right at this minute, I'd like you to stop tearing into me with vague accusations.

Why should I take the blame for every imagined thing that's wrong between us?'

'Because I've done all I can to make it work and you're not bloody well helping.'

'Don't swear at me. It shouldn't be an effort. Either it works for us or it doesn't—'

'And you've decided it doesn't?'

'Don't put words into my mouth.'

'The way you're acting suggests you've given up, that being married to me is the most God-awful bore.'

'And so it is, when you're being sanctimonious like now.'

'Thank you for your honesty,' he said with deep sarcasm. 'Now we're getting somewhere.'

'You're trying to make me into someone I'm not.' She marched to the sink and flung in her sticky spoon with a crash. 'You're trying to meld us both together, to make us into a like-thinking whole. You can't, we're different, you are you, and I am very definitely me. Me!' she said loudly, swinging round on him.

'You're talking cock.'

'I am *not* talking cock. That's why I went away, to find some sort of identity.'

'I'm sick of hearing about your identity. You left without warning, without a thought for anyone's feelings, because whenever life gets tedious or doesn't go your way, that's how you deal with it, by running away.' He heard his voice getting louder. He could not remember losing his temper.

'Shut up! You're shouting.'

'We're both shouting. It's a relief after days and nights of living with someone who shows as much emotion as a zombie, in bed and out.'

She stared at him, her face white now, eyes bright with tears of fury. 'You're a shit, Rick!'

'And you, Laura, are turning into a first-class bitch.'

In one swift movement she grabbed the nearest object to hand and flung it at him across the kitchen. The wet dishcloth hit him in the chest and fell into the mixing bowl. She leant on the work surface, panting. He removed the cloth between thumb and finger; then, with great precision poised a large dollop of stuffing on the spoon and let fly as with a catapult. The mixture landed in the middle of her face and stuck there, a gluey mass like a badly applied mud-pack round mouth and eyes and nose, out of which she glared in sheer astonishment. For seconds they both stood transfixed, he by the accuracy of his aim, she in shock. He began to laugh.

'I suppose you think that's funny.' She turned to the sink trying to wipe away the worst of it with her fingers and catching sight of herself mirrored in the windows. Her shoulders began to shake; she sank onto a stool and covered her face with her hands, gasping with either tears or laughter, he wasn't sure which.

'Don't cry.'

'I'm not crying.' She gave a snorting giggle. 'I'm laughing, and I don't want to because I'm furious with you.'

'Likewise. Shall we call a halt?'

He tore off a wad of kitchen paper and began to clean her face carefully, tilting it upwards with one hand. When he had finished, he bent his head and kissed her. 'You taste of sage and onion,' he said, grinning.

'It's so unlike you,' she said, 'flinging stuffing about like a child. You're so in control as a rule.'

'Perhaps I should do it more often in future. I've a feeling you admire that sort of thing.'

'I'm not forgiving you for the things you said,' she warned him. Her skin was pink and shiny from his administrations.

'Let's go to bed,' he said, 'and discuss it there.'

'The brandy butter, the stuffing—'

'Hell take them both.'

They did not discuss anything in bed, as it happened, too engrossed to talk. It was strange, Laura thought afterwards, how something as basic and disturbing as a row could relieve tension instead of building on it. She lay in the crook of Rick's arm and felt no longer at war with herself, for the first time for many months. There had been nothing particularly new about their love-making, but the familiar could be oddly comforting when rediscovered, like having a warm bath after the water had been cut off for days. Her only fear was that her appreciation might slip away with the passage of time, and she determined to hold on to it and to remind herself how the familiar had been put at risk. She could not forget Rick's words spoken in anger, but she had to admit that a lot of them were true.

Later they wrapped themselves in dressing-gowns and ordered a takeaway, and sat eating it messily at the kitchen table.

'We used to do this before we were married. D'you remember?' she said. 'Why does one stop doing those sorts of things, I wonder?'

'Because of the children, I suppose,' he answered, 'and the necessity of giving them good, nourishing meals.'

'You sound like Mrs Thatcher.'

'Perish the thought.'

'Working mothers turn to convenience foods. Their offspring seem quite healthy.'

'Talking of work, shouldn't you be thinking seriously of Gerard's offer?' he asked. 'He won't keep it open for you for ever.'

'I have thought, and I've turned it down.'

281

'Is that wise? I think you need the stimulus.' He looked worried. 'I don't want you—'

'You don't want a bitchy, discontented wife, is that it?'

'I don't want you bolting again, I couldn't bear it. Promise me you won't.'

'I promise.' She smiled at him. 'Besides, I'm not going to sit and do nothing. I'd like to do something connected with mental illness; something to help the Joes of this world. I don't know what exactly, since I'm not qualified, but I'm going to find out.'

'Fund-raising?'

'It's too remote. I'd like to be in contact with them, in some way.' She paused. 'They're moving Joe to a London hospital soon,' she said. 'Would you come and visit him with me?'

'I don't know that I'd have the right approach.'

'I think you'd be very good at it,' she told him encouragingly. 'And you'd be able to see for yourself how difficult it was not to become involved with him.'

He started to stack the takeaway cartons together. 'I enjoyed that. No washing up, either. I never really imagined he was the sole reason that kept you in Cornwall,' he added calmly, carrying the débris to the garbage bin.

She watched his back, her heart suddenly pounding with apprehension. 'What else could there possibly have been?' she asked.

'I know about Mark.' He sounded casual, as if the knowledge did not worry him unduly. 'Let's take the wine upstairs and finish it there.'

In the drawing-room he settled himself in an armchair, pulling her down to sit on the floor between his knees. 'I knew when I saw you together at the wedding,' he said.

'How?' The word slipped out of her involuntarily before she could stop herself.

'The way you were together; body language. I don't want to know about it, unless—'

'Unless?'

'Unless it's important.'

She sighed. 'There's nothing to tell, really. His wife died, he was alone and unhappy, and I wasn't particularly happy either. I suppose it made us kindred spirits, that's all.'

'It hasn't made him any happier, from what I saw.' He stroked her hair absently. 'He's in love with you.'

'A little, perhaps.'

'You can't be "a little in love". You either are or you're not,' he pointed out. 'And you?'

She thought of the day they had visited the church at St Just, the beginning of it all, and of subsequent days she had spent fighting a losing battle. There were times when it was justifiable to lie and this was one of them.

'No,' she answered, and then more honestly, 'Mark wasn't the cause of my not wanting to leave. On the contrary, I ran away, ran home, before he had a chance to become important to me.'

He said gently, 'But you didn't quite get away in time, did you?'

She did not reply, and they sat in silence for a moment. 'I don't want to turn this into an interrogation,' he said eventually. 'I only want to know if you are going to think about him continuously, as you've been doing for the past weeks. Part of you has been elsewhere; I'd very much like it if it returned. Will it, do you think?'

She twisted round to face him. 'Do you really have to ask me that after this evening?'

He shook his head. 'Do I get it for keeps?' he asked, kissing her.

'Yes,' she promised. 'It won't disappear again.'

Much later that night, she found herself unaccountably wide awake. To give herself something to do, she took Rick's Christmas present from its hiding place and stood it with the others under the tree, and switched on the tree candles. She had given him Joe's painting of the seagull in flight; the other one of the falcon she had sent to Mark a week ago, unframed and carefully wrapped between two sheets of cardboard. A letter had been enclosed, muddled and ambivalent, leaving the way open to the future. She sighed. As from this evening, all routes were closed now except for one. Cornwall seemed like another world to her, remembered in sounds: the sea on the rocks below her window, Brutus's tail thumping the floor, Jeremy's cheerful laugh, a series of voices and snatches of conversation. She thought of Mark alone in his farmhouse, and then recalled that he would be with Francie and Jeremy, almost a family, and felt happy for him. Perhaps, who knew, there would be the cementing of an old relationship. The Christmas tree, illuminated in dead of night, had a mystical quality about it, seemingly standing for some sort of essential goodness which was too much for her to bear.

She turned off the lights and stood for a moment in darkness, thinking, remembering, realizing that this sort of moment would come again from time to time. There was nothing to be done about it. She had not, after all, promised to forget, for memories were impossible to extinguish; and Rick would never ask her again because he would not want to know the answer. Some things were better left unsaid.

THE END

The Fifth Summer
Titia Sutherland

Every summer the Blair family went to Italy – to the villa in The Garden, a lush wilderness of cypress trees and bougainvillea tumbling down to the sea. Phoebe, who owned the villa and lived close by, loved the Blairs – of all her summer guests they were the ones who gave meaning to her life. She was possessive, enigmatic, manipulative, but Will and Lorna never really minded – until the fifth summer.

Something was wrong even before they arrived. There was a tension, a distance between Lorna and Will, something strange that Lorna could not quite define. The children were equally off-balance – Debbie overweight and rebellious, Fergus tortured and falling in love for the first time. And into this uneasy gathering of friends, family, and lovers, burst Bruno Andreotti, handsome, greedy, selfish, much loved by women but giving nothing of himself to any of them. Bruno was to prove the catalyst that blew the fifth summer apart, making Will and Lorna and the two children reassess and finally rebuild the structure of their lives.

'THE STANDARD OF WRITING IS HIGH, EACH CHARACTER IS WELL DRAWN, RELATIONSHIPS AND FEELINGS ARE BELIEVABLE. YOU CAN PRACTICALLY FEEL THE WARMTH OF THE SUN ON THE PAGES'
Sue Dobson, *Woman and Home*

'SUTHERLAND SCORES FULL MARKS . . . A FIRST NOVEL OF PROMISE AND SOME DISTINCTION'
David Robson, *Sunday Telegraph*

0 552 99460 X

BLACK SWAN

Out Of the Shadows
Titia Sutherland

The house was one of the most enduring influences
in Rachel Playfair's life. It was really too large for one
woman, but she liked the memories it held, the graceful
garden, and even the amiable resident spirit who lived on
the top floor. When Rachel's authoritative and somewhat
pompous son tried to persuade her out of her house,
she decided to make changes in her solitary life. With
three children who needed her only spasmodically, and
a small lonely granddaughter who needed her quite a
lot, she made plans, first of all to take in a lodger and
then, with the help of the unhappy Emily, to research
the past of her house. Both decisions were to shatter the
structure of Rachel's tranquil life.

The lodger proved to be a beguiling but disturbed
man who was instantly fascinated by his cool landlady,
and the delving into the past reopened a moving
and poignant wartime tragedy that held curious
overtones of events in Rachel's own life.

'AN EVOCATIVE STORY . . . GENTLY TOLD, ENVELOPS
YOU COMPLETELY'
Company

0 552 99529 0

BLACK SWAN

Accomplice of Love
Titia Sutherland

When Leo Kinsey bought 'Girl with Cat' – the painting
of a nude whose auburn hair was the same colour as the
cat's fur – he had no idea how deeply involved he was
to become with both the artist, and the model. Josh Jones
was a huge rugged bear of a man. He was also one of
the most talented painters Leo had ever discovered and,
very quickly, Leo and his wife, Josh and Claudia – the
girl with the auburn hair – formed an uneasy friendship.
Leo was to give Josh a one-man exhibition in his elegant
and distinguished gallery, and Josh invited Leo down
to their cottage in the country. In spite of Josh's heavy
drinking and the tension between him and Claudia a
careful *status quo* was preserved.

It was when unexpected tragedy smashed Leo's
comfortable and orderly life, that the relationship
changed. For Claudia, Josh's volatile, exciting, exotic
wife, became all-important to Leo. Between them
flared a dangerous spark that threatened to disrupt
the lives of everyone about them.

0 552 99574 6

BLACK SWAN

A SELECTION OF FINE TITLES
AVAILABLE FROM BLACK SWAN

THE PRICES SHOWN BELOW WERE CORRECT AT THE TIME OF GOING TO PRESS.
HOWEVER TRANSWORLD PUBLISHERS RESERVE THE RIGHT TO SHOW NEW
RETAIL PRICES ON COVERS WHICH MAY DIFFER FROM THOSE PREVIOUSLY
ADVERTISED IN THE TEXT OR ELSEWHERE.

☐	99564 9	**JUST FOR THE SUMMER**	*Judy Astley*	£5.99
☐	99537 1	**GUPPIES FOR TEA**	*Marika Cobbold*	£5.99
☐	99593 2	**A RIVAL CREATION**	*Marika Cobbold*	£5.99
☐	99467 7	**MONSIEUR DE BRILLANCOURT**	*Clare Harkness*	£4.99
☐	99367 5	**TIME OF GRACE**	*Clare Harkness*	£5.99
☐	99590 8	**OLD NIGHT**	*Clare Harkness*	£5.99
☐	99506 1	**BETWEEN FRIENDS**	*Kathleen Rowntree*	£5.99
☐	99584 3	**BRIEF SHINING**	*Kathleen Rowntree*	£5.99
☐	99325 5	**THE QUIET WAR OF REBECCA SHELDON**	*Kathleen Rowntree*	£5.99
☐	99561 4	**TELL MRS POOLE I'M SORRY**	*Kathleen Rowntree*	£5.99
☐	99529 0	**OUT OF THE SHADOWS**	*Titia Sutherland*	£5.99
☐	99460 X	**THE FIFTH SUMMER**	*Titia Sutherland*	£5.99
☐	99574 6	**ACCOMPLICE OF LOVE**	*Titia Sutherland*	£5.99
☐	99494 4	**THE CHOIR**	*Joanna Trollope*	£6.99
☐	99410 3	**A VILLAGE AFFAIR**	*Joanna Trollope*	£5.99
☐	99442 1	**A PASSIONATE MAN**	*Joanna Trollope*	£5.99
☐	99470 7	**THE RECTOR'S WIFE**	*Joanna Trollope*	£5.99
☐	99492 8	**THE MEN AND THE GIRLS**	*Joanna Trollope*	£5.99
☐	99549 5	**A SPANISH LOVER**	*Joanna Trollope*	£5.99
☐	99548 7	**HARNESSING PEACOCKS**	*Mary Wesley*	£5.99
☐	09304 2	**NOT THAT SORT OF GIRL**	*Mary Wesley*	£5.99
☐	99355 7	**SECOND FIDDLE**	*Mary Wesley*	£5.99
☐	99393 X	**A SENSIBLE LIFE**	*Mary Wesley*	£6.99
☐	00258 5	**THE VACILLATIONS OF POPPY CAREW**	*Mary Wesley*	£5.99
☐	99126 0	**THE CAMOMILE LAWN**	*Mary Wesley*	£6.99
☐	99495 2	**A DUBIOUS LEGACY**	*Mary Wesley*	£6.99
☐	99591 6	**A MISLAID MAGIC**	*Joyce Windsor*	£4.99